"You aren't go[...]
until you come home with me,"
Julia burst out frantically.

"I watched my brother get bushwhacked this evening," she continued. "I don't even know if he's alive. If you'll agree to come with me, I will make it worth your while."

Lone Wolf peered into her mesmerizing eyes and felt himself caving in.

There was no question that he had other places to go. But the damnedest thing was that Julia had impressed the hell out of him. Plus no one had ever stood up for *him* before. Ever. It was that one unexpected deed of courage that refused to let him send her off alone in the darkness.

"Okay, I'll saddle my horse and make sure you get home safely," Lone Wolf finally said.

Damn good thing he wasn't planning to spend more than a couple of hours with her. Even if she was a one-of-a-kind female he had no intention whatsoever of getting emotionally attached.

Not to her or anyone else.

* * *

Lone Wolf's Woman
Harlequin Historical #778—November 2005

Praise for Carol Finch

"Carol Finch is known for her lightning-fast,
roller-coaster-ride adventure romances that are
brimming over with a large cast of characters
and dozens of perilous escapades."
—*Romantic Times*

Praise for previous titles

The Ranger's Woman
"Finch delivers her signature humor,
along with a big dose of colorful Texas history,
in a love and laughter romp."
—*Romantic Times*

Texas Bride
"Finch delivers another well-paced western with likable,
realistic characters, a well-crafted backdrop
and just enough history and sensual tension
to satisfy western and romance readers."
—*Romantic Times*

CAROL FINCH

Lone Wolf's Woman

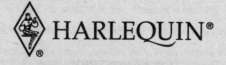

TORONTO • NEW YORK • LONDON
AMSTERDAM • PARIS • SYDNEY • HAMBURG
STOCKHOLM • ATHENS • TOKYO • MILAN • MADRID
PRAGUE • WARSAW • BUDAPEST • AUCKLAND

ISBN 0-373-29378-X

LONE WOLF'S WOMAN

Copyright © 2005 by Connie Feddersen

This edition published by arrangement with Harlequin Books S.A.

® and TM are trademarks of the publisher. Trademarks indicated with
® are registered in the United States Patent and Trademark Office, the
Canadian Trade Marks Office and in other countries.

www.eHarlequin.com

Printed in U.S.A.

Please address questions and book requests to:
Harlequin Reader Service
U.S.: 3010 Walden Ave., P.O. Box 1325, Buffalo, NY 14269
Canadian: P.O. Box 609, Fort Erie, Ont. L2A 5X3

This book is dedicated to my husband, Ed,
and our children, Christie, Jill, Kurt, Jeff, Jon and
Shawnna. And to our grandchildren, Brooklynn,
Kennedy, Blake and Livia.
Hugs and kisses!

Chapter One

Dodge City, Kansas
April 1880s

Vince Lone Wolf swore a blue streak when he heard the clatter of hooves on the wooden bridge a quarter of a mile away. "Damn fool brat," he muttered as he skulked away from his campfire to conceal himself in the darkness and monitor the rider's rapid approach.

He had a pretty good idea who the intruder was— because of the confrontation he'd had an hour earlier. He had stopped at a saloon on the south side of the railroad tracks in Dodge City to purchase a bottle of whiskey to tide him over during his jaunt to Colorado. *Big mistake,* he mused as he crouched in the underbrush beside the river to watch the rider thundering toward his camp. A peach-fuzz-faced kid at the bar had tried to square off against him because of his reputation as a gunfighter and bounty hunter.

Cowboys and saloon girls had scattered like buckshot when the kid challenged him to see who was the fastest on the draw. The wannabe gunslinger kept tossing insults, trying to bait him.

Lone Wolf had perfected lightning-quick reflexes and honed his instincts through practice and experience. They were his strong suits. Tact and diplomacy were way down the list. Instead of trying to talk the mouthy brat out of his insistence on a quick-draw contest that might get innocent bystanders shot, Lone Wolf had knocked the kid's feet out from under him and laid him out flat on his back in the middle of the saloon.

Then Lone Wolf had loomed over the wide-eyed pest like the flapping angel of doom. "You wanna die before you reach twenty, kid? That's your business," he had snarled ominously for effect. "Just don't waste *my* time while you're trying to get yourself killed. I've got bigger fish to fry than some scrawny tadpole that's still wet behind the gills."

Then he had confiscated the kid's sidearms, grabbed the bottle of whiskey and stalked from the saloon.

No doubt, the kid's bruised pride and temper had sent him rushing headlong into camp tonight. He had undoubtedly come to retrieve his confiscated hardware and demand another showdown.

"Just what are you trying to prove, kid?" he muttered as he watched the rider race closer to camp. "That you're utterly fearless or just plain stupid?"

Lone Wolf sighed heavily. His legendary reputation, which had somehow escalated from fact to fiction, was a standing invitation to every would-be shootist who wanted to advertise his skills with a six-shooter. Lone Wolf found it tiresome that half the folks he knew wanted to gun him down to save their worthless hides from a jail sentence, or to establish names for themselves as gunmen.

The other half treated him like a social outcast. They went out of their way to avoid contact with him because he was a half-breed, and a bounty hunter to boot. But he got paid handsomely to rid the world of ruthless murderers and thieves that so-called decent folks were afraid or unwilling to risk their charmed lives to remove from society.

Call him a hopeless cynic, but he swore the criminals he tracked down weren't much better than the snooty, two-faced folks he had encountered in proper society. The socialites were just more discreet about getting what they wanted. They were, however, more than obvious about their distaste for his mixed breeding and disreputable profession.

Which was why he camped outside of town instead of renting a room at one of the local hotels. He preferred to avoid encounters with the snooty folks in Dodge City as much as possible.

The truth was that Lone Wolf had the same use and respect for those uppity hypocrites as they had for him. Which was none whatsoever.

His thoughts trailed off as the rider plowed through the darkness, headed straight for the campfire. Lone Wolf hunkered down, poised to spring into action when the kid came within striking distance. He damn well intended to scare the bejesus out of him once and for all.

Lone Wolf's abrupt whistle startled the winded horse. When the mount sidestepped, he launched himself at the kid like a pouncing panther. Before the kid realized what was happening Lone Wolf jerked him roughly from the saddle. He took amused satisfaction in hearing the surprised squawk that erupted from the kid's lips when he cartwheeled across the ground.

Before the kid could catch his breath, Lone Wolf plunked down on top of his sprawled body. He laid a knife to the kid's throat and pressed his hand to his heaving chest to hold him securely in place.

"What the hell…?" Lone Wolf snatched back his right hand when he unexpectedly made contact with the feminine breasts that were concealed beneath the oversize jacket.

He was still gaping at his captive in disbelief when the owner of those full breasts walloped him upside the head with both hands at once.

"Get off me!" she shrieked in outrage.

Lone Wolf sank back on his haunches—still sitting astride the woman who had left both his jaws stinging.

"Get off me *now!*" she yelled while her arms swept upward again to slap him silly.

He caught her wrists in a vise grip. "I'll get off when you calm down," he snapped gruffly.

Teeth clenched, she reared up her head. "I'll calm down *after* you get off me!"

Lone Wolf was sorry to say that he became momentarily distracted when her oversize hat tumbled sideways and a riot of frothy red-gold curls cascaded around her shoulders. The shiny tendrils caught flame in the campfire light and her livid green eyes fixated murderously on him.

Breathtaking did not accurately describe the woman's facial features. Her spiky lashes, pert nose, full lips and elegant cheekbones were an intriguing study of light and shadows. Lone Wolf simply gaped at her for what seemed like several minutes, wondering how he could have mistaken this lovely female for the drunken brat that had invited a gunfight an hour earlier. But now that he could see her for who and what she was, it was difficult *not* to respond to the sight and feel of her lush body so close to his.

It took considerable willpower to rein in his wandering thoughts and pay attention to business. He told himself that while this female was disguised in a man's hat, jacket and breeches, he should have been able to tell the difference, even in the darkness. But he supposed that since she rode as expertly as a man she had thrown him off track, especially since he had been expecting someone else to show up.

Lone Wolf shifted sideways to sit down cross-legged beside his unexpected guest, then he squinted disapprovingly at the fetching female. "Next time you decide to come charging into my camp like a bat out of hell, *don't*. In my business, I make it a policy to act first and ask questions later—*if* I get around to it." He glared at her. "Now what the devil are you doing out here alone? Any woman with a brain in her head should know better than to do what you just did. I guess we know what that makes you, don't we?"

"Thank you so much for the insult," Julia Preston snapped as she levered herself into a sitting position to dust off her jacket. "I never would have thought that your type would turn out to be so preachy."

She bit her lip, annoyed with herself for sniping at the hard-edged man when she desperately needed his help. But she had been swinging wildly on an emotional pendulum for almost two hours. She was worried sick about her injured brother and she was frantic to return to the ranch to check on him. First, however, she had to persuade this tough-as-nails bounty hunter to come with her.

Snarling at Lone Wolf was *not* going to gain his co-operation.

Having the wind knocked clean out of her, and having a man's hands planted on her chest had done nothing for her deteriorating disposition and her temper. It was difficult to be diplomatic and charming when her world had been turned upside down—again—and she felt the overwhelming need to lash out to vent her grief, anger and frustration.

None of her problems were Vince Lone Wolf's fault. She knew that, but she was in such turmoil that she was about to explode. He, unfortunately, was in the direct line of fire.

"I need your help, and damn it, I will have it!" she all but shouted at him. "I need you to come home with me."

He cocked his head and stared curiously at her. Julia dragged in a restorative breath and tried to get herself under control. It was impossible.

"I need—" Her voice broke. The memory of her brother being blown out of the saddle, and dropping to the ground like a rock, descended on her like a tormenting nightmare.

Every ounce of inner strength and adrenaline that had sustained her while she raced off to summon the doctor, and then locate Lone Wolf—as Adam had demanded in a pained whisper—gushed out like a deflated balloon. Her emotions had been running so high and swift that she burst into humiliating tears. She dropped her head in her hands and let the pent-up frustration bleed out of her.

"I—I'm s-sorry," she blubbered helplessly.

She heard rather than saw the bounty hunter rise to his feet and walk away. Hard-hearted bastard, she thought. He probably didn't care if she cried herself dry, as long as she didn't do it in front of him.

Julia was taken by complete surprise when she felt Lone Wolf's lean fingers curl around her hands to pry them away from her face. He surprised her a second time when he pressed a tin cup to her lips.

"Here. Drink this. It'll make you feel better."

Maybe he had a heart, after all, she allowed as she clamped her shaking hands around the cup, then took a gulp.

She realized too late that she had ingested a huge swallow of whiskey, not water. Fire burned her throat and she gasped to draw breath. While she sputtered and wheezed he whacked her between the shoulder blades until she could inhale air.

"Take another sip," he insisted.

Julia frowned dubiously at the contents of the cup, then took a cautious drink. She was amazed to discover the liquor, once it finished burning the lining of her throat, had a calming effect. She took another swallow, then another.

When she glanced up to thank Lone Wolf for his unexpected kindness, the words stuck to the roof of her mouth. She found herself staring into his bronzed face, noting the braid of midnight hair—adorned with blue beads—that dangled beside his high cheekbones. A half-moon scar left a noticeable indentation on the curve of his stubbled jaw. Hazel eyes, encircled with flecks of gold, stared intently at her.

Her appraising gaze dropped to his sensuous lips, then drifted to the beaded necklace that was decorated with some sort of Indian talisman. She noticed that his shoulders seemed as broad as a buffalo's and his black shirt stretched tightly across his muscled chest.

He crouched down in front of her, his buckskin breeches clinging to his powerful thighs, his scuffed black boots indicating hard use. Julia found herself thinking this legendary shootist dressed to portray exactly what he was—the product of two opposing civilizations. His garments were a combination of Indian and white cultures and he didn't seem to favor one style over the other.

Whatever he found the most comfortable and practical, she suspected.

Although Julia had heard tales of Lone Wolf's impressive feats against the worst criminals in western society, she had never seen him until now. Her first impression was that he was a tough, competent warrior, and an intimidating force to be reckoned with.

He probably saw her as a weepy lunatic of a female. At the moment his opinion wasn't too far off the mark.

"You about done bawling so we can talk?" he asked.

Another wave of mortification crested over her. It was beyond embarrassing to fall apart in the presence of a man known for his fearlessness and impressive survivor skills. There were those in polite society who would condemn this man because of his mixed heritage, his dangerous reputation and his socially unaccepted profession. But Julia Preston would have given her soul if she could borrow his unflinching nerve and practiced skills for just one night.

Nothing would have made her feel better than to repay her ruthless neighbor for what he had done to her brother and for what he constantly tried to do to undermine their ranch.

The clatter of hooves on the bridge brought Julia's head up. She heard Lone Wolf mutter, "Well, hell. More company. Just what I don't need right now."

He sprang to his feet and darted off to scoop up the rifle he had left by the campfire.

Julia watched Lone Wolf turn sideways to steady the butt of his rifle against his muscled shoulder. She noted that he stood at an angle, refusing to give the approaching rider a wide target—just in case the man was gunning for him.

Lone Wolf definitely knew how to minimize the risk of taking a direct shot.

Too bad that her brother hadn't been able to do the same thing before the sniper had fired at him.

"That's close enough, kid!" Lone Wolf bellowed. "Stop your horse or I'll drop it out from under you."

Julia frowned, bemused, when the rider came close enough for her to recognize him. "Harvey Fowler? Is that you?" She stared incredulously at the rail-thin, frizzy-haired young man in homespun clothes.

Harvey swiveled in the saddle to gape owlishly at her. "What are you doin' out here with this half-breed bastard?" he asked in a slurred voice. "Was he trying to molest you?" His narrowed gaze bore mutinously into Lone Wolf. "Gimme back my pistols, you sidewinder. I plan to fill you full of lead for touchin' her. You don't even deserve to breathe the same air she does!"

Julia didn't know what Harvey thought he was trying to accomplish by hurling insults or why he thought he needed to defend her honor. But only a suicidal fool would purposely try to provoke Lone Wolf into a showdown.

Furthermore, she didn't need Harvey's interference. His arrival was causing an unnecessary delay and costing her valuable time.

"I have urgent business with Lone Wolf," she told

Harvey as she marched over to stand directly between the men. "Does your mother know you're out here issuing drunken threats to the wrong person?"

Harvey thrust back his bony shoulders and tilted his head to an aloof angle, obviously offended that she had brought his mother into the conversation. "I'm here to have it out with the half-breed redskin. He made a fool of me at the saloon."

Behind her, she heard Lone Wolf snort. "Give yourself full credit, kid. You made an ass of yourself without any help from me." He took Harvey's measure down the sight of his rifle barrel. "Let's just cut to the chase, shall we? I'm faster on the draw than you are. That's a fact. I've got years more experience. You don't stand a snowball's chance in hell with me right now. Go home and practice on fence posts and empty bottles. If you're still all-fired determined to face me down in a year or two then you can look me up."

"No," Harvey spouted off. "I want to finish this right now! Unless you're too much of a yellow-bellied coward to face me with six-shooters."

Julia gasped at the foolhardy young man who was two years her junior. She remembered Harvey well enough from their school days to recall that he was a fatherless child who had a chip on his shoulder. He wanted to be recognized as a man, even though he continued to behave like a troublesome child.

Annoyed, Julia set her hands on her hips and stared up at her former school chum. "Now you listen to me, Harvey. Squaring off against a gunfighter of Lone Wolf's caliber is a very bad idea. If you don't turn that horse around and go home I will tell your mother what you tried to do. You're lucky Mr. Lone Wolf has a strong sense of honor, restraint and integrity." At least she hoped he did. "Otherwise you would find yourself shot full of holes, jackknifed over the saddle and hauled to Boot Hill for burial."

Harvey puffed up like a toad. He glowered at Julia, then growled at Lone Wolf. "Gimme my pistols."

"No." Lone Wolf flatly refused. "You can pick up your firearms at Sheriff Danson's office after you've cooled down and sobered up."

When Harvey didn't budge from the spot, Julia hitched her thumb over her shoulder. "Go home, Harvey, and for Pete's sake show enough sense not to come back."

Snarling in irritation, Harvey wheeled his horse around and galloped off.

Julia's shoulders sagged in relief. "Well, that's one person who won't get shot today," she mumbled.

"What's that supposed to mean?"

Julia flinched when Lone Wolf's deep resonant voice came from so close behind her. Sweet mercy, the man moved as silently as a shadow. She hadn't seen or heard him coming.

Summoning her composure, she pivoted to find that she had to tilt her head back to meet his gaze. The man stood at least six foot three, she guessed. She felt like a dwarf beside him.

Dragging in a deep breath, she squared her shoulders and said, "My brother wants to hire you as a bodyguard and detective. He said to tell you that you can name your price, Mr. Lone Wolf. He also said that you owed him a favor. Can we go now?" she asked impatiently. "Time is wasting."

When Lone Wolf shook his head, his raven hair

drifted across his shoulders, gleaming blue-black in the firelight. Julia had the insane impulse to run her fingers through those shiny strands to test their thickness and texture.

Where had that ridiculous thought come from? she asked herself. She had just met this man. Because she found him intriguing wasn't important at the moment.

Julia gave a mental shrug, presuming the shock and turmoil caused by Adam's ambush this evening had turned her emotions topsy-turvy. That was the only plausible explanation for her curious fascination with the rugged bounty hunter. She wished she possessed his unflappable composure and gunfighting talents so she could resolve the problems facing her.

"Despite this supposed favor I owe your brother, I already have an assignment. I'll be busy for the next few weeks," Lone Wolf informed her. "I have a saddlebag full of bench warrants that I picked up from Sheriff Danson this afternoon. I have a long ride to Colorado in the morning to track down the three thieves that robbed one of the banks in Newton, Kansas."

When he turned away, she grabbed his arm. "You aren't going anywhere until you come home with me," she burst out, frantic for his cooperation. "I made a promise to my brother, and I intend to keep it."

He half turned to stare pointedly at the fingers clamped around his elbow. When she didn't take the hint and release him, he sent her a steely glance and peeled off her fingers one at a time. "*No*. I can't take your assignment until I finish what I've started."

Julia groaned in frustration. Somehow she had to make this man understand that she was desperate and that he had to come with her. *Now*.

"I watched my brother get bushwhacked this evening. I don't even know if he's still alive because he made me promise to fetch Doc Connor, and then come to get you. He insisted that I leave him in the care of our ranch foreman and the other cowboys."

She stared pleadingly at him. "If this turns out to be my brother's last request to me, then I intend to honor it. I will make it worth your while if you'll agree to come with me, as he asked."

Lone Wolf studied her determined stance. He also marveled at her resilience. He had to admire the woman's spirit and gumption, even if he did have to turn down the assignment.

Learning that she had been an eyewitness to her brother's ambush explained her rapid mood swings and fiery behavior. And he was impressed by the way she had pulled herself together and by her relentless attempt to gain his assistance. She had defied danger by riding straight through the wrong side of town and clattering over the bridge to reach his camp.

The thought made him frown disapprovingly.

"You should have swerved around the wrong side of Dodge to reach my camp, even if you were in a rush to find me." He flashed her a stern glance. "You took one helluva risk. The south side of the tracks is the last place decent folks should be, especially at night. Especially if you are a woman. Even your boy's clothing is no guarantee against trouble. Don't do that again."

He saw her shoulders stiffen, saw her delicate chin tilt upward. "I told you that my brother was bushwhacked." Her voice wobbled, but to her credit she shored up her jumbled emotions and went on. "I didn't want to face any delays taking the long way around to reach your camp, because I'm anxious to check on Adam. He wants to hire you until he gets back on his feet."

He peered into those mesmerizing green eyes and felt himself caving in.

Well hell, he reckoned that she deserved something for all the trouble of looking him up. The least he could do was accompany her back home to check on her wounded brother.

He pivoted on his heels. "Okay, I'll saddle my horse and make sure you get home safely."

"Thank you." Her voice quavered and he thought he heard a muffled sob. "Now *I* owe *you* a tremendous favor."

Chapter Two

A few minutes later, Lone Wolf mounted his piebald pony and watched Julia swing gracefully into her saddle. "Which direction are we heading?" he asked.

When she pointed east he took the lead to use the cross-country shortcut that bypassed town. Considering what a skilled rider she was he didn't think she would have trouble keeping her seat while moving over the uneven terrain.

"I'm sorry if I seem as much of a nuisance as Harvey Fowler," she said as she followed behind him. "My brother keeps telling me that I don't know when to shut up and back off. I didn't mean to sound so pushy and demanding, but this is very important to me. My brother is all I have left."

"What's your name, daredevil?" he asked as he reined his gelding into a rock-strewn ravine.

"Julia Preston. My brother is Adam."

"Doesn't ring a bell."

So, why am I riding off into the night with you? he asked himself bewilderedly. There was no question that he had other places to go, come morning. He could use some shut-eye. But the damnedest thing was that Julia had impressed the hell out of him when she had faced off against that pesky kid. Plus, no one had ever stood up for *him* before. Ever.

It was that one unexpected deed of courage that refused to let him send her off alone in the darkness. He might have earned the reputation of being the toughest son of a bitch in the state—which was probably the reason her brother wanted to hire him—but he wasn't so hard-hearted that he could completely disregard a desperate woman.

It was a fact that Julia was the prettiest female he'd ever laid eyes on. Her admirable character traits and strength of will appealed to him as much as her physical attributes. She was pure and wholesome and he found that altogether irresistible.

Nothing would come of his temporary fascination, of course, but she was easy on the eye.

"Just one thing, Miss Preston." He drew his horse to a slower pace so she could ride beside him.

"What's that?"

"Although you proved yourself to be daring more than once tonight, don't plant yourself between me and a potential threat again," he said. "If that drunken brat named Harvey had decided to draw down on me—with the firearm that he probably didn't think I saw tucked in the waistband of his breeches—you could have gotten your head blown off. That wouldn't have done your brother much good."

Julia sighed heavily. "Sorry. I haven't been thinking straight since Adam got shot two hours ago."

She still wasn't thinking straight, he decided as he

studied her shadowed profile. Because of her situation, she was treating him as an equal, a potential friend. Her kind usually regarded him as a second-class citizen and steered clear of him. Ordinarily, he could have cared less, but he had the instinctive feeling Julia was one of a rare breed of woman.

Damn good thing he wasn't planning to spend more than a couple of hours with her. Even if she was a one-of-a-kind female he had no intention whatsoever of getting emotionally attached. Not to her or anyone else. He had accepted his life for what it was and he was comfortable with it.

He cast his shapely companion a sidelong glance, then decided a short-term diversion wouldn't hurt before he rode off to Colorado tomorrow.

"How bad was your brother hit?" Lone Wolf asked five miles later.

"He suffered a serious chest wound."

"Did you get a look at the sniper?"

She nodded. "I was standing on the front porch when he appeared from a copse of cottonwood trees to the west, just as my brother approached the ranch house. The sniper was wearing a long canvas coat and wide-brimmed hat. He was riding a dun horse with three white stockings and a white blaze on its muzzle.

"I wanted to storm up to the man that I suspect is responsible for the shooting and repay him in kind, but Adam sent me to fetch you. I suspect he was trying to divert my quest for revenge and shoo me away, in case his condition worsened," she added sourly.

"Smart man, your brother," Lone Wolf praised. "You might have played into your adversary's hands."

She huffed out her breath. "That's what Adam said. But if he doesn't survive—"

He could tell by her quivering voice that she was holding onto her composure by a slippery thread so he changed the subject. "I need background information, Miss Preston. What do you think prompted this ambush?"

"Julia. Call me Julia." She managed a watery smile. "When a woman bawls her head off in front of man and exposes all her weaknesses she should be on a first-name basis."

When she glanced sheepishly at him he caught sight of her features. He felt another thud of unnamed emotion thump him in the chest. Lone Wolf fiercely resisted the unfamiliar sensation and turned his attention to the business at hand.

He watched Julia inhale a restorative breath and gather her thoughts. His traitorous gaze dropped to her breasts and he hurriedly jerked his attention back to her face. Which didn't help much because, damn it, he found himself studying each enchanting feature.

"We have been involved in a feud with our nearest neighbor for three years," she stated, her voice growing steadier with each word. "It began when my father and our neighbor's wife were found dead in our wrecked wagon at the bottom of a ravine. Our neighbor was as overwrought as Adam and I were."

Or did her neighbor simply pretend to be overwrought because he was the one who'd orchestrated the murders to repay his wife's infidelity? Lone Wolf wondered.

"The scandal turned him bitter and vindictive," Julia continued. "He swore our father had humiliated and cuckolded him. He wanted to buy our ranch, sell every head of cattle with the Preston brand on it and wipe away the family name, along with the ugly memory of the supposed affair."

"You don't sound convinced that something sordid was going on between your father and your neighbor's wife."

Julia shook her head emphatically. Moonbeams glowed in the curly cascade of red-gold tendrils. Lone Wolf looked the other way when another jolt of unwanted awareness shot through him. This woman was too distracting.

"My father was devoted to my mother," Julia maintained. "After my mother died from cholera, Papa spent the next four years until his death devoted to raising Adam and me. He showed no interest in other women."

She shrugged helplessly. "I can't explain why Papa and our neighbor's wife were together that night. Neither do I know why her buggy was left beside the road after she had ridden into town to be a midwife for her friend. But I do not believe for one minute that my father was romantically involved with Rachel."

Lone Wolf didn't comment. He couldn't say for sure but it sounded as though Julia's undying loyalty and love for her father had clouded her judgment. He thought there was a strong possibility that a clandestine affair might have been going on, whether Julia wanted to accept it or not.

"Adam and I were determined to hold the ranch together, but it hasn't been easy. Incidents of rustling began not long after Papa died. We had no substantial proof that our neighbor was involved, but he was our prime suspect. He seemed to hate us."

Julia continued. "To complicate matters, our neighbor's daughter was our childhood playmate, and he refused to allow her to associate with us. Still the affection between his daughter and Adam remains. She grew up loving my brother and he has always felt the same way about her."

It sounded to Lone Wolf as if history was trying to repeat itself. Julia's bitter neighbor, however, was having none of that. Not after he had lost his wife to another man. The prospect of losing his daughter to the son of his wife's lover was obviously intolerable. Especially if Adam was using his charm on the neighbor's daughter to retaliate.

"I know what you're thinking," she surprised him by saying.

"Do you? Then you would be the first," he countered drily. "I try very hard not let anyone know what's running through my mind. It's bad business when dealing with cutthroats who like to get the drop on you."

"You're thinking Adam is trying to get back at our neighbor by turning his charms on his daughter," Julia guessed correctly. "But you couldn't be more wrong. Maggie and Adam were childhood friends, and then they became sweethearts. That was long before the hint of scandal."

"Maggie?" Lone Wolf grew very still. His focus settled intently on Julia.

"Maggie Griffin. Sol Griffin's daughter," she explained, unaware of the suppressed emotion roiling through Lone Wolf.

Tormenting memories flashed through his mind, then exploded like fireworks. Old hurt and the raw pain of rejection threatened to swamp him. For a moment he was transported back to a time when he had been a weak, desolate and vulnerable teenager.

"Despite Sol's unfair decree, Maggie and Adam continued to see each other secretly," Julia reported. "Maggie has rejected every marriage proposal that Sol approved. When she stood up to him and informed him that if she couldn't wed Adam then she would never take a husband, Sol sent her to Saint Louis to stay with his cousin's family. She has been home for two months and she and Adam have gotten very good at sneaking away so they can be together."

"Maggie must have a great deal of determination and gumption," Lone Wolf remarked.

Julia bobbed her head and smiled fondly. "She does, in her own ladylike, dignified way. Which is why we are steadfast friends and always have been."

"And Sol Griffin is one bitter, obstinate man," he murmured.

When Julia stared curiously at him, Lone Wolf shrugged as nonchalantly as he knew how. "I know of Sol Griffin."

Know of him? Hell, he was Sol Griffin's blood kin, a fact that he would not acknowledge or accept under the circumstances. Sol had made that known eighteen years ago.

"If you know of Sol, does that mean you won't help my brother and me because you don't want to get on his bad side?" she asked anxiously.

"I was born on his bad side," Lone Wolf muttered under his breath.

"Pardon?"

He clenched his teeth, stifled the onrush of resentment, and said, "I don't allow personal sentiment to get in the way of business. *If* I decide to take an assignment, then I represent the client who is paying me. No one else."

"You will be exceptionally well paid if you agree to take this assignment," Julia assured him. "I want that sniper brought to justice for the murder attempt on my brother's life. If the man I saw firing his rifle at Adam is remotely connected to Sol, I want to see them both locked in jail with no chance of parole— Oh, God... Maggie..."

Her voice trailed off and her shoulders slumped in frustration. "I can't get word to her about what happened to Adam. And though she resents Sol's demand to keep her distance from Adam, I doubt she will believe her father would go so far as to have Adam shot to end their courtship."

She raked her hands through her hair and sighed. "I'm sorry. I feel as if I'm telling you all my problems. It's bad enough that I practically bled tears on your shirt. I don't expect you to figure out how I'm going to break the bad news to my dearest friend."

"Not a problem," he said with a casual shrug of his broad shoulders. "I get paid to solve other people's dilemmas. That's difficult to do without all the facts."

Julia glanced at the powerful-looking bounty hunter who sat a horse so impressively. He seemed detached, even more distant than before. And why shouldn't he be? He wasn't embroiled in the upheaval of her life.

She was just another prospective client to him.

Her thoughts trailed off when she spotted the glow of lights in the distance. Almost home... Soon she would find out if Adam had survived his gunshot wound.

With tension coiled inside her, she promptly picked up the pace. She had her horse in a full gallop by the time she reached the dirt path that led to the ranch house.

Lone Wolf was right on her heels. When she skidded her horse to a halt and bounded from the saddle, his lean fingers closed around her forearm to waylay her. She looked up at his inscrutable expression and wished she possessed the same iron-willed self-discipline. She felt as if she were on the verge of scattering in every direction at once, while he was a bulwark of physical and emotional strength.

"Take a breath, Julia," he ordered firmly. "A deep one."

She did as she was told.

"Again," he demanded.

Julia sucked in a huge gulp of night air and tried to get herself under control.

"You won't accomplish a damn thing by walking in there and falling apart. Whatever happens, I'll be here to take care of things. Save the tears and tantrums for later. Do you understand? Don't give your brother or your employees something else to worry about right now."

She peered into his angular face, into those intense hazel eyes that bored straight into her. "Does that mean that you *will* take this assignment?" she asked hopefully.

When he nodded, Julia embarrassed herself by flinging her arms around his neck and practically squeezing the stuffing out of him. She buried her head against the solid wall of his chest and savored the sense of security that overcame her. Although she was aware that he didn't reciprocate—except to drape his brawny arm awkwardly around her shoulder—she absorbed his strength. She clung to him for comfort and support for several moments, wondering why she had developed an instant attachment to a total stranger.

Maybe it was because she had poured her heart out to him and he had listened, then agreed to help. Maybe it was because she was desperate to anchor herself to something strong and solid.

Vince Lone Wolf was definitely that. Rumor had it that he was hell on outlaws, ruthless when necessary and unyielding as granite. Legend also had it that no one that he was sent to apprehend ever walked away to brag about escaping from him. He was the justice system's last resort, and he accepted the difficult challenges no one else wanted.

This was definitely the man Julia needed on her side.

Summoning her composure as best she could, Julia stepped back, then wheeled toward the front porch. When she opened the door and was met with silence, another wave of apprehension swooped down on her. She took comfort in Lone Wolf's presence as he hovered over her, close as her own shadow.

She headed up the steps to Adam's room, wondering what her acquaintances in Dodge City's elite social circle would think of her association with Lone Wolf. No doubt, they wouldn't approve. But Julia had been raised not to be judgmental and presumptuous. Furthermore, her brother's life and the future of Preston Ranch were at stake. She would be damned if she was influenced by the dictates of society. She and Adam had a hired gun on their side in this feud and she didn't give a flying fig what anyone thought of that.

Lone Wolf might be hard-edged, gruff and emotionally detached, but if he could help her put her life back together and end this dangerous fight with Sol Griffin then she would be forever in his debt. Plus, she wouldn't think twice about paying whatever price Lone Wolf demanded for his expert assistance.

Her thoughts trailed off and her footsteps stalled as she stared at the closed bedroom door. With Lone Wolf's words of advice whispering through her mind, Julia inhaled a steadying breath, then grabbed the doorknob.

She prepared herself for the worst…and prayed for the best as she entered the room.

Chapter Three

The moment Lone Wolf stepped into the room behind Julia his attention settled on the deathly pale patient whose chest was wrapped in bandages. When Julia rushed to her brother's side to clutch his hand, Lone Wolf noted her visible relief.

After studying Adam's pale face and sandy-blond hair for a long moment, Lone Wolf recalled their one and only meeting. Near as he recollected it was about a year ago, when he was in a saloon on South Side in Dodge. He hadn't gotten the name of the man who had casually leaned toward him at the bar to confide that one of the ruffians playing poker had a pistol resting against his thigh beneath the table.

It was trained on Lone Wolf's back.

Lone Wolf had murmured, "I owe you one," before he strolled up behind the hombre he had been sent to arrest for robbing a dry goods store in Abilene. If memory served, Adam Preston had tripped up the criminal when he tried to bolt and run, saving Lone Wolf the trouble of tracking him down.

"How bad off is he?" Julia asked as she half turned to stare inquisitively at the stout, gray-haired physician who had scooped up his medical bag.

The doctor smiled gently. "Lucky to be alive, but I think he'll make it. He's going to require lots of bed rest."

Lone Wolf watched Julia's shoulders slump in relief, saw the wash of tears that filled her luminous green eyes. But when she looked in his direction she regathered her composure, just as he'd ordered her to do.

Because of Adam's injured condition, a mountain-load of responsibility fell on Julia's shoulders, along with a heaping mound of traumatic emotion. But she seemed to be made of sturdy stuff. The determined set of her jaw indicated that she intended to meet the challenge of managing the ranch until her brother's condition improved.

Damn, she was something—as much as he wished he hadn't noticed. It had taken every ounce of self-control he could muster not to respond when Julia had flung herself into his arms on the front porch a few minutes earlier. The feel of her luscious body pressed against his caused fierce need to spear through him.

When another ripple of desire tried to overtake him, Lone Wolf reminded himself that Julia Preston was a client—too damn attractive and intriguing for his peace of mind but a business client nonetheless. He didn't want or need the slightest personal involvement with her. He was a man who needed no one. With that in mind he concentrated on the problems at hand.

"I managed to dislodge the bullet," Doc Connor reported as he came to stand at the foot of the bed. "Adam should come around in a few minutes. But don't tire him out." He handed Julia a bottle of laudanum. "Give him another dose to help him sleep and keep him sedated for several days."

Five minutes after Julia had introduced Lone Wolf to the men who had congregated in the room, the physician bid them good-night and promised to return the following day. Frank Slater, the foreman, and two of the cowboys eyed Lone Wolf cautiously before they also took their leave.

A moment later Adam's eyes fluttered open.

Julia pressed a kiss to his peaked forehead. "Hey, big brother." She smiled affectionately. "I'm glad to hear that you're going to be all right. That is, if you follow doctor's orders and rest while I take care of things for you. I get to boss you around. I've always wanted to do that."

The faintest hint of a smile trailed across Adam's ashen lips. Then he fixed his dazed eyes on Lone Wolf. "Make sure no harm comes to Julia," he wheezed. "But I need to warn you—" he paused to swallow and lick his lips "—she can be a handful."

Lone Wolf didn't doubt it. Even when Julia was at her worst, overcome with grief and anguish, she had spunk, spirit and courage in spades. She had braved the dangers of South Side to find him quickly. Plus, he remembered well how she had retaliated when he had accidentally touched her in an inappropriate manner.

"I'll be on my best behavior while Lone Wolf is underfoot," Julia promised. "You won't even recognize me."

Adam's smile faded and his eyes drooped. "You need to tell Maggie—"

"You can tell her yourself later," Julia cut in as she

offered him a dose of the sedative. "Right now you need to rest. I'll be back to check on you after I get Lone Wolf settled in for the night."

He swallowed dutifully as his focus drifted to Lone Wolf. "Thank you for coming to help. Now *I* owe *you* one."

When Adam drifted off, Julia heaved herself to her feet. She looked exhausted but mightily relieved that her brother had survived. Lone Wolf wondered what it felt like to be loved so devotedly. The affectionate bond between brother and sister fairly radiated in the room. No doubt, they had grown very close after losing their mother, and then their father.

Aware of the strong attachment and family connection the Prestons shared made Lone Wolf realize something was missing from his life. It had been almost two decades since he had felt as if he belonged anywhere. He had also gotten used to knowing that he was probably the only one who gave a damn whether he even existed. But at least he was the master of his own soul. There was a lot to be said for that.

"I'll show you to your room," Julia murmured as she breezed past him. He tried very hard not to get lost in her feminine scent again. But it was difficult, especially when the aroma of jasmine clung to his clothes after she had hugged him gratefully.

"No need for a room," he insisted, following her into the hall. "I'll camp outside."

Julia stopped short, spun around then tilted her head to stare up at him. "No, you will not," she countered firmly. "The whole point is for you to be close at hand in case Sol decides to send his henchman to finish the job on Adam."

Lone Wolf's eyes widened. "You want me under the same roof with *your* kind?" He snorted at that. "You'd be laughed out of town by your highfalutin friends. Half-breed bounty hunters aren't prized houseguests so don't bother trying to be noble. I don't miss what I'm not used to."

Julia looked him squarely in the eye and said, "Do you want to hear the truth, Lone Wolf?"

"Yeah, don't mind if I do. That would be a refreshing change, considering the ruthless, backstabbing, two-faced liars I usually have to contend with in my line of work."

Julia studied him consideringly, trying to imagine what his life was like, knowing he had been stigmatized for reasons beyond his control. No matter what anyone else thought of him, she admired the countless talents and skills that had earned him the reputation as one of the most formidable shootists and capable trackers in the West.

She also wondered if the fact that her emotions had been all over the place the past few hours accounted for her unexpected attachment to him. She certainly hadn't developed an interest in any of the fortune hunters who had tried to charm her into marriage the past few years.

But her connection with Lone Wolf was different. *He* had been there when she needed a shoulder to cry on and had offered her moral support when she returned to the ranch. He had also helped her brace for the worst before she climbed the steps to determine if Adam had survived.

Of course, it was pretty clear that he didn't want any involvement with her, but he had been there for her whether he'd wanted to be or not. That made him special to her.

"Well, the truth is," she said belatedly, "that my maternal grandfather didn't think my father was good enough for my mother, which was, of course, ridiculous. Snobbery, society's dictates and prejudices are wasted on me. I have been encouraged to think and speak for myself and to stand up for what I believe in. I'm not, nor have I ever been, a shrinking violet who is easily controlled. You need to know that from the start."

His low, rumbling chuckle startled her. She grinned when she saw him smiling wryly at her.

"I figured out that you had gumption and spunk, right off." He rubbed his stubbled jaw. "You also pack a mean wallop. I didn't think I had that retaliation coming since it was unintentional. You weren't who I was expecting."

Julia blushed furiously, remembering the feel of his hand on her breast. She had reacted instinctively, unaware that he had mistaken her for Harvey Fowler. "You're right," she admitted. "You didn't deserve those hard slaps. I apologize. It was just my self-preservation instinct kicking in." She returned to the matter at hand. "You will be using my suite during your employment. No argument."

He scowled.

Julia lurched around to stride down the hall before he had the chance to protest again. "I want you next door to Adam. On the same side as the balcony, in case someone sneaks up on him. That is sensible and practical."

"And where will you be sleeping while I'm lounging in your bed?" he asked, close behind her. "What makes you think this mysterious sniper isn't coming after *you* next—because you can identify him. I need to know exactly where you are if trouble arises."

The comment caused her to jerk up her head, and she noted his grim countenance. He might be right, but she refused to cower, even if she *and* her brother might be targets of Sol's revenge.

"I'll be in the guest room across the hall," she said, gesturing over her shoulder.

Lone Wolf opened the door then gave a low whistle as he surveyed the palatial suite that surpassed anything he had ever seen. Expensive furnishings lined the walls. Velvet drapes cascaded beside floor-length windows that provided a view of the moonlit gallery and the rolling hills beyond. These were definitely accommodations fit for royalty.

But he was as far from royalty as you could get.

"Nice place, Julia. I always wondered what the lap of luxury looked like."

"You're going to know what it feels like, too," she told him determinedly. "You are staying here. We will speak of it no more. I already told you that you could name your price for helping Adam and me." Her arm swept out in an expansive gesture. "These are the fringe benefits. A nice room and home-cooked meals. This is what Preston hospitality looks like, so get used to it."

Lone Wolf chuckled. He didn't have reason to laugh very often. But Julia had provoked his amusement twice in a matter of minutes, not to mention the reluctant smiles she had drawn from him since they'd met.

Obviously she was as generous as she was spirited and intelligent. He liked that about her. Liked the fact that she knew her own mind and stood up for what she believed in. That separated her from the ordinary masses and drew his respect. He wondered, however, how she was going to react when he named the fee he intended to charge for taking this assignment.

He predicted her attitude toward him would change drastically when she was asked to pay his price.

"Very well, I'll bunk here if that's what you want," he acquiesced.

"Good. I'm glad we don't have to waste time arguing over that issue." She pivoted around to fetch her nightgown and a clean set of clothes from the marble-top dresser and intricately carved wardrobe closet.

"As for your fee, I don't know how you prefer to conduct business. Am I to pay a partial sum now and the remainder later?" She clutched the pile of clothes to her chest, then strode up in front of him. "I have cash on hand, but if it isn't enough I will make a withdrawal from the bank tomorrow."

Lone Wolf stared down into her vibrant green eyes and watched the lantern light gleam on that mass of shiny gold hair. She was cooperation and good cheer right now, but that was about to change.

"Name your price," she offered generously.

"I will take this assignment," he affirmed. "But if I've learned nothing else in life it is that there is always a catch."

She shrugged, unconcerned. "My brother is still alive and you're here to make sure he stays that way. Whatever this *catch* is, I'm sure Adam and I will abide by it." She smiled wryly. "Unless you want the deed to our property in exchange. Which, incidentally, is what I think Sol Griffin ultimately wants. But he is not going to get it and neither are you."

"I will forgo the usual traveling fee since I'll be staying here. But I *insist* on marriage. The pretense of it.

With you," he stated firmly and succinctly. "*Or* the public announcement of our betrothal at the very least."

Sure enough, her eyes popped and her jaw sagged on its hinges. The clothes she had clutched in her arm dropped to the toes of her boots.

"That is the catch, Julia." He stared challengingly at her. "Take it or leave it."

He knew she couldn't possibly understand his reasoning and he wasn't in the habit of explaining himself to anyone. She hadn't a clue what had prompted his unexpected stipulation and he was anxious to hear her response. He was forcing her to put her noble ideals on the line. Right here. Right now. She claimed that she didn't judge a man by his mixed heritage and less-than-respectable occupation.

This was the decisive moment when he found out if she meant what she said. He really expected her to fail the test.

She stood there staring up at him so intently that he felt the urge to squirm. She sized him up for a long moment then frowned. No doubt, she was trying to figure his angle.

"A pretend marriage. To me," she repeated pensively. "That's the catch?"

"Yes," he confirmed with a sharp nod.

She cocked her head, appraising him from another angle. "Just what is the reason behind this?"

"Smart as you are, you'll figure it out for yourself after you've given it some thought."

"You're giving me too much credit."

No, he gave her all she deserved. He'd seen her in several telling situations tonight and she'd held up remarkably well. "You're bright and you're gutsy and that counts for a lot in my book," he said.

"Am I? Did you notice that *between* the humiliating moments while I was ranting, desperate and bawling my head off?"

He shrugged lackadaisically. "That was just about letting off steam. You were entitled."

He waited while she mulled over his request. He couldn't help but wonder how she saw him. Half-civilized? Unattractive? Unworthy of the pretense of a romantic involvement with her? Just what did Julia Preston see while she was looking him over so critically?

Not that he cared, of course. He was just curious.

Julia bent at the waist to scoop up her clothes, then tossed him another contemplative glance. "I'm assuming that I will have the night to consider this stipulation." She arched a challenging brow. "A woman shouldn't be too hasty when accepting or declining a marriage proposal, should she?"

She didn't mention that she had rejected the last three proposals in two minutes flat.

"The *pretense* of marriage," he corrected quickly.

"Or the *announcement* of a betrothal."

"At the very least."

She ambled to the door, then glanced back at him. "If you were one of the three suitors who asked for my hand recently, I would know your angle immediately."

"Only three?" His thick brow arched. With her brains, beauty and wealth, he would have guessed more.

A mischievous grin pursed her lips. "According to my suitors, I'm not society's traditional female. Much too unconventional when it comes to fashion," she added as she gestured toward her attire. "Too headstrong and willful. And that was the catch they hadn't counted on." She stared pointedly at him. "Beware, Lone Wolf, *you* might get more than you bargained for."

"I'll take my chances." He chuckled, finding that he enjoyed negotiating with this feisty female. "Getting more than I bargain for is a hazard of my profession."

"You will have your answer later," she said before she closed the door behind her.

Lone Wolf wondered if she might slam the door with a vengeance to show her displeasure with his shocking request. Then he remembered that Adam was asleep in the next room. Julia wouldn't think of disturbing him.

Admiring the expensive furnishings, Lone Wolf peeled off his clothes, then set the bowie knife—which he kept strapped to his left thigh—and both pistols on the nightstand. He placed the derringer that he sheathed in his shirtsleeve under the fluffy pillow and laid the long-barreled boot pistol on the empty space beside him.

He had learned the importance of keeping his arsenal of weapons within easy reach, no matter where he was.

Even while lounging in this fancy suite.

He recalled the names of several dead lawmen who hadn't heeded that good advice.

Lone Wolf sprawled on the bed and immediately became enshrouded in the feminine fragrance that clung to the luxuriant bedding and mattress. He lay there staring up at the frilly canopy, trying to estimate how long it would take his quick-witted client to figure out the primary reason he had suggested a pretended marriage.

She, of course, wouldn't have a clue what other reasons had prompted him to make the stipulation. But for now, one reason was enough. Astute as Julia was, he didn't think it would take her long to puzzle it out.

Three hours later, after Julia had stopped by Adam's room, she purposely barged unannounced into her suite. She skidded to a halt when she heard the click of two triggers. The low, threatening growl warned her that she was treading on dangerous ground.

Whatever else Lone Wolf was, he was not a man caught off guard easily. She was relieved to know that, glad to see that he was armed to the teeth and that he was capable of protecting her brother and himself instantaneously.

"You should have knocked and announced yourself," he grumbled.

Heat flamed across Julia's face when she saw him flip the sheet over his hips then heard the pistols clang against the nightstand. The legendary bounty hunter slept naked, she realized. Had there been more moonlight spraying through the floor-length windows she would have seen that clearly for herself.

Drawing herself up to full stature, and careful not to allow her gaze to dip below his shadowed face, she padded closer to the bed. "I came to—"

"Is Adam all right?" he cut in worriedly.

"Yes, thank you for asking. He is still in pain and chattering like a magpie in his drug-induced dreams. I changed the dressing on the wound and the bleeding is under control."

"Good. Now turn your back so I can slip on my breeches."

"And not have you at the same sort of disadvantage that I faced when you dropped that 'there's just one catch' in my lap?" Julia scoffed. "You deserve to sit there feeling awkward. Turnabout is fair play."

"Your brother is right," she heard him mutter. "You *are* a handful."

"Thank you. I pride myself in being a man's equal, not the extension of his opinions and his will."

"Why am I not surprised to hear that?"

Julia clutched her robe together, then crossed her arms under her breasts. "I think I have figured out why you want the pretense of a marriage during this assignment."

Her first thought had been that he wanted to take full advantage of the situation, but she'd reminded herself that she was trying to measure him against the yardstick of ordinary men. "You aren't like the fortune hunters I've encountered."

"Are you asking or telling?" he said wryly.

"I'm telling you what I've learned about you already."

"Just don't try to find qualities in me that aren't there," he warned. "I am what I am. Nothing more or less. Nothing admirable. Nothing special."

But he was certainly all man, she mused as her betraying perusal slid down from his bare chest to his lap. She couldn't decide if she was relieved or disappointed that darkness concealed his masculine body.

"Get to the point, Julia," he said impatiently. "It's the middle of the night and I'm only dressed for the kind of social call that you and I are *not* going to participate in."

She winced at his brisk tone and her gaze returned to his face—from which it never should have strayed in the first place. She inhaled a quick breath and said,

"The pretend marriage is your attempt to protect my reputation while we're working closely together. Am I right?"

"Partially," he murmured. He would get to the more-than-a-mite-selfish reasons later.

"If Sol Griffin thinks we're married, he might try to go through you to get to me. You would become one of the obstacles he would have to remove to get his hands on Preston Ranch. And three murder attempts would arouse the sheriff's suspicions and launch an official investigation."

"Bingo. Smart lady," he praised.

"Thank you. However, a betrothal would accelerate an attempt on my life," she remarked.

Damn, she was right, he realized. He had given her credit for her sharp intellect, but he still had underestimated her.

"Therefore," she went on to say, "I intend to spread the word of our marriage as soon as I inform Adam of our plan. If anyone asks I will insist that after several chance meetings between us, I realized you suited me perfectly."

Which he did, Julia mused. This man had agreed to put his life on the line to protect Adam. He didn't harbor ulterior motives like her other beaux. She trusted him. She liked him. She was attracted to him, even when she knew nothing permanent would come of the arrangement. She certainly didn't need a husband to complete her, and he didn't need a wife, with his tumbleweed lifestyle.

"And so," she added belatedly, "I will agree to your little catch, because it is an ingenious solution."

Lone Wolf smiled to himself. He would like to be on

hand when Sol Griffin received the news of this supposed marriage to Julia Preston. That would go a long
way in compensating for the hurt and rejection he had
suffered at Sol's hands.

A fleeting shadow on the gallery put Lone Wolf's
senses on full alert. He bounded to his feet, reacting instinctively to the potential threat that descended on
Adam. Behind him he heard Julia's sharp intake of
breath—and he remembered that he was still naked.

"Well, hell." Muttering, he snatched up the sheet and
tucked it around his waist. He scooped up his pistols on
the way to the balcony. "Stay here," he gritted out when
he heard Julia scurrying along behind him.

"But—" she protested.

"Stay in here," he snapped in a tone that invited no
argument.

To his relief, Julia screeched to a halt.

Lone Wolf slipped silently out the door.

Chapter Four

While the cloaked figure breezed toward Adam's room, Lone Wolf moved into position to pounce. The would-be assailant never knew what hit him. Lone Wolf had a stranglehold on the intruder's throat and a pistol pressed threateningly against his temple before he could react.

To Lone Wolf's frustration, however, Julia flagrantly disobeyed his order by darting across the gallery to position herself in front of his captive. He made a mental note to sit this foolhardy female down later and read her every line and paragraph of the riot act. He had specifically told her to never again put herself between him and a potential threat.

And damn it, she had done it twice in the same night!

"Jules, it's me!" came the chirping voice.

Lone Wolf frowned when Julia gestured for him to release his captive.

"It's Maggie," Julia informed him.

"Maggie?" Lone Wolf stepped back a pace then expelled an exasperated snort. "I would sincerely appre-

ciate it if the women around here would wear dresses so I can tell who's who."

When Maggie Griffin pivoted to face him, he went very still. Her wide-eyed focus trailed down his bare chest to survey the white sheet that glowed in the moonlight. Then she glanced bewilderedly back and forth between him and Julia. When her attention shifted to the door that led into Julia's bedroom, he knew exactly what she was thinking. Hell, he could practically *hear* her thinking it.

"Maggie Griffin, meet my husband, Vince Lone Wolf," Julia introduced without missing a beat.

"Your *what?*" Maggie croaked as she staggered back a pace. "The Lone Wolf who—" She clamped her mouth shut, then blinked owlishly at him…and at his state of undress. "The legendary bounty hunter? *That* Lone Wolf?"

He nodded, clamped both pistols between his side and left elbow, and then reached out to shake her hand. "Pleased to meet you." He had waited years to make her acquaintance, to see what she looked like, to see how she reacted to him.

She didn't move, just stared at his hand.

Eventually she pulled the concealing cap off her head to let a thick mane of sable hair tumble around her shoulders. Finally she offered her hand and a tentative smile. "Nice to meet you, Mr. Lone Wolf. Vince was my grandfather's name."

Lone Wolf studied her trim statuesque figure, enchanting face and long-lashed blue eyes. She reminded him of the memory he carried of his mother, the white captive who had caught the rapt attention of his Cheyenne father.

He interrupted his assessment to look at Julia, who was frowning at him. For the life of him he couldn't figure out what he had done to annoy her. But the instant she saw him staring curiously at her she manufactured a smile, then slipped her arm around Maggie's shoulders and turned her toward Adam's room.

"What are you doing here at this time of night, Mags?" Julia asked.

"Adam was supposed to meet me at the usual place at ten o'clock. When he didn't show up I came looking for him." Her accusing gaze settled on Julia. "Why didn't he mention your wedding? Was it tonight? I would have found a way to attend if I had known. Is that why he didn't meet me?"

Julia flung up her hand to halt the barrage of questions. She turned to Lone Wolf. "Why don't you get dressed, *dear,* while I explain things to Maggie."

When he wheeled around and disappeared into the bedroom, Julia tossed aside the foolish stab of envy she had felt when her supposed husband made such a thorough study of Maggie. Julia knew she paled in comparison to Maggie Griffin, who was the picture of feminine grace, deportment and refinement. Julia had never had a problem concealing her insecurities before, and no man's opinion or interest in her had mattered until she met Vince Lone Wolf. But suddenly she was disappointed that he took his sweet time appraising her best friend's startling blue eyes, peaches-and-cream complexion, winsome smile and dainty figure. Julia had thought he found her mildly interesting…until Maggie arrived.

Now Julia was just an afterthought.

She wanted to punish him for making her feel less

than feminine and desirable compared to her oldest and dearest friend.

Would you listen to yourself! came a scolding voice inside her head. Her brother had barely escaped death this evening and she was inwardly stewing over her inappropriate and ill-fated fascination with this bounty hunter. She was a poor excuse for a sister if she couldn't keep her mind focused on Adam and his difficult recovery from a gunshot wound.

"Why didn't you tell me that you were getting married?" Maggie demanded. "When and where did you meet the bounty hunter? Last I heard there were three other suitors on bended knee, trying to get you to agree to marry them."

Julia waved off the rapid-fire questions then grabbed Maggie's hands in her own. Small hands that were devoid of calluses. While Julia jumped in with both feet to assume the duties at their ranch, Sol had forced Maggie to play the genteel hostess and reigning princess at Griffin Ranch.

Of course, that did not imply that Maggie approved of her lot in life. It only meant that Sol held unrealistic expectations for his only daughter and expected her to follow his dictates. Maggie had learned to be discreet and inventive in order to remain true to her nature and her heart's desire.

Julia drew a calming breath and tried to think of a delicate way to tell Maggie what had happened. There wasn't a good way to sugarcoat this disaster so she simply spit it out. "Mags, my brother couldn't meet you this evening because he was bushwhacked."

"Oh, my God!" Maggie gasped as she lurched past Julia to check on Adam.

From out of nowhere Lone Wolf appeared to clutch Maggie's arm and tow her backward. "Adam was seriously wounded," Lone Wolf said gently.

"Oh, God…oh, God," Maggie chanted.

"I'm going to give you the same advice I gave Julia," he hurried on. "Don't fall to pieces in front of a man who's racked with pain and shot to hell. He needs to see optimism, a show of inner strength and encouragement. He needs to see your confidence that he is going to pull through. Can you do that for him?"

Maggie bobbed her head, sniffled, then drew a shaky breath. "You're right, of course. Yes, I can do that. I *have* to see him." She gathered her resolve and stiffened her spine. "I would like to hire you to track down the dastardly man who did this to Adam."

Julia inwardly grimaced as she and Lone Wolf exchanged discreet glances. She did not relish sharing her suspicions with Maggie. Just how did she tell her dearest friend that her father had most likely ordered the execution attempt on Adam?

When Maggie eased open the door to Adam's room, Julia was one step behind her, ready to offer the kind of moral support Lone Wolf had provided for her.

She swore she was viewing her own startled reaction to Adam's fragile condition. It was all there on Maggie's delicate features. The fear, anguish and frustration. She eased down on the edge of the bed to clutch Adam's hand and hold it next to her heart. Then she brought his fingertips to her lips.

"I love you, Adam. More than life itself. I cannot imagine how I could survive without you."

Julia cast Lone Wolf a sidelong glance, noting that he was surveying Maggie intently. When he smiled faintly, Julia frowned, completely bemused. What the devil was he thinking? she wondered. More to the point, what was he *feeling?*

She could have sworn this swarthy bounty hunter had taken one look at Maggie's enchanting face, shapely figure, polished manners and had become bewitched. But his expression seemed to hold something more than masculine approval, which left Julia confused.

Her perplexing thoughts trailed off when Adam's eyes fluttered open. "Mags..." he said raggedly.

"Thank God you're all right," Maggie murmured as she brushed his knuckles against her cheek. "Julia told me what happened."

Not all of it, Julia silently amended. She really was dreading that upcoming conversation.

"You know I can only slip away from home at night," Maggie whispered as she reached out to brush Adam's sandy-blond hair away from his forehead. "But I will be here to check on you every evening until you're back on your feet."

When Adam slumped against the pillow, Maggie's breath caught and she valiantly battled to keep from bursting into sobs. Julia hoisted her to her feet, then steered her onto the terrace.

"I'll make sure you get home safely," Lone Wolf volunteered as he came up behind them. "Adam is getting what he needs to fully recover. Plenty of rest. Julia will see that he follows doctor's orders."

While he shepherded Maggie across the balcony toward the staircase, Julia trailed behind them. A host of insecurities rose inside her when her supposed husband wrapped a protective arm around Maggie's shoulders to guide her down the dark steps. She reminded herself that he had also shown her the same kindness and support while she was distraught.

Just because she had developed an infatuation for Lone Wolf did not imply that he had the slightest romantic interest in her. And just because they had agreed to pretend to be married didn't mean she was more to him than just another paying client.

This was a business arrangement, she told herself as she reversed direction to enter her bedroom. It wasn't his fault that he'd preyed heavily on her mind since the moment she found herself flat on her back, staring up into that rugged, bronzed face.

Julia flounced on her bed and muttered at the confusing jumble of emotions that had hounded her all evening. She shouldn't trust any of these feelings that bombarded her. Adam's attack had put her into a mental confusion and kept her there.

When Lone Wolf had suggested this marriage, she realized it would work to her advantage as well. Everyone in her social circle knew she would inherit a trust fund when she married. That was why she had been inundated with so many proposals. She had given up on finding a man who wanted her simply for who she was on the inside. If spreading the word that she had married Vince Lone Wolf resolved that problem alone, Julia was all in favor of it.

Maggie had dealt with the same influx of proposals and refused to accept any because she had given her heart away years earlier. But at twenty-one Julia hadn't encountered a man who turned her head or piqued her interest. Hadn't found a man she could trust to be honest in his intentions toward her.

Then she had run headlong into Lone Wolf and

known instantly there was something intriguing about him that called out to something inside her. She was physically attracted to him and impressed by him. He made her feel safe, secure and protected in the midst of a storm of turbulence.

Julia rolled to her side and fluffed her pillow. She had never expected to meet a man who didn't have hidden motives, but it was a welcomed change. She had even been so presumptuous to think that Lone Wolf liked her for herself. He had praised her intelligence, her gumption and her spirit.

Then Maggie showed up and all of Julia's insecurities and inadequacies came rushing to the surface, making her outspokenness and unconventional manner glaringly apparent.

Lone Wolf could see for himself that Julia wasn't as appealing as Maggie. Any man could.

Muttering, Julia flopped onto her back and pulled the pillow over her head. Lord, she was such an imbecile for getting sidetracked by these rare feelings that Vince Lone Wolf inspired in her. And it hadn't helped when he had bolted up earlier without a stitch of clothes to pounce on the supposed intruder. Dark though the room had been, Julia had gotten a revealing peek at his masculine body. The shadowed vision dancing in her head refused to go away.

"Stop thinking about that!" Julia muttered under her breath. She had only two objectives, she reminded herself sensibly. One, she had to make certain Adam recovered. Two, she needed to ferret out the sniper to determine if he had any connection to Sol Griffin.

This unexpected attachment to Lone Wolf was the result of distress, roiling emotion and feminine curiosity, she convinced herself. She was simply reaching out to find someone reliable and trustworthy while her world was in upheaval.

She wasn't wasting precious time wondering if Lone Wolf found her lacking and unappealing. She was simply going to shut her eyes and go to sleep so she could be alert and energetic enough to care for Adam.

Her brother needed her. He was all the family she had left and she wouldn't fail him. And that was that.

Lone Wolf slipped silently into Julia's bedroom suite and stopped short when he realized she was asleep in the bed she had assigned to him. Now what was this supposed to imply? he wondered. He stared at her shapely form and the glorious mass of curly blond hair that splayed across the pillow. His fingertips itched to stroke those silky tendrils and he longed for another whiff of her enticing feminine scent.

Was this an unspoken invitation?

Because if it was, she wouldn't have to ask him twice.

Even while his body hardened with anticipation, guilt slammed into him like a freight train. As much as he wanted to slide into bed beside this bewitching, feisty female, the fact that he hadn't been completely honest with her about his motives for a pretend marriage stopped him cold.

This was a woman who valued honesty and trust, he reminded himself. She would be outraged with him if she learned the truth that he had conveniently omitted.

Despite all that, here she was in his assigned bed. There was no denying that he wanted her. What man wouldn't? Julia was full of fire and spirit and she had an irrepressible passion for life that utterly beguiled him. She was every man's secret dream. Even a man who, according to Harvey Fowler, wasn't fit to breathe the same air that she did.

Unfortunately Harvey spoke the truth. Lone Wolf lived in a world where violence was a weekly occurrence. He was used to it, but Julia wasn't. It was plain to see that she had become rattled by her brother's brush with death.

To him it was business as usual.

Which meant they had nothing in common. Plus, she wasn't his type. Hell, he didn't have a type. What he had was the occasional sexual encounter to scratch an itch. It didn't get more complicated than that and it was going to stay that way.

Yet…temptation was right under his nose and tantalizing thoughts of Julia Preston were dancing in his head. Scowling, Lone Wolf braced his hands on the side of the bed and stared at the tormenting vision of beauty, wishing he knew for sure what Julia was doing in his designated bed.

Was it by accident or on purpose?

"Woman, if you are trying to drive me crazy…it's working."

Silently he gathered his hardware and pulled the quilt from the foot of the bed. In one minute he had fashioned a pallet on the floor—directly between Julia and the terrace door. If anyone tried to get to her or Adam they would have to go through him.

And after all, wasn't that his only reason for existence? To resolve other people's problems? Half-breeds had difficulty acquiring respectable jobs. As a bounty hunter and bodyguard, he was a dispensable commodity that protected decent folks from criminal elements of society. He was the last defense between good and evil.

If Julia hadn't needed him to solve her problems she probably wouldn't have given him a second glance. Yet, for a few hours he had felt he belonged somewhere, helping put a family back together after tragedy struck.

This was something different than tracking ruthless murderers and thieves through the wilderness—while trying to avoid getting himself shot in the process.

Lone Wolf rolled onto his side and stared at the bed that had felt so incredibly comfortable earlier. There was a lot to be said for luxury. Even more to be said for snuggling up to the soft feminine body that was just beyond his reach.

Another blast of lust hammered him. He wondered if the self-restraint he had spent thirty-two years perfecting was going to hold up around Julia. Then he asked himself why a woman like her would possibly want a man like him.

She wouldn't, he assured himself realistically. Whatever she was doing in that bed it was not meant to be a subtle invitation, he decided.

Maybe she had tried to wait up for his return to make certain Maggie had gotten home safely and had fallen asleep. Maybe she had simply forgotten that she had offered the suite to him. But whatever the reason, he was going to wait until morning to find out.

In the meantime he had placed himself in the perfect position to protect her from an intruder. Until this feud was resolved, Lone Wolf promised that he was going to be the Prestons' bodyguard and hired gun.

Furthermore, he was not going to forget his place. If

he did, society would certainly remind him of it quick enough. So-called decent folks had been doing it for years. He just hoped Julia could withstand the strain of censure that was sure to come her way because of their pretend marriage.

Another wave of guilt buffeted Lone Wolf. Damn it, he never should have stipulated a pretend marriage, even if it was a practical way to protect Julia and to satisfy his personal vendetta against Sol Griffin.

Lone Wolf made a pact with himself to find another way to protect Julia. He would retract his request come morning. He simply didn't have the heart to seek vindication on Sol at Julia's expense. In addition, Julia needed to know the truth about his connection to Sol. The longer Lone Wolf waited the worse her reaction would be.

He would tell her in the morning, and she would send him packing because of his family ties to her worst enemy.

Lone Wolf cast one last glance at the intriguing woman in bed, sighed in exasperation and told himself to go to sleep. Tomorrow he would be on his way to Colorado and she would find someone else to resolve her problems.

The next morning Julia came slowly awake. She stared up at the overhead canopy—and realized that she had plopped onto her own bed instead of the one in the guest room. Alarmed, she peeked to see if Lone Wolf had assumed she was issuing an invitation for him to sleep with her.

She sagged in relief when she noticed the other side of the bed had not been disturbed.

Tossing back the sheet, she sat up to survey the room. Nothing was out of place and Lone Wolf was nowhere to be found. Julia dressed in her shirt and breeches, then hurried in to check on Adam. She stumbled to a halt when she saw Lone Wolf straddling a chair backward, visiting with Adam, who was propped up on a pile of pillows, sipping coffee. There was a tray of bread and canned peaches beside him. Obviously Lone Wolf had been tending the patient and was taking his duty as bodyguard seriously.

"Morning, sleepyhead," Adam said with a wobbly smile.

She returned her brother's grin, then cast Lone Wolf an awkward glance. His expression was carefully neutral. If he was wondering what she had been doing in the bed she had offered to him it didn't show on his ruggedly handsome face.

"Adam has been giving me more background information on the rift with your neighbor," Lone Wolf remarked. "He agrees that Sol Griffin is the most likely suspect. But we aren't going to limit our search to just him."

"And we aren't going to breathe a word of this to Maggie until we know for certain," Adam declared adamantly. "No sense turning her world upside down until absolutely necessary."

Julia glanced out the window toward Griffin Ranch, which sat in the distance. Her eyes narrowed and she muttered furiously when she spotted a man wearing a long canvas duster and wide-brimmed hat. He had emerged from the shadows of a grove of cedar trees that lined the spring-fed creek on Preston property. Although he was riding a sorrel gelding this time, she suspected he was the same man who had shot Adam.

"He's back. The vulture is probably trying to find out if he managed to kill Adam last night." Julia wheeled around and took off like a shot.

"Damn it, Jules, be careful!" Adam called out hoarsely.

Julia paid him no heed. She was intent on tracking that sidewinder cross-country to see if he headed to Sol Griffin's house. She didn't hear but rather felt Lone Wolf's presence behind her as she bounded down the steps.

"Slow down, woman," Lone Wolf grumbled. "Think. That sniper might be trying to lure *you* out."

"Maybe dashing off half-cocked isn't the wisest course of action," she muttered. "But I want revenge so badly I can almost taste it."

"Back door." He clutched her arm and herded her down the hall. "Better yet, *you* stay here and let *me* track the hombre."

"No, I'm going with you and that's that."

He noted the determined tilt of her chin and remembered that Adam had told him Julia had run wild after their father's death. She had become daring, reckless and impulsive while she dealt with her grief.

Judging by the look on her face, she refused to be frightened off by the thought of personal danger. He'd have to resort to tying her up to prevent her from going with him.

Julia burst ahead of him to lead the way across the back lawn. "I didn't mean to take your bed last night," she blurted out. "Old habit, I guess. Where did you sleep?"

"On the floor so I could keep an eye on you and Adam," he replied as he grabbed her hand and sprinted toward the barn.

To his surprise she didn't bother to saddle a horse, just grabbed a bridle and bit. Lone Wolf was willing to bet this wasn't the first time Julia had galloped off bareback. Not that he minded, of course. He had grown up in a Cheyenne camp, learning to ride expertly at a young age.

He grabbed her reins and led both horses through the back exit of the barn. "We'll circle to the south so our friend won't realize that he's being tracked."

"He's no friend of mine," Julia muttered bitterly. "He and Sol became my sworn enemies when they blew Adam out of the saddle last night."

Lone Wolf winced inwardly. He couldn't delay telling Julia about his connection to Sol Griffin. But considering her present frame of mind, he didn't think *now* would be a good time.

After boosting Julia onto her horse, Lone Wolf swung onto his pinto. Giving Julia a direct order to follow behind him, he headed for the underbrush and willows that lined the creek.

"He's still there," Julia scowled, glaring at the silhouette that lurked in the trees. "Maybe we should just wing him a couple of times then fire a few questions at him."

Lone Wolf swallowed a smile. "Don't you think it would be wiser to figure out if the sniper is working alone first?"

She grumbled sourly, "I suppose you're right."

Julia simmered down a bit as they picked their way along the creek bank. Five minutes later the unidentified rider had disappeared completely from sight.

"There. You see? This is what comes of being cautious," she muttered in disappointment. "He's vanished again."

"But he left tracks," Lone Wolf said encouragingly. "Sometimes that's better than the direct approach."

"I would be a dismal failure in your profession," Julia admitted. "Absolutely no patience."

"Most of the deceased bounty hunters I used to know had the same flaw. This profession separates men from their mistakes. You have to learn to outwait and outwit your quarry." He sent her a pointed glance. "If you can't do that then go home where you should have stayed and let me handle this alone."

She kept quiet while he slid from his horse to study the hoofprints. "He's almost the same size as I am," he informed Julia.

She blinked, baffled. "How do you know that?"

"Depth of the indentation and the stride of the horse. Your horse can manage long strides because of your smaller size. Mine can, too, because I selected this piebald pinto for his muscular strength, stamina and agility. White men don't always take that into consideration."

"You leave nothing to chance, do you? I'm impressed," Julia murmured.

"Don't be. I'm not telling you anything that any self-respecting Cheyenne warrior didn't learn before he was ten years old."

Lone Wolf swung onto his paint pony, then followed the trail that seemed too obvious, what with all the broken branches on small seedlings. The tracks led down to the creek bank, leaving deep indentations in the mud.

Lone Wolf's senses went on alert.

"Trap," he whispered as he snaked out his hand to push Julia down on her horse.

Chapter Five

They barely had time to duck before a bullet whistled past the place where her head had been. The second shot sailed over Lone Wolf's shoulder—missing him by mere inches.

But he found out what he wanted to know.

The sniper wasn't working alone. The second shot had come from a different location in the thick grass that lined the winding creek.

Lone Wolf slapped Julia's horse on the rump, then dug in his heels to send his mount racing back in the direction they had come. Two minutes later they emerged from the creek. Julia looked a mite bewildered. He figured it was the first time someone had taken potshots at her.

It was not *his* first time. He had been a target more times than he cared to count.

"Sol has finally lost his grasp on reality," she said, and gulped. "He was serious when he said that he wanted to wipe the Preston name off the face of the earth. Doesn't he realize that he's going to turn his own daughter against him when she learns the truth?"

"Lesson number two," Lone Wolf murmured as he circled behind a rolling hill for protection. "Do *not* jump to conclusions. We don't have proof that either ambush is tied to your feud with Griffin, no matter how much you might want them to be."

Julia gnashed her teeth. "Easy for you to give him the benefit of the doubt, but not for me. Your brother wasn't warned away from his true love and he didn't get shot. Nor have you been battling rustlers since your father's death. This is another example of Sol trying to make our lives miserable so we'll give up, sell out to him and move away.

"And why are you defending him?" She huffed. "Because you've developed an interest in Maggie?"

Lone Wolf gaped at her in astonishment. "Where in the hell did that come from?"

"Are you saying that you don't find her attractive?" Julia demanded. "That would make you the first man I've met who doesn't."

Obviously getting shot at had rattled Julia more than she realized. This incident was reminiscent of the nightmare that left Adam bedridden. Suddenly she was spouting comments without thinking first, because her emotions were all over the place again.

"Of course I think Maggie is attractive." Lone Wolf chuckled and shook his raven head. "But if you're under the impression that I'm interested in her then you're wrong."

"Am I?" she challenged.

"Yes, you are," he insisted.

He shifted uneasily on horseback and looked away. Julia frowned at his peculiar behavior and wished she knew exactly what he was thinking. But Vince Lone

Wolf was a master of self-disciplined stares that gave away none of his emotions.

"There's something you need to know." He took a deep breath, which made his broad chest expand noticeably. "Sol Griffin is my uncle and Maggie is my first cousin," he said in a hurried rush.

Her mouth dropped open and her eyes popped. "Your *what?*"

Julia had no idea what she had expected him to say, but that wasn't even on the list! Well, that explained a lot. No wonder he was reluctant to pin the shooting on Sol.

She suddenly recalled that Lone Wolf had refused her request for help until *after* he learned that Sol was involved. Alarm flared inside her. "What is this? Some kind of double cross? Are you working with the snipers?"

She recoiled from him, staring at him as if he were a dangerous threat rather than a trusted ally. Her first thought was that he meant to kill her where she sat, and then claim that someone else had attacked her.

Just what was in this for him? she wondered suspiciously. Partial ownership in her ranch after she and Adam were dead?

The frightening realization that this *was* a trap and that Lone Wolf was part of the conspiracy sent adrenaline pumping through her veins. For one wild moment Julia wondered if the reason Lone Wolf had volunteered to accompany Maggie home last night was so he could consult privately with Sol.

Dear God, she thought frantically. They were in cahoots and she had blundered headlong into disaster.

Instinct demanded that she run for her life before

Lone Wolf grabbed his pistol and aimed it at her. Frightened, Julia took off like a rocket, using the technique of sprawling atop her horse to reduce her chances of being shot.

"Damn it, Julia," he growled as he chased after her.

She cursed him back as she rode hell-for-leather toward the safety of home. He intended to betray her, she thought mutinously. The one man she thought was different from the rest of his gender. The one man who aroused her interest without trying. The man she had decided to pretend was her husband. The first man she wasn't averse to having underfoot because she actually liked and respected him.

Curse it, she would never trust her judgment of men again!

Julia scowled when she heard the thunder of hooves close behind her. Swift as her mount was, it was no match for the powerful black-and-white paint gelding and its exceptionally skilled rider. Julia shrieked in alarm when Lone Wolf clamped his hand around her forearm. Before she could fight back he snatched her off her horse while at full canter and she found herself suspended in midair momentarily.

Her breath gushed from her lips when he clutched her against his muscular body. Julia squirmed defiantly while he forced her to straddle his thighs. She stared at the traitor face-to-face and wished him a fast trip to perdition.

"Simmer down," he snapped as he reined his pinto to a walk.

"Like hell I will!" She spit the words at him and struggled valiantly for release—for all the good it did.

"Didn't I just get through telling you not to jump to conclusions? Lesson number two, remember?"

Her gaze filleted him and he reciprocated in kind. She decided that when Lone Wolf was irate he could be very intimidating. He looked ominous and foreboding, just as he had last night when he'd yanked her off her horse and followed her to the ground to lay a knife at her throat.

The mistaken sense of security and comfort that she felt when she was with him shattered in the face of his thunderous scowl and the unyielding hold he had on her. The man certainly made a frightening enemy, she decided.

Julia knew she was as good as dead, because Lone Wolf had to be in a league with Sol. Her bitter neighbor was going to win this feud and his gun-toting nephew would make sure of it.

"You tricked me," she said furiously. "You *used* me. And when you kill me I will find a way to come back and haunt you for the rest of your days—"

To her astounded amazement he angled his head and kissed her. To shut her up, no doubt. He couldn't use his hand to cover her mouth because both arms were clamped around her waist to hold her still. So he kissed her. Hard.

Stole her breath out of her lungs was more accurate. He crushed her so tightly against him that she couldn't move. He kept on devouring her lips—and any woman with a lick of sense in her head would have continued to resist. Instead she melted against his powerful body and focused on the tantalizing taste of him, the unexpected pleasure that unfurled inside her.

She blamed her impulsive response on the emotional carousel her life had become. Plus, no man had ever dared to grab her and kiss her breathless, for fear of offending her and losing the potential meal ticket she represented. But Lone Wolf was nothing if not bold and daring and she had witnessed several examples of those dominant traits during their short acquaintance.

When he finally allowed her to come up for air she swore her eyes had crossed and he had robbed her of the ability to speak and think straight. She simply stared at him—at his sensuous mouth, to be specific—and wondered why she wanted him to kiss her like that again.

Obviously she had gone crazy. It was the only explanation for wanting to kiss a man who had turned out to be her worst enemy.

"Don't make me do that again, Julia," he growled at her.

Something fragile and unfamiliar that had just burst to life inside her—some unique sensation she couldn't adequately identify—died a quick death. He was letting her know straight away that he had only kissed her to silence her…and nothing more. It wasn't personal.

Curse the man! He was crushing to her feminine pride.

When he lifted his hand to curl it around her throat she wondered if he had decided to choke her instead of shoot her. But his fingers didn't close viciously around her windpipe. He simply tilted her head back so he could stare her squarely in the eyes.

"Are you listening now?" he asked gruffly. "No thinking allowed. No presumptions, either, wildcat. Just listen."

"Answer one question first," she muttered rebelliously. "Do you plan to kill me when you're through talking? If so, I want to have the last word instead of hearing your lies."

Lone Wolf sighed audibly. A *handful* did not begin to describe this high-strung, headstrong woman. She was sassy and defiant and kissing her into silence had been a bad idea.

He had enjoyed it too damn much.

He had been afraid that would be the case.

Sure enough, one taste of her and he had wanted much more. He had been a little rough and greedy and he sincerely regretted that. But she was completely mistaken if she thought that was the kiss of a man who wanted her dead.

What he wanted was to have her beneath him, to be inside her…and if she couldn't feel his arousal then she wasn't paying attention.

And damn it, this was not a good time for him to discover that his reaction to Julia was not something easily controlled or ignored.

"I'm not trying to kill you, although you're going to manage that feat by yourself if you go haring off like you tried to do earlier," he snapped, angry with himself for being so vulnerable to this woman. He had spent years teaching himself to be invincible. And poof! This five-foot-nothing female got to him in every way imaginable. "I'm trying to keep you alive, but you have to cooperate!"

Her reply was a disbelieving snort.

"If you think I have an allegiance to my uncle then you are very much mistaken." He nudged his horse forward to retrieve Julia's mount, which had stopped to graze a few yards away.

He deposited her on her horse. "I didn't tell you about my kinship to the Griffins right off because I figured you would overreact." He stared meaningfully at her. "The way you are overacting now."

"So you waited until I actually began to trust you," she accused harshly. "And here I thought you were different from other men. Obviously you're all the same—devious and manipulative."

Lone Wolf hadn't intended to go into detail about his history with Sol, but Julia was staring at him with those luminous green eyes that reflected hurt, betrayal and indignation. He couldn't bear that, not from her.

Sappy fool that he had suddenly become, he longed to see the look of trust and approval again. It had made him feel good about himself, made him feel worthy of respect. Now he felt as if he had lost something precious and unique and he instinctively struggled to regain whatever it was about Julia that lured him to her against his will.

Whatever the hell it was, he was glad that he had the good sense not to examine it too closely.

"My mother was Sol's younger sister. Her name was Isabella," he elaborated as he rode toward the barn. "She was captured by a Southern Cheyenne raiding party when she was sixteen."

"Your mother was Sol's sister?" She stared owlishly at him, as if having trouble accepting the notion.

"Yes," he affirmed solemnly. "My father became intrigued by my mother and he took her as his wife. She adopted his culture and made a place for herself with the Cheyenne. I believe that she was happy with him."

Julia listened intently, apparently waiting for him to continue. He was relieved to note that she had set aside her anger and frustration—temporarily at least.

"One winter, when George Custer was just a colonel, trying to make a name for himself as a soldier, he attacked our encampment on the Washita River in Indian Territory," Lone Wolf informed her. "He massacred our people, women and children included. First I watched my father and Chief Black Kettle die, then my mother, who wasn't far behind because she had found a safe hiding place for me in the underbrush."

Julia's heart went out to Lone Wolf. She knew how it felt to watch someone you loved being shot down. But she could only begin to imagine the extent of anguish he had suffered. The nightmare of watching his family and friends being murdered must have been devastating.

"I'm sure what you felt was even more horrible than the feelings that bombarded me after losing my father, only four years after Mama's passing," she murmured. "I was angry, lost and disoriented. I fiercely denied the scandalous report of Papa's secret liaison with Rachel Griffin because it felt like a betrayal to my mother."

"Grief makes you say and feel crazy things," Lone Wolf agreed. "It's hard to know what you're supposed to feel."

Julia gave a self-deprecating smirk. "It definitely made *me* go a little crazy. I tried to outrun everything by throwing myself into duties on the ranch. I was willing to try anything, no matter how dangerous or unladylike. Anything to keep my mind occupied and hold all those hounding emotions at bay."

Lone Wolf nodded in understanding as he stared into the distance, as if looking through a portal in time. Julia saw his jaw clench, noticed his fist knot around the reins. Although he usually appeared calm and unflappable she could tell that the tragedy of his youth still affected him deeply.

"My mother survived her wounds for a few hours

after the soldiers rode away." His voice was brisk and clipped. "She insisted that I leave the reservation and make use of the fact that she had taught me to speak fluent English and that I was half white.

"I wasn't sure that I wanted to abandon my people and the only way of life I understood," he admitted. "But I had lost all family ties in that brutal massacre. I got to thinking that anywhere had to be better than living in that valley of death and walking over those graves."

His mouth twisted in bitter irony. "At least Custer paid dearly for his unprovoked attack on our camp. The surviving Cheyenne put a curse on him and chanted to the guiding spirits to give them revenge. To this day our people swear it was that curse that led Custer into disaster at the hands of the Sioux and the Northern Cheyenne at the Battle of Little Bighorn."

"Where did you go after the massacre?" Julia asked gently. "You couldn't have been but a young teenager when this happened."

"I was fourteen," he reported. "My mother made me promise that I would find her brother in Kansas and ask him to take me in. It was her dying wish that I unite with her white family and make a fresh new start in life."

Julia watched his countenance change to an expression of resentment and torment. She knew what he was going to say even before he told her what happened. "Sol rejected you."

He nodded stiffly. "I went to him, carrying the heart-shaped necklace my mother always wore as proof of my ancestry. I told my uncle that my mother had died trying to protect me and that she sent me to him for help."

Lone Wolf scoffed sourly. "Sol was outraged that I

had the nerve to show my face on his ranch. He shouted me off his property and told me not to come back. He said he wanted nothing to do with 'the spawn of a savage.' He swore that if I tried to make contact with him, his wife or his infant daughter that I would end up dead like the rest of my clan."

Julia reached out to comfort him, as he had comforted her in her hour of need. She wasn't sure he even noticed her hand folding consolingly around his rigid forearm.

"I had no choice but to live off the land like a scavenger," he went on bitterly. "Without my training with the Cheyenne I would have starved to death. I didn't want to go back to the confinement of the reservation. I couldn't bear to come face-to-face with the grief and torment all over again, either."

His expression turned as hard as granite. "I survived like a wild animal, if only to infuriate and defy Sol Griffin with my very existence. For those first three years I lived for no other purpose than to show Sol that he could deny me, but I was out there somewhere, waiting for the right moment to make his life as miserable as he made mine."

Julia groaned inwardly at the thought of a young boy growing up so alone, alienated and cruelly discarded.

"I trained myself to be tough and competent enough with every weapon so I could withstand the ridicule and defend myself when I reentered white society."

He laughed humorlessly as he glanced at Julia. "The irony of all this is that instead of heading west I decided to headquarter in this particular area. When I came here eight years ago, Dodge City was a fledgling town that had sprung up around the buffalo-hide business.

"Criminals showed up to rob and swindle traders and merchants and I was sent to track them down. I made plenty of money because business was brisk. But deep down inside I knew the reason I set up camp here was to let Sol know that I was never so far away that he could forget I existed. I wanted to be the ever-present thorn in his side."

Julia smiled faintly. She could understand Lone Wolf's need to prove himself to the world—to Sol in particular. He never wanted Sol to forget the injustice and rejection.

Julia didn't blame him one bit. She figured she would be tempted to do the same thing.

"As much as Sol hates me for who and what I am, he and Maggie are my only family link. I'm not sure why that seems important to me, because I still want to be the reminder to Sol that he might have run me off but he will never be rid of me."

"You were pulled in two directions at once," she murmured pensively.

"Yes," he said, and managed a slight smile. "Strange how the need to belong is so hard to overcome. But I have had a small measure of revenge over the years. My reputation with a gun offers the kind of intimidation Sol once used to run me off. I'm no longer that half-starved, gangly kid who came looking for protection, only to encounter hatred and rejection."

Julia disliked Sol Griffin more with each passing minute. Only a man without a heart or conscience could be so cruel as to turn his back on his long-lost sister's son.

A shadow of doubt suddenly crossed her mind. She wondered if Sol's wife *had* sought out Julia's father for comfort and passion. Maybe Sol's inherent bitterness had driven Rachel into the arms of another man. What if her father had stolen another man's wife? The possibility forced Julia to question her steadfast belief that her father and Rachel hadn't turned to each other to appease their loneliness.

"Meeting Maggie was an unexpected pleasure," Lone Wolf remarked as he drew his steed to a halt near the rear entrance to the barn. "I can see some of my mother's physical characteristics in Maggie."

So that's why Lone Wolf had looked Maggie over so carefully, Julia realized. He had noticed a family resemblance, felt a connection that he had been deprived of for years on end.

"The next part of the story isn't much easier to tell," Lone Wolf said, his eyes moving away from her inquisitive stare. "While it's true that our pretend marriage will offer you protection and hopefully complicate Sol's attempt to overtake your ranch, you need to know that I have an ulterior motive. I've been feeling as guilty as hell about it, too."

Julia realized what he meant before he had a chance to explain. Instead of being insulted she chuckled, which must have surprised him because he did a double take.

"You sly devil," she teased. "I can see why using a pretend marriage to confound Sol was too good for you to pass up. What better way to get Sol's goat than to supposedly marry his enemy."

"It's more than that," Lone Wolf admitted as he dismounted. "It is also meant to assure him that even though he rejected me, *you* consider me good enough to marry."

Julia stared down at his chiseled features, noting a hint of vulnerability, a need to be accepted. She wanted to curse Sol soundly for making his nephew feel unwanted, unloved and forcing him into emotional isolation.

Furthermore, she didn't have the heart to hold a grudge against Lone Wolf because of his hidden motive. She suspected that she would have done the same thing. She had a fierce craving for revenge herself, so who was she to judge him?

This was just one more reason for Julia to detest Sol Griffin. What a shame that Maggie might have to suffer for her father's many sins. Like Lone Wolf, Maggie was a victim of circumstances beyond her control. To hurt Sol would inflict pain on Maggie. She would be left twisting in the wind, torn between her love for Adam and her feelings of obligation to her father.

Julia's thoughts trailed off when Lone Wolf lifted her from the horse and set her to her feet. She peered up at him, understanding him, sympathizing with him, caring about him in a way she had never cared about those pretentious fortune hunters who tried to charm her into marriage.

Yes, Lone Wolf wanted to use her to infuriate Sol Griffin. And yes, his motivation was a bit self-serving. But then, so was hers, she mused. Lone Wolf was risking his life to protect her and Adam. Already Lone Wolf had been shot at because of his association with her. Plus, he was in double jeopardy because of his previous clash with Sol.

"I should have been completely honest with you at the start," he said as he stepped away. "A pretend marriage is still an effective solution to complicate Sol's plans, if he is indeed responsible for the ambushes." He smiled wryly. "The fact that I am your hired gun and supposed husband will serve to focus his anger on me. If we're lucky, news will reach Sol soon and he will decide to deal directly with me, once and for all."

Impulsively Julia laid her hands against the solid wall of his chest. She pushed up on tiptoe and gave him quick, smacking kiss. She rather liked that she surprised him and left him blinking at her in amazement.

"What was that for?"

He backed away from her, placing a respectable distance between them, as if to remind her that their association wasn't personal.

Fighting feelings of rejection, Julia shrugged and glanced away so he wouldn't notice her hurt expression. "Sorry, I simply got carried away. As for your dealings with your uncle, I don't begrudge you the chance to annoy him with our marriage charade. You deserve your own vindication."

Leading the way into the barn, they returned the horses to their stalls. Then they headed toward the house. "We need to inform Adam of our wedding plans before we ride into town to notify the sheriff of the ambush attempts."

"Your brother isn't going to approve," Lone Wolf predicted as he fell into step beside her.

"Adam is in no condition to object, but I will make him understand this is necessary." She halted on the front steps then turned to him. "Just one thing."

He arched a thick black brow. "What's that?"

"From this moment forward I want you to be completely honest with me. Understood? I would like to think there is one man, aside from my brother, that I can trust implicitly. Deal?"

He cocked his head. "Even if the truth isn't always what you want to hear?"

"Even if," she insisted before she pivoted around and hiked up the steps. "I never again want to doubt that I can trust you with my life… and everything else."

"Everything else? Like what?" he questioned.

My heart, if I'm not careful. But I hope it won't come to that.

"Julia?" he prodded. "Your life and what else?"

"My brother's life, of course," she said evasively. "He's all I have and I don't want to lose him."

And she was going to make sure Adam was safe and protected, she vowed. At least Adam was going to find happiness. Somehow she was going to see to it that Adam and Maggie were allowed to marry instead of sneaking around to be together.

Sol Griffin was not going to stand between two people who had been in love for more than half their lives, not if Julia had anything to say about it.

And she intended to have plenty to say about it!

Chapter Six

"Well? Did you track down that bushwhacker?" Adam asked the moment Lone Wolf and Julia came through the bedroom door.

"No, it was a trap." Julia sank down on the edge of the bed to lay her hand on Adam's forehead. "Still feverish. You should try to sleep."

Adam's eyes widened in alarm. "Are you telling me that the sniper shot at *you,* too?"

Once again, Lone Wolf witnessed a display of fierce devotion between brother and sister. Adam didn't like knowing that his sister had been in harm's way.

Lone Wolf wondered how it would feel to have someone in his life that cared so much about him.

"Missed us by a mile," Julia said with a dismissive flick of her wrist.

Adam slumped against the pillows. "That's a relief."

Lone Wolf's brows jackknifed. Missed them by a mile? Hell! It was a wonder they didn't have new parts in their hair. Obviously Julia had taken him very seriously when he advised her to project a positive attitude in Adam's presence.

Julia handed her brother a cup of water, then shoved a teaspoon of laudanum against his lips. "Lone Wolf and I have a plan," she declared.

Adam made a face and swallowed the sedative. "What plan?"

"If Lone Wolf is not only our bodyguard and detective, but also my husband then Sol won't think he can get his hands on our property, even if he gets rid of us."

"Husband?" Adam croaked, frog eyed.

"Pretend husband," Lone Wolf quickly inserted then stared curiously at Julia.

What was she trying to do? Give her brother apoplexy on top of all else?

"We will plant the rumor of a marriage and make Sol believe it," Lone Wolf explained. "Considering my reputation as a shootist, he might think twice about trying to pick all three of us off. He certainly has more than one reason to believe that I would come after him, especially if something happened to my new wife."

"What other reason?" Adam questioned, puzzled.

Julia sent Lone Wolf a glance that said, *We'll get into that some other time.*

"What he meant was that going up against a gunfighter with his reputation would not bode well for Sol," Julia interjected as she tucked the sheet around her brother's shoulders. "We can discuss this in detail later. You look worn out, big brother."

Adam sighed heavily. "I can't stay awake for more than ten minutes without feeling exhausted." He looked worriedly at Lone Wolf. "Are you sure a pretend wedding is the best way to handle this feud with Sol?"

"Absolutely," Julia inserted confidently. "Lone Wolf would actually be doing me a favor. You know I'm fed up with marriage proposals aimed to latch onto my trust fund and partial ownership in our ranch."

Julia blinked, suddenly distracted by an inspiration that bombarded her thoughts. She wondered how Lone Wolf would react to the unexpected request she decided to make when they were alone.

"I thought you *enjoyed* rejecting all those pretentious fortune hunters," Adam said, dragging Julia back into the conversation.

"No more than Maggie does," she said pointedly.

The comment wiped the teasing smile off Adam's ashen lips in nothing flat. His face scrunched up in a scowl. "I'd like to marry Maggie in secret. That would put a stop to Sol's attempts to handpick her husband."

"If Sol found out about it, you might become the victim of another sniper attack before you recover your strength and can fight back," Lone Wolf remarked. "Then half this ranch would probably wind up under Sol's control. You and Julia seem to think that laying claim to this property is his ultimate objective. I'm the outsider here, the wild card that he can't trump. In addition, the sheriff is my business acquaintance. If something happens to me he will come looking for answers."

Adam nodded pensively. "Are you going to report our suspicions about the bushwhackings to the sheriff?"

"Yes. That's where I'm headed next," Lone Wolf assured him. "Since I'm working for you, I also need to return the bench warrants to Sheriff Danson. He will have to find someone else to track the band of thieves that headed for the Colorado hills."

Lone Wolf could tell that Adam was quickly losing ground. His eyelids were at half-mast and his shoulders sagged noticeably. Plus, what little color he had regained in his face was fading fast.

"Just rest, Adam," Julia insisted as she patted his hand comfortingly. "Lone Wolf and I will take care of everything. Maggie promised to return after dark to check on you. I'm sure you wouldn't want to sleep through her evening visit."

She barely got out the comment before Adam's eyes drifted shut and his chin sagged against his chest. She smiled affectionately as she traced his pallid features. "A pity, isn't it, that Adam never had eyes for anyone but his worst enemy's daughter? Why does life have to be so messy and complicated?"

"I don't know…it just is," Lone Wolf said cynically. "It has never been anything but an uphill battle with live ammunition coming at you from every direction at once."

"I couldn't have put it better myself," she said as she came to her feet. "Since Papa died and this feud with Sol erupted, nothing has been easy. There was no time to grieve, just dive into taking charge of the ranch and uphold my share of the responsibility."

She smiled ruefully. "Plus, I lost constant contact with my best friend. We needed each other when the world came crashing down on both of us." Julia frowned, disgruntled. "I can tell you for certain that I would be a lot happier if Maggie wasn't Sol's daughter."

"I'm not the least bit pleased to be his nephew," Lone Wolf muttered on his way out the door. "Too damn bad that you can't pick and chose your kinfolk…."

His voice dried up when he heard footsteps echoing on the stairs. His gaze narrowed on the well-dressed

man who had arrived unexpectedly. Lone Wolf esti-
mated that the visitor was three or four years his senior.
Obviously the man hadn't led the rough-and-tumble
life that was Lone Wolf's existence.

"Julia, I came as soon as I heard the news," the man
said as he reached the head of the steps. Obviously he
wasn't in peak physical condition because he grabbed
hold of the banister for support and huffed and puffed
for breath.

His disapproving regard landed squarely on Lone
Wolf who returned the look with equal distaste. This
gent was much too delicate looking and self-important
for his tastes. The sooner he left the better Lone Wolf
was going to like it.

"I've seen you around town," the man wheezed.
"Aren't you—?"

"He's my husband," Julia broke in as she curled her
hand around Lone Wolf's elbow. "Thomas Whittaker,
this is Vince Lone Wolf. Thomas is our family lawyer.
He has been managing our business affairs since before
we lost Papa."

"Your *husband?*" Thomas chirped, goggle-eyed.

"Yes," Julia confirmed. "And I do wish everyone I
tell wouldn't look so surprised. I am well pleased with
my choice. I have rejected my share of offers that did
not suit me. I know precisely when one does and this is
it."

Whittaker didn't extend his hand in greeting. Neither
did Lone Wolf. He suspected Whittaker had a personal
interest in Julia and that he was dismayed by the news
of her wedding. Of course, what would-be suitor would
be pleased to learn that this wealthy beauty was off the
marriage market?

"When did the nuptials take place?" Thomas questioned, his attention bouncing back and forth between husband and wife.

He looked as if were trying to picture them as a couple and found the prospect inconceivable. The disdainful glare directed at Lone Wolf implied that he was nowhere near good enough for Julia. But Lone Wolf was accustomed to condescension.

It had ceased to disturb him years ago.

"Actually we were married last night." Julia smiled so brilliantly that Lone Wolf swore he had been momentarily blinded. "Vince was so very supportive when Adam was wounded. He suggested that we postpone the wedding, but I insisted on holding the ceremony after Adam's condition stabilized."

"Adam approves of this match?" Thomas asked doubtfully as he paced back and forth in front of them, then pulled his watch from his vest pocket to check the time.

"Oh, yes," Julia gushed enthusiastically. "He met Vince a year ago and he was as impressed by him as I was."

Thomas's frown deepened as he snapped the elaborate gold timepiece shut. "Just how long have you two known each other?"

"Six months." To make a convincing show of affection, Lone Wolf curled his arm possessively around her waist then dropped a kiss to the crown of her curly reddish-gold head.

"*Where* did you meet?" Thomas grilled him intensely as he went back to pacing, as if striding back and forth in front of a witness on the stand in court. "No offense intended—"

No offense intended, my ass, Lone Wolf thought.

"—but *that* sort of information would have circulated on the grapevine of gossip in town."

When Julia peered up at Lone Wolf from beneath that thick fringe of long lashes and flashed him a dazzling smile, he swore his knees turned to jelly. Good Lord, she was breathtaking. If he wasn't careful he could get lost in those sea-green eyes and forget where he was. How was he supposed to remain distant and standoffish while playing this charade for Whittaker's benefit?

Damn, he couldn't afford to get too attached to Julia. For her sake, as well as his own, he had to seal off his emotions, just as he had when he lost his parents.

"Really, Thomas," she said, shifting her attention to the brown-haired gent. "There is no need for this third-degree interrogation. You sound like a lawyer."

"I *am* a lawyer," he huffed as he went back to his pacing.

"But you are first and foremost a family friend. And as a friend I will confide that the first time I met Vince he took my breath away."

Lone Wolf swallowed a snicker. That wasn't exactly a lie, he supposed. He had mistakenly jerked Julia off her horse and pinned her to the ground so quickly that it had knocked the breath clean out of her.

"When I looked up at him for the first time, I must confess that he demanded my complete attention and I couldn't see past him."

Of course, she couldn't. He had been right in her face—with a dagger at her throat. That would nab anyone's attention pretty damn quickly.

"And do not spread this around town, Thomas," she

insisted confidentially, "but we have been meeting secretly each time Vince returned from an assignment."

Lone Wolf wasn't sure what prompted him to make another possessive display of bussing a kiss over her cheek. Maybe it was to stake his imaginary claim on Julia. Maybe it was because she made their pretend marriage sound like the perfect fairy tale and he wanted to be a part of it. For a few moments at least.

Whatever the case, he went so far as to brush the pad of his thumb over her lush bottom lip. He had the wildest urge to kiss her, right there and then, too. Not the way he had earlier, but slowly, thoroughly and gently. He felt the overwhelming need to compensate for his forceful attempt to quiet her down so she'd listen to what he had to tell her.

"And I'm crazy about Julia," he murmured huskily. "Maybe the rest of the world thinks I don't deserve her, but I'm bewitched to the point that I don't care."

Then he yielded to the reckless impulse and pressed his lips to hers while the disapproving lawyer watched. He felt Julia tense up momentarily but, impressive little actress that she'd turned out to be, she melted against him and kissed him back. She even draped her arms around his shoulders and hugged him close.

For one dizzying moment Lone Wolf forgot that he was putting on an act to convince the family attorney that he was hopelessly devoted to Julia. He simply savored the intoxicating taste of her. He wished he *did* believe in fairy tales and that she could be part of his life long enough for him to discover if there *was* something that he had been missing the past decade.

"Ahem."

Lone Wolf raised his head to see Whittaker glaring

reproachfully at him. Better men than this dandified gent had glared reproachfully at him for years on end. But this was the first time Lone Wolf could honestly say that he had enjoyed annoying so-called decent folks.

Ordinarily he just didn't give a damn.

"Oh, sorry." Julia tried to look properly embarrassed as she licked her lips and rubbed sensuously against him.

The gesture made Lone Wolf groan in unfulfilled torment.

Hell! He was really getting carried away with this charade. This was make-believe and Julia was playing along to add credence to their pretend affection that had resulted in marriage. That was the beginning and end of their association, he reminded himself sternly. Wishful thinking would only complicate their lives. They were too different, and getting lost in the feel of her tantalizing body and inviting lips would only bring him torment.

"Yes, well, I'm obviously interrupting so I will be on my way to see Adam," Whittaker mumbled as he retrieved his watch again, checked the time then repocketed the fancy timepiece.

When he tried to veer around Julia, she clutched the sleeve of his expensive pin-striped jacket to waylay him. "Adam is asleep and I don't want to disturb him. I'll tell him that you dropped by."

Whittaker pivoted on his spindly legs and tossed Lone Wolf another disparaging glance as he passed.

"Now that I have met the criteria of the trust fund that my maternal grandfather left for me, I will stop by your office sometime soon," Julia remarked. "Please have the papers ready for me to sign."

"What?" He jerked his attention from Lone Wolf to Julia. "Yes, of course, the trust fund. I'll take care of it," he murmured before he hurried down the steps.

Lone Wolf frowned as the lawyer scuttled through the door and out of earshot. "You got a little carried away with that last part," he chided. "Don't you actually have to be married with the certificate in hand to collect your trust?"

"Oh dear, did I forget to mention there was just one *small catch* in our arrangement?" She grinned mischievously when his eyes narrowed warily. "This marriage will have to be legal. I want control of the trust so I can cover the losses from rustling that have cut into our profits."

"When did you arrive at that conclusion?" he choked out.

"The inspiration struck while we were talking to Adam a few minutes ago," she informed him. "I decided to resolve another problem facing us right now. A shortage of funds."

"This is not as simple as marriage and divorce arrangements in the Cheyenne culture," he reminded her. "A woman has only to invite a man into her tepee and announce that they are married. If she wants a divorce she simply tosses his belongings through the flap and that is the end of their union."

"I think I like the Cheyenne approach," Julia said. "No fuss. I especially like the fact that the choice is up to the woman." She frowned unhappily. "I think I was born into the wrong culture and probably two decades ahead of my time."

He waved off her sassy comments. "I'm serious, Julia. Getting a divorce isn't simple or readily accepted by whites. I'm not sure this is a good idea."

She cocked her head and studied him curiously. "Have you had a better marriage offer?"

"No, I haven't proposed to anyone. Hadn't planned to. And I have never been proposed *to,* either."

"Well, I have," she replied. "I rejected all the others because I had more to lose and my suitors had much to gain. Furthermore, even if you and I are married, I won't make any unreasonable demands on you. Naturally, you will be free to come and go as you please after Adam is back on his feet and we apprehend whoever is responsible for the shooting. I think this is a convenient solution that resolves several problems effectively and I intend to follow through with it."

Lone Wolf curled his forefinger beneath her chin. "I think," he said very deliberately, "that the turmoil surrounding your brother's injury has skewed your ability to reason. You don't want to be legally married to a man like me. You can toss my belongings on the front lawn at some point in the future and I will take the hint to skedaddle and never come back. But in the white culture we will still be married." He studied her intently. "What if you meet someone and decide you want to spend the rest of your life with him?"

I think I already have, she thought as she stared at his striking features and got sidetracked by those intense hazel eyes. "I'm twenty-one years old, Lone Wolf. I have been courted for four years and I have yet to encounter a man who meets my expectations." *Except for you,* she tacked on silently.

Julia continued. "This is a practical solution, especially since we will have to enter and exit my bedroom to keep up appearances. Servants gossip, you know. They also gab to servants in other households. If we aren't sharing the same room then eventually word will spread and Sol will become suspicious."

Lone Wolf frowned curiously. "What if the time comes when you decide you want a child?"

"Then that obligation will fall to you," she replied.

She stifled a gurgle of laughter when he stared at her as if she had two heads—neither of which was equipped with a brain.

"Do you find that prospect distasteful?" she challenged.

"Hell, no, but…" His voice fizzled out and he angled his dark head to stare suspiciously at her. "Why do I get the feeling that I'm missing something here?"

She shrugged nonchalantly and said, "Because you are." Julia broke into a smile, delighted that she had the chance to toss his words back in his face. "Smart man that you are, I'm sure you'll figure this out soon enough."

She pivoted toward her room. "I'll go change so we can contact the sheriff and take care of the marriage license."

Julia snickered as she closed the door behind her. The stunned expression on Lone Wolf's face was priceless. She knew he wasn't a man who was surprised very often. In his line of work he was accustomed to contemplating every possibility and angle. It was immensely gratifying to know that she had managed to shock him by announcing her stipulation.

She peeled off her shirt and breeches, and then she winced when she realized that *she* had manipulated Lone Wolf into a marriage he didn't want or need. But since he hadn't objected too strenuously she suspected he saw this as an official method of infuriating his uncle.

In addition, the citizens of Dodge City who treated Lone Wolf like a second-class citizen needed to know that Julia didn't share their ridiculous belief that the boundaries of social classes were not to be breached. It also annoyed Julia that Lone Wolf was one of the main reasons dangerous criminals had been brought to justice and decent folks could safely walk the streets.

Why were people so reluctant to acknowledge that?

Besides his contributions to safeguarding society, he was also an honorable man with a conscience and a good heart. It tormented Julia to no end that he'd been rejected by his white family and left to fend for himself at a young age.

She wanted it known that she was nothing like Sol or the other self-important socialites in Dodge who didn't treat Lone Wolf with the respect and consideration he truly deserved.

If nothing else, Julia was going to return the tremendous favor the bounty hunter was doing for her family. He was placing himself in the line of fire to protect Adam and the ranch. That counted for a great deal in her book and she appreciated the gesture.

If she was going to take a husband then it would be a man she could admire and respect. In addition, she could look forward to not being hounded by more fortune hunters, who offended her with their hidden agendas.

Plus, after that incredibly amazing kiss he had bestowed on her for Thomas Whittaker's benefit, she had discovered what physical desire felt like…and she wanted more. Even if Lone Wolf was reluctant to pursue the attraction she felt for him.

A warm tingle skittered down her spine as she fastened her gown. She definitely had met a man who inspired unfamiliar longing inside her. She was beginning to understand the emotions and sensations her brother and Maggie shared. She had just discovered that she had been missing something intense and overpowering.

Julia twisted her hair atop her head in a fashionable coiffure, then stared critically at her reflection in the mirror. Did Lone Wolf find her the least bit desirable? She doubted any man would turn down an invitation to intimacy, but could he really care for her? Or would it matter which woman was in his arms?

Wheeling away from the mirror, Julia told herself that her decision to make the marriage legal was for her benefit. It was also sensible and practical. Given her suspicions toward Sol, the complication of Maggie caught in the middle of this feud and Adam's weakened condition, this wasn't the time to stew about whether Lone Wolf might actually like her to the same degree that she had come to like him.

"First and foremost this is a business arrangement," she reminded herself as she padded barefoot across the room to retrieve her kid boots.

Just because she could easily fall for Lone Wolf was not his problem. She was not going to make it his problem, either. There was no rule stating that when a woman stumbled upon a man she found fascinating and arousing that he had to return those feelings. In fact, Lone Wolf usually made it a point to keep his distance, refusing to let himself become physically or emotionally involved.

Always the detached professional, she mused, disappointed. However, she understood that she and Lone Wolf had enough on their plates. He was strapped with the difficult job of bodyguard, while collecting evidence that would identify the mastermind behind the attacks. As for Julia, she needed to concentrate on caring for Adam and keep her eyes peeled so she could locate that elusive bushwhacker.

While Julia was getting dressed, Lone Wolf stood in the hall, trying to figure out what the hell had just happened. Had Julia Preston, who could wed any man she chose, just proposed to him? Had she just asked him to father her child when she decided to start a family? Was she insane?

Never mind that both prospects flattered and appealed to him. That wasn't the point. And even though he had never considered marriage, this feisty, intelligent female would be his first choice.

That was also beside the point.

How could a real marriage be good for her? Certainly, she would acquire her trust fund—however much that was—but she would also acquire a husband who was considered a social outcast by her friends and acquaintances in polite society.

Flustered, Lone Wolf wheeled toward Adam's room then eased open the door. "Good. You're awake."

Adam blinked groggily as he massaged his shoulder. "I hate that laudanum. Makes me feel like I have cobwebs in my head and cotton in my mouth." He gestured toward the glass of water on the nightstand. "Could you grab that for me? And what's going on? I thought you were headed to town."

"We're leaving after Julia changes clothes," he replied.

Adam frowned worriedly. "Damn, Lone Wolf, you look rattled. What's wrong?"

"Nothing much." Lone Wolf handed Adam the glass. "Except that your sister is insane."

A grin crinkled Adam's waxen features. "I tried to warn you about her. She's headstrong and willful. Papa doted on her and I wasn't much better after she became my responsibility. Neither of us had the heart to break her spirit. I learned years ago that, whatever his reason, God made my sister unique. Whatever she's done to rattle you is just *Julia being Julia.*"

Adam took a sip of water. "Save yourself some time and frustration and simply accept that fact. It will make your life a lot easier."

"Are you saying she's a hopeless cause?" Lone Wolf asked in amusement as he strode over to retrieve the saddlebags he had stashed in the corner that morning.

Adam grinned. "Pretty much. Fortunately she seems to like you reasonably well so maybe she'll go easy on you." His expression turned somber. "I can't bear the thought of seeing Julia hurt. She's my sister and I feel responsible for her. I can't even imagine a world without Julia in it."

Lone Wolf couldn't either and that was starting to bother him. A lot.

"When Sol sent Maggie to Saint Louis to keep her away from me, it was Julia who made the loneliness bearable. Sometimes I think she purposely threw herself into working jobs on the ranch that are better suited to men just to keep my mind occupied by lecturing her on the dangers she might encounter."

"She became even more of a hellion and daredevil to distract you?" Lone Wolf asked then watched Adam nod his ruffled head.

Oddly that made sense, knowing Julia as he did. And

it hadn't taken long to get to know a lot about her, he realized. She had a dominant, exuberant personality. She seemed to like being in constant motion, testing herself, pushing her limits and defying the restraints of conventional womanhood.

Lone Wolf glanced down at Adam, noting that he was about to doze off again. He wondered if he should nudge the man awake and inform him that his sister had decided to make the marriage legal. He mulled over that thought while he changed into a fresh set of clothes, then decided to let Julia give her brother the unexpected news.

Hell, he was having trouble recovering from the shock of Julia's *just one little catch* himself.

Chapter Seven

Lone Wolf nearly swallowed his tongue when he glanced up to see Julia perched at the head of the steps a quarter of an hour later. She was dressed in a bright yellow gown that emphasized the small indentation of her waist and her full breasts. Red-gold ringlets coiled around her oval face.

Damn, she was so incredibly attractive. But then he had also found her utterly alluring when her hair was in disarray and she tramped around in her breeches and shirt. It was easy to understand why her would-be suitors flocked to her.

Julia was mistaken if she thought that money was the primary reason men pursued her. He wondered if she had any idea how breathtakingly beautiful she was. Probably not. Vanity wasn't one of Julia's shortcomings.

When she smiled and started down the steps, Lone Wolf heard that voice in his head yelling, *You can't marry this woman! She's bright and shining like the sun and you are the dark side of the moon. You are out of your mind if you go through with this.*

Earlier, Julia had challenged him to figure out why she insisted on marrying him. Well, he hadn't figured it out.

He obviously wasn't as smart as she thought he was.

"I half expected you not to be here," she said as she stepped down beside him.

"Why's that?" he asked, cursing himself soundly for his inability to take his eyes off her.

"Cold feet?" she teased.

Leaving Frank and two cowboys standing guard over Adam, Lone Wolf took her arm and shepherded her out the door to assist her into the waiting carriage. "Yeah, well, you're the one who should be running scared. I don't know beans about being a husband."

"I thought you did well enough when you portrayed the devoted husband for Thomas Whittaker's benefit."

Lone Wolf wasn't sure it had been an act. And that made him extremely twitchy. It was one thing to wed Julia as a practical and sensible solution to the problems she faced. It was another matter entirely to get caught up in his role.

He had encountered dozens of dangerous assignments, but this one had disaster written all over it because Julia was such a beguiling distraction, and he'd be a fool if he made more of the arrangement than what it was.

Moreover, if he didn't keep his wits about him and his senses attuned to trouble, Julia could get hurt. If anything happened to her because he wasn't paying close attention, he couldn't forgive himself.

His thoughts trailed off when a buggy approached. His senses went on immediate alert and he took the precaution of laying his six-shooter beside his hip on the buggy seat.

"It's only Benjamin Clement, the banker," Julia said. "His daughter, Audrey, is a former schoolmate. He's harmless."

Lone Wolf wasn't going to accept the fact that Benjamin was harmless until he was damn certain of it. He carefully surveyed the round-bellied gent who carried an air of arrogance and self-importance similar to that of Thomas Whittaker.

"Julia." Benjamin nodded his balding head and blatantly ignored Lone Wolf. "I heard that you had trouble last night."

"Where did you hear that?" Lone Wolf asked suspiciously.

"From Doc Connor." Benjamin squared his thick-bladed shoulders. "I came to make another offer for your ranch. And to check on Adam, of course," he added hastily.

"The answer was no after Papa died and the answer is still no," Julia told him.

Benjamin's full jowls crinkled in a placating smile. "Come now, m'dear, your life would be easier if you and Adam took the money and left business decisions to someone else."

Lone Wolf eyed the banker speculatively. As much as he wanted to pin the attacks on Sol, the arrival of Benjamin Clement was suspiciously well timed. The banker could certainly afford to pay some thug to do his dirty work as easily as Sol could.

And while he was assigning possible blame, he couldn't overlook the lawyer, who might be harboring hidden motives. No doubt, there were several people in Dodge who would like to get their greedy hands on this fertile ranch land and its valuable water resources. It was going to take the process of elimination to figure out who was behind the Prestons' woes.

"Let's go, Lone Wolf," Julia insisted. "We have business to attend and I'm not interested in Benjamin's offer."

"At least think about it," Benjamin called out. "You know where to find me if you change your mind."

"Nothing like having the local vultures circling after disaster strikes," Julia grumbled.

"I consider your banker a potential threat."

Julia blinked, startled. "You think he wants this ranch that bad?" When Lone Wolf nodded, Julia shrugged. "Fine, but I still think Sol's motives make him our prime suspect."

"I'm all in favor of him myself. But as I said before, jumping to conclusions gets you nowhere fast. I'm going to sniff around and see what turns up."

Forty minutes later, they climbed down from the buggy and walked toward the justice of the peace's office. "It isn't too late to change your mind," he felt obliged to remind her.

Julia tilted her curly head and looked him squarely in the eye. "I've made up my mind. This is what I want."

He grinned wryly. "Ah, the steel trap snaps shut."

Julia snickered good-naturedly. "That's one of the things I like about you. No pretentious flattery. No premeditated charm. Just simple honesty. Promise me that I will always have that from you."

He nodded agreeably. "You look incredible in yellow, by the way."

"Thank you. You look incredible. Period."

Lone Wolf wasn't accustomed to praise. Criticism?

Yes. Scorn? Certainly. A compliment from Julia did wonders. It dawned on him as they entered the office that her opinion of him was the only one that mattered.

When had that happened?

His thoughts trailed off when a stocky, white-haired gent appeared from the living quarters behind the office. He jerked to a halt and his bewildered attention leaped from Julia to Lone Wolf. Here was yet another example of folks taking one look at him and deciding he didn't belong in Julia's company.

Well, they were right, but here he was nonetheless.

"Julia?" the man bleated. "What are you doing here? Is he with you?"

"We want to get married," she said, ignoring his startled expression. "Earnest Calloway, this is Vince Lone Wolf."

"I know who he is, but I—" Earnest's voice trailed off and he tugged nervously at his cravat. Then he stared warily at Lone Wolf. Obviously the man had serious reservations about this match, but he hesitated to speak.

"We're in a bit of a rush," Julia pressed on. "I don't know if you've heard yet, but my brother was shot last night. I don't want to be away from him for too long."

"*Shot?* No, I hadn't heard. That's perfectly dreadful!" Earnest commiserated as he opened a file cabinet to retrieve the license. "I hope Adam is doing all right."

"Much better this morning." Julia glanced expectantly toward the hall. "I was hoping your wife could witness the ceremony. Is she here?"

"Yes, I'll fetch her." Earnest lurched around and lumbered off.

Lone Wolf noted the shocked expression on the woman's plump face when she came forward. The consensus was that Julia was marrying beneath her station. She seemed to be the only one in town who didn't give a fig.

Never having attended a wedding—much less been the *groom* at one—Lone Wolf wasn't sure what he expected. But it was a quick and painless procedure. The I-dos only took a few minutes. And suddenly Julia was his wife. Julia Lone Wolf? *Wife?* He was *married?* To *her? Unbelievable!*

Why had he allowed this ridiculous scheme to go this far? he asked himself. Obviously he was as unbalanced as Julia was. Or maybe she had made him so insane that he couldn't reason.

But there you had it. Married. Husband and wife. For however long she decided to keep him to resolve her problems.

"Now if you will just sign your names this will be official," Earnest said as he handed over the certificate.

Still dazed, Lone Wolf penned his name then gave the document to Julia.

"Keep them preoccupied while I change today's date to yesterday's," she whispered as she kissed his cheek.

Lone Wolf floundered for a topic of conversation while the older couple regarded him nervously. Honestly, you would have thought they expected him to gun them down if they looked at him the wrong way. Hell, he wasn't even carrying hardware.

Well, not that anyone could see. After all, the ordinance in Dodge City stated no firearms were allowed on the north side of the tracks. That was the respectable side of town. Since he wasn't here in an official capacity as a deputized lawman he had left his holsters in the buggy.

"Fine stretch of weather we're having," he commented for lack of anything else to say. "Although last week's dust storm was a real… bother." Small talk was not his forte. Obviously. "Of course, we could use some rain."

The Calloways bobbed their gray heads, saying nothing. To his everlasting relief Julia handed a copy of the certificate to Earnest then tucked her copy in her reticule. The moment they swept out the door to the boardwalk she huffed a sigh of relief.

"I don't think they will notice the change of date," she said as she surged toward the sheriff's office. "They will be too busy spreading the news around town. This way my lawyer can't argue with the signed and dated document. I should have no trouble obtaining the trust fund now."

"Irony at its finest," Lone Wolf smirked. "I've been chasing criminals for years. Now I'm married to a woman who lies to her lawyer the same day she forges a legal document."

Julia laughed then curled her hand around his elbow. "Look on the bright side, *dear.* I'm exactly what you're used to."

She was nothing like what he was used to, he silently corrected. Which was why he had allowed himself to be talked into this marriage, he supposed. Still, it was a bad idea.

His thoughts flitted off and a frown clouded his brow when he saw Harvey Fowler—dressed in his shabby, homespun clothes and brown cap—looking noticeably hungover.

Harvey's bloodshot eyes narrowed on Lone Wolf. "I told you to keep your distance from Julia," he muttered.

Before Lone Wolf could put the disrespectful kid in his place, Julia surged in front of him like a human shield.

"Harvey, you are making a nuisance of yourself again," she chided. "I am married to Lone Wolf. I don't want you to call him out every time we meet on the street. Understood?"

"*Married* to him?" Harvey hooted. "Why would you go and do a fool thing like that? He ain't even one of us."

Julia crossed her arms over her chest and raised a challenging brow. "One of us? And just *who* are *we*, Harvey?"

"White, for starters." Harvey glanced over Julia's head to focus his distaste on Lone Wolf. "He's a halfbreed redskin and a bloodthirsty bounty hunter to boot."

To Lone Wolf's amusement Julia got right in the kid's face. "We are all the same, Harvey," she insisted. "Two eyes, a nose and mouth." She stared pointedly at him. "Some of us, I will admit, have oversize mouths and don't know when to keep them shut."

She stared down Harvey like a gunfighter at twenty paces. "Now kindly step aside. I want us to remain friends, but if you continue to exhibit rude behavior that won't be possible."

Julia clasped Lone Wolf's hand and smiled radiantly at him. "Come on, sweetheart. We have errands to run this afternoon." To Harvey she said, "Tell your mother hello for me. Is she still working at Landau's Café?"

Harvey bobbed his fuzzy head then opened his mouth—and apparently thought better of hurling another insult. But he did glower at Lone Wolf once more for good measure before he veered around them and stalked down the street.

"Charming kid," Lone Wolf commented as they continued down the boardwalk. "What's the whole story on him?"

"His father turned to thievery because he thought it would be easier than putting in a hard day's work plowing fields on their farm," Julia reported. "He was killed by a bounty hunter when Harvey was thirteen. Helen Fowler was left to provide for her son."

"So the kid is taking it out on me because of my profession," Lone Wolf muttered.

"Apparently so. Harvey definitely needs some positive direction, but there is no one around to guide him. His mother is trying, but he has a rebellious streak that won't quit."

Julia frowned thoughtfully. "When I acquire the extra money from my trust perhaps I can hire Harvey. Frank Slater would be a positive influence on his life. Our foreman took Adam and me under wing after Papa died. Frank might be able to get him under control."

Lone Wolf grinned teasingly. "He didn't do much of a job of getting you under control though, did he?"

When Julia smiled at him, her green eyes sparkling with irrepressible spirit, Lone Wolf felt forbidden hunger gnawing at him. Before he could stop himself he reached out to trail his forefinger over her creamy cheek. He glanced sideways to notice the disapproving stares directed at him because Julia was on his arm and he had dared to touch her in public.

She didn't seem to care that passersby were staring. In fact, she wasn't paying the slightest attention to anyone but him. You had to admire an independent-minded woman who didn't allow the dictates of society to define her or disturb her.

It occurred to him a moment later that Julia Preston—Lone Wolf, he silently corrected himself—was *too* independent and unconventional to become the wife of a gentleman. Their expectations for women would be too confining to suit her active and energetic approach to life. But he pretty much accepted her for what she was and let her do as she pleased—unless she put herself in harm's way.

"So that's it," he mused aloud.

Julia glanced at him and frowned. "What's it?"

"You married me because you don't think I'll hold you back or demand a certain kind of behavior that men from your social circle might expect."

"That's only a fringe benefit," she said with a shrug, and then nodded to an acquaintance who gaped at her in shock when he passed by. "But that's not the reason why."

Befuddled, Lone Wolf followed Julia into the office and saw Sheriff Danson thumbing through wanted posters. He glanced up, took one look at Julia then frowned at Lone Wolf.

"Oh for heaven's sake, not you, too, Sheriff Danson," Julia scowled. "It amazes me how deep prejudices run, even out here on the outpost of civilization. Lone Wolf and I are married and I am perfectly satisfied with the match. I don't see why everyone else can't be, too."

Dumbfounded, Milton Danson gaped at her.

Lone Wolf swallowed a snicker. Julia had become his champion. It was hardly necessary, but it was amusing to watch her in action. He decided if his new wife ran short of money she could sell sass by the barrel. Plus, she seemed to delight in shocking folks out of their comfortable ruts.

This woman was definitely a new breed, he decided. The world was no more prepared for the likes of Julia than it was for a social pariah like him.

"Married? The two of you? Well, I'll be." The sheriff sank back in his chair, stared at them for a contemplative moment. Then he smiled wryly. "Interesting."

Lone Wolf reached into his back pocket. "I stopped by to return the bench warrants."

"A shame that. Where am I going to find someone of your caliber to take on those thieves that headed west?" He glanced teasingly at Julia. "He can't be replaced, so that makes you guilty of obstructing justice, young lady."

"Perhaps that's true," she tossed back playfully, "but a man on his honeymoon is not expected to go tramping off to Colorado and leave his adoring wife behind."

When Milton glanced at him then frowned pensively, trying to figure out why he had taken the warrants if he had planned to marry, Lone Wolf scrambled to offer a plausible explanation. "We decided to move up our wedding after Julia's brother was bushwhacked. The incident changed my plans."

"Bushwhacked?" The sheriff shot to his feet. "When?"

"Last night," Julia reported. "I saw a man wearing a long duster and dark, wide-brimmed hat appear from the trees. He was riding a dun-colored horse with white markings. He surfaced again this morning, mounted on a sorrel, and tried to lure us into an ambush. If not for Vince's sharp instincts the results might have been disastrous."

While Milton wrote down the description Julia offered and filled out a report, Lone Wolf surveyed the wanted posters tacked up in the office. But he saw no one that seemed to fit Julia's vague description.

Whoever the sniper was, he made certain that he was difficult to identify.

No doubt, the mastermind didn't want his henchman to be tracked down easily. He was lying low until he struck again.

"I assume you want to handle this investigation yourself." Danson reached into his desk to retrieve a deputy badge, then tossed it to Lone Wolf. "You've been deputized several times before so consider yourself officially deputized again. If you need my assistance let me know."

After the sheriff took the statement, Lone Wolf escorted Julia outside. He veered into a shop to purchase matching gold bands, despite Julia's protest that it was unnecessary.

"It *is* necessary," he told her determinedly. "There should be visible evidence that this is an official marriage."

"My, you bounty hunter types are big on evidence, aren't you?" she smirked. "But you're wasting your hard-earned money. News travels fast in Dodge and we're providing visibility by being seen in each other's company."

He stared her down. "Nevertheless, there will be wedding bands. You might think you can ride roughshod over me, but on this issue I am standing my ground."

"Fine, but I will pay for my—"

His hand clamped over her reticule when she tried to reimburse him. "No," he said sternly. "Don't argue with me."

"I was wondering when the tyrant would rear his ugly head," she teased. "A man gets a wife and suddenly he thinks he is the boss and master. I do believe we need to sit down to establish a few ground rules when we get home."

The devilish twinkle in her eyes assured him that she hadn't taken serious offense. Her smile faded away when he slipped the plain gold band onto her finger. An unfamiliar sense of possessiveness overcame him as he held her hand in his and the impact of their union hit him full force.

If he wasn't careful he was going to make more of this marriage than was intended. It was a charade, he told himself for the umpteenth time. That was all it could ever be. Anything else was out of the question. He couldn't let himself forget that.

During the ride to the ranch, Lone Wolf reminded himself that Julia now had the protection of his reputation as a professional gunfighter. Also, she had gained the legal certification needed to receive her trust fund. That provided an additional obstacle in Sol Griffin's attempt to purchase the ranch. In addition, if the Prestons weren't desperate for money, it might foil Sol's scheme. Or Benjamin Clement's scheme, he tacked on, determined to keep an open mind about possible suspects.

He wished he could convince himself that he didn't want something more from this arrangement than to protect the Prestons from a forced takeover. His selfish motives had put the marriage into motion and selfish motives had him visualizing all sorts of intimate benefits. Hard as he tried to prevent it, he wanted Julia in the worst way.

He cast Julia a discreet glance as they rode over the knoll of ground to see the ranch house sitting in the lush valley below. A blow of lust lambasted him. Damn, he wanted his new wife as his lover, forbidden though she was to him.

Lone Wolf blew out a frustrated breath. He knew Julia demanded honesty from him, but he wasn't sure he could tell her *that.*

A movement in the shadows of the trees caught his attention and he quickly switched mental gears. Years of instinct and reflexes flared to life in less than a heartbeat. Even before he heard the crack of a gunshot he saw the puff of smoke rise from rifle barrel that glinted in the sunlight.

"Ambush! Get down!" he yelled urgently at Julia.

Chapter Eight

Lone Wolf cursed viciously as he flung himself sideways. Julia was sitting between him and the oncoming bullet and he felt as though he was moving in slow motion. Frantic, he hooked his hand around the back of her neck and all but shoved her to the floorboard. When he tried to follow her down a searing pain blazed through his right arm.

"Vince?" Julia scrambled onto her knees. "Are you—?"

Her wild eyes focused on the bloody wound on his upper arm. Fury exploded through her, transporting her back to the moment when she had watched her brother collapse as the result of a sniper's bullet.

Oh, God, not him, too, she thought wildly.

"Stay down, damn it," Lone Wolf scowled as he pushed her sideways.

Another bullet whizzed over his head as he grabbed the reins and sent the horse and buggy racing downhill in a zigzag pattern that made it difficult for the bushwhacker to get off a clear shot. Clinging to the seat, Julia braved a look to the west. Sure enough, the sniper sat astride his horse near the grove of trees.

This time he was riding a bay with black mane and tail.

Julia was beginning to think that three different men had been sent to ambush them. Or did Sol want her to think he had hired an army of sharpshooters to gun down her family? Was that supposed to terrify her into selling out and leaving the area? Or had Benjamin Clement arranged this ambush to frighten her into accepting his offer?

And why this sudden push to acquire Preston Ranch?

Another report from the rifle split the air and thudded into the dirt near the carriage. When the sniper moved in closer for the kill, Julia cursed him to hell and gone. She grabbed one of Lone Wolf's six-shooters— he had the other one clamped in his left hand. Together they blasted away at the sniper until he wheeled around and plunged into the trees.

Heart pounding, Julia focused her attention on treating the pulsating wound on Lone Wolf's right arm. She tore a strip from her petticoat to use as a tourniquet.

"I am never going to forgive you for thrusting yourself into the path of that bullet that might have been meant for me." Fear and frustration made her voice sharp as she popped the reins over the horse to head home.

"You're welcome," he gritted out sarcastically.

"Damn it, Vince—"

"It's my job to protect you," he cut in gruffly. "It's what I'm paid to do. That's why you hired me. Remember?"

"Adam hired you," she clarified, "and I'm firing you.

I don't want to see you hurt because of me. And furthermore, we have no way of knowing if you were the primary target now that word has spread of our marriage. I might simply have been sitting in the wrong place and the sniper was trying to fire *over* my head to get to you."

"Whatever the case, it looks like this is going to be the shortest marriage on record," he smirked as he clamped his injured arm against his ribs. "I'll gather my belongings and clear out when we reach the house."

Julia sent him a withering glance. "You are not fired from being a husband. You are stuck with that indefinitely. But your services as my bodyguard are over. I'm dispensable. If anyone should be wounded, it's me, not you! You are here to protect Adam!"

"Julia, I'm fine. Really," he murmured.

"You are not fine," she railed. "I've become the curse of your life and that's the last thing I want!"

"You need to simmer down," he recommended. "Try taking a deep, calming breath."

"No, I want to pitch a fit. Damn it, this is the last straw!" she erupted. It helped to relieve the pent-up emotion that had her near to bursting apart at the seams.

"Now take a breath," he ordered, a hint of amusement in his voice and a twinkle in those green-gold eyes.

Julia took his advice and sucked in a huge gulp of air. She watched a lopsided smile uplift the corner of his mouth as he stared at her. How could he smile and offer support when he was injured and bleeding? Did nothing faze this tough, hard-edged man? How had he learned to adjust to being shot at constantly? And how many times did you have to get shot at to make you immune to fear, as Vince Lone Wolf obviously was?

The thunder of hooves indicated that some of the hired hands had heard the shots and had come riding to the rescue. When Lone Wolf tried to commandeer a horse from one of the cowboys, Julia clutched the collar of his shirt and yanked him back down on the carriage seat.

"You aren't going anywhere until we have treated that wound," she said in no uncertain terms. She turned to one of the cowhands. "Bill, see if you can find the empty casings from the sniper's rifle cartridges. But don't put yourself or the other men in danger. That scoundrel might be waiting to pick you off."

Bill Forrester nodded grimly then looked to Lone Wolf, as if awaiting his nod of approval. Julia was accustomed to giving orders at the ranch, but suddenly Lone Wolf—because of his reputation, she suspected—had become the higher authority.

Although that realization rankled, she supposed it was important that Lone Wolf commanded the respect of the hired hands since he was now her husband, as well as one of the most sought after bounty hunters and shootists in the state.

When the cowboys galloped off, Lone Wolf popped the reins to urge the horse forward. "For what it's worth, I would have given your men the same instructions." A wry smile quirked his lips. "When you aren't ranting like a banshee you show a great deal of common sense."

Despite the fact that she was frustrated with the alarming turn of events she managed a smile. How could she not? The stimulating effects of his grin mesmerized her. She wished he would smile more often. But considering the life he led, she doubted amusement and pleasure were common occurrences. If she provided him with a little amusement and enjoyment then she had made a positive impact on his life.

"Feeling better now?" he asked as he eased down on the brake and brought the buggy to a halt near the front door.

"Yes, but I'm still mad at you for getting yourself shot on my behalf." Julia bounded to the ground then scurried around the buggy to clutch his good arm. "In case you have other ideas, you are off duty for the rest of the day," she said authoritatively.

Looking around, Lone Wolf asked. "Where's that marriage certificate?"

She frowned, bemused, as she propelled him through the front door at a fast clip. "Why do you need to see it?"

"Just wondering where it says that *you* get to boss *me* around."

She flung him an exasperated glance as she towed him up the staircase. "I'm simply taking charge. I've done it for years. It's second nature."

Julia called out to Nora Dickerson, the housekeeper, to boil water and bring bandages up to her room. Lone Wolf bit back a grin as Julia half dragged him down the hall. He had never been fussed over before. It was rather comforting, even if Julia was half-snarly and out of sorts. It was obvious that she had a bit of a temper. In every tense situation she got scared for only a few moments then she went straight to mad.

As for Lone Wolf, he was still feeling the aftereffects of fear. *For her.* She'd come dangerously close to getting shot. Better him than her, he decided as she tugged him to the bed.

His thoughts scattered when she unfastened his shirt.

He watched her hands stall when they skimmed his bare chest. He saw heat suffuse her cheeks before she stiffened her resolve and helped him ease his injured arm from the shirtsleeve.

He looked the other way, willfully ignoring the sexual tension that radiated between them.

Julia didn't appear to be offended by the puckered scar from a knife wound that bisected his belly. She didn't even flinch when she noticed the indentation from a bullet hole that scarred his left shoulder. She overlooked his unsightly souvenirs of battle as easily as she disregarded his mixed heritage and profession, as if they were no consequence in forming her opinion of him. That still amazed him.

"How did you get those scars?" she asked as she guided him down to the edge of the bed.

"Shoot-outs against lopsided odds."

He glanced down at the bloody wound that left four inches of jagged flesh on his upper arm. Damn, it felt as bad as it looked. It was deeper than he had first thought, too. The slug hadn't grazed muscle; it had nestled beside the bone.

Hell, this was going to slow him down for a few days.

"How lopsided were the odds?" she quizzed him.

"Four to one." He hitched his thumb over his shoulder. "My saddlebags are in Adam's room. There's a tin of poultice, an Indian remedy, I use on wounds. Fetch it, will you?"

He blinked, startled, when she framed his face in her hands and dipped her head down to stare directly at him.

Her scent filled his nostrils. The feel of her hands on

his skin had the most amazing effect on him. Those sensuous lips were a hairbreadth away and he was craving the taste of them.

Hungry desire clenched in his belly. The pain in his arm didn't seem so severe for those few moments while he was lost in her fragrance and the depths of those luminous green eyes.

"Thank you for what you did out there," she whispered. "It was brave and courageous and I'm humbled by your selfless deed." Her mouth brushed his in the softest caress imaginable. He felt ten times better until she said, "But if you ever do that again I swear *I* will shoot you myself!"

"Why does it bother you so much?" he asked, baffled.

"Because you matter. To me." A smile twitched her lips. "Furthermore, I don't want the distinction of being involved in the shortest marriage on record, either. I have my heart set on keeping you alive and kicking."

And then she sailed off to fetch the poultice, leaving his aroused body vibrating like a tuning fork. He chuckled and shook his head as he braced himself up on his left hand.

Adam Preston was right on the mark when he said that his sister was bursting with spirit and vitality. She was as impossible to predict and control as a thunderstorm. He liked that about her, oddly enough.

Life with Julia would never be mundane or boring.

Watch it, Lone Wolf, came that pesky little voice of reason again. *Don't get too comfortable here. Every job you've undertaken has been temporary. Nothing is permanent and neither is this whirlwind marriage.*

* * *

Julia swore she had been surviving on adrenaline for the past four days. She had tramped back and forth between Adam and Lone Wolf's bedsides to make sure both men were resting comfortably. After the ambush that occurred on the way home from the wedding, she had sent for Doc Connor to dig out the bullet that was lodged in Lone Wolf's upper arm. She had also sent three cowboys into town to report the most recent shooting to Sheriff Danson.

Since then she had fulfilled several necessary duties as ranch manager and had collapsed in exhaustion every night to regenerate energy so she could face another day.

After several exasperating disagreements with Lone Wolf about staying in bed so he could heal, she decided that he was a less cooperative patient than her brother. Although Doc Connor had told her Lone Wolf had lost a considerable amount of blood and that he needed to stay off his feet, Lone Wolf kept pacing restlessly around the house. Short of tying him down she couldn't get him to stay put and recuperate.

And so she had resorted to drastic measures. She had laced his meals with enough laudanum to ensure he slept entire days away, and the nights.

After checking on Lone Wolf that evening, Julia decided it was high time that she confronted the man she held responsible for her angry frustration. As a precaution, she tucked Lone Wolf's derringer into the pocket of her breeches then tiptoed onto the dark gallery. She descended the back steps to retrieve her horse. Tonight she intended to be on hand to determine how Maggie sneaked undetected from her house to visit Adam. Maggie didn't think twice about scurrying off alone in the darkness and neither did Julia. She was going to use that same route to enter the house to issue her own warning to Sol Griffin.

Thirty minutes later Julia crouched in the underbrush, watching a posted guard circle the back of the Griffin ranch house. Immediately thereafter Maggie appeared on the upper terrace, dressed in dark breeches and a shirt.

A muffled chuckle tripped from Julia's lips as she watched her dainty friend perform a series of agile maneuvers, after hoisting herself onto a sturdy tree limb that hung an arm's length away from the wrought-iron railing.

Although Sol had done his best to make sure Maggie was first and foremost a dignified lady, he hadn't been able to counter Julia's hoydenish influences on his daughter.

Watching Maggie maneuver down the tree, Julia knew it was a strong indication that she was a woman who was willing to go to extremes to be with the man she loved.

Julia approached the house after Maggie scurried through the underbrush to fetch the horse that she'd hitched to a pasture gate. Impatiently she monitored the guard as he made his rounds. When he turned the corner she dashed over to shimmy up the branches and begin her ascent to the balcony. She glanced down to note that the lantern light blazing through the open window of Sol's study provided him with a clear view of the balcony steps.

No wonder Maggie used the tree as her escape route. Sol would have seen her make her late-night exits if she tried to scamper down the back steps.

Julia muttered a curse when she discovered Maggie had locked her bedroom door. The doors leading to three guest bedrooms were also bolted shut. She kept checking locks until she turned the knob to Sol's spacious suite.

"Dear God," Julia murmured when she noticed that all of Rachel Griffin's combs, brushes and jewelry were exactly where she had left them three years ago. She had the unshakable feeling that Rachel's clothes were still hanging in the wardrobe as well. If this wasn't a sure sign that Sol hadn't let go of the past, and still kept his wife's memory alive, Julia didn't know what was.

No wonder Sol had never forgiven the Prestons. He hadn't moved on, just remained suspended in time. He spent every night in this room, which stood like a shrine to his departed wife. The very same wife that he convinced himself had been lured into trysts with Julia's father.

Julia's thoughts trailed off when she noticed a yellowed photograph sitting on the dresser. She didn't recognize the young girl, but there was something familiar about her. She reminded Julia of—

She halted in mid-step when she realized who the young girl probably was. Her breath stalled when she noticed the heart-shaped locket Lone Wolf had mentioned. This had to be Lone Wolf's mother. This was Isabella, Sol's younger sister. Sol had created another shrine and kept it in plain view.

The man was either extraordinarily sentimental or tragically obsessed. It was the latter, no doubt, considering that he had rejected his own nephew and turned the resentment caused by his wife's death on the Prestons. In Sol's tormented mind, anyone named Preston was personally responsible for his misery.

Julia exited the room and tiptoed downstairs. She paused in the hall when she heard the murmur of voices in the study.

"Everything is going as planned, Sol," she heard an unidentified man announce. "The necessary papers should be drawn up, signed and ready to post shortly."

"Good. I want the arrangements carried out quickly and discreetly," Sol insisted.

Julia clenched her teeth. Damn the man! What was he planning? Other than the obliteration of the Preston name?

"What about the other matter?" the visitor asked.

Julia muttered under her breath, wishing she could identify Sol's associate. Unfortunately she would have to move directly in front of the open door to do that.

"That particular matter is going to require more finesse," Sol remarked. "My daughter is being difficult again. We had another confrontation this afternoon and she isn't speaking to me. But she'll come around eventually."

Don't bet on it, Sol, thought Julia. Maggie had a mind of her own and she knew how to use it, much to Sol's frustration.

"Are you still expecting the wedding to take place in Abilene in two months?"

Julia's eyes popped. Wedding? Whose wedding? Was Sol getting married? Surely not, considering the shrine in his bedroom suite. He must be referring to Maggie. Curse Sol for trying to marry Maggie off against her wishes! The bastard was probably waiting for Adam to expire from his chest wound. While Maggie was grieving and desolate Sol would arrange the wedding of his choice.

Impulsively Julia tapped the derringer she had tucked in her pocket. She would do the world a favor if she gave Sol a taste of his own medicine. The prospect of using him for target practice was beginning to have tremendous appeal.

The scrape of a chair put her senses on alert and indicated that one of the men had come to his feet.

Julia recoiled behind the door.

"I'm going back to town to see what else I can find out."

"I'm paying you to be discreet so be certain that you are," Sol demanded.

Julia heard the outside office door creak open, then shut. She was disgruntled that she hadn't been able to identify Sol's accomplice. When she heard Sol rummaging through his desk and shuffling of papers, she decided it was time to make her entrance.

She took immense satisfaction in seeing Sol jerk upright and gape at her in shocked surprise.

Chapter Nine

"How the devil did you get in here, you little witch?" Sol darted an uneasy glance at the door where his mysterious accomplice had exited a moment earlier.

Julia gave no indication that she had eavesdropped on the conversation. "I flew in on my broom," she said flippantly. "I had no other choice since I am no longer welcome to enter through your front door."

"You aren't welcome here. Period." His brows swooped down in a sharp vee. "You better not have disturbed my daughter. I've made it clear that she is to have no association with you."

"I didn't come to see Maggie. I came to see you."

"Did you come to seek my advice, Julia?" he smirked. "If so, I advise you not to break into my home because you might get shot."

The smug smile that thinned his lips did nothing to enhance his appearance. Julia had once thought Sol was a distinguished-looking man with his tailored clothes, salt-and-pepper hair and tall, dignified stature. Now he was just an embittered man who lived for revenge.

"I'm getting used to people shooting at me, thanks to you." She reached into her pocket to retrieve the shell casings the cowboys had found at the site of the second ambush. "I think these belong to your henchman. Careless of him not to pick them up."

Sol leaned back in his chair, his shoulders rigid, his expression defiant. "Are you implying that I am responsible for the recent bushwhacking? If you try to pin it on me then you're going to find out what trouble really is, young lady."

"The name is *Mrs. Vince Lone Wolf,*" she took grand satisfaction in announcing. "I guess that makes you my uncle, too, doesn't it?"

The scowl that swallowed his features testified to the extent of his outrage. "I'm not claiming him *or* you as family," he snapped, his hands curling into tight fists. "You always were impetuous and too daring for your own good, Julia. Marrying that ruthless half-breed gunfighter will do nothing to improve your reputation as a reckless hoyden."

"I didn't come here seeking your approval." Her gaze narrowed on him. "I came here to issue a warning, Sol. Call off your hired assassins. I informed the sheriff that if anything else happens to Adam, to my new husband or to me that *you* are to be arrested as the prime suspect."

"How dare you suggest I'm involved in your run of bad luck." His arm shot toward the door. "Get out of here before I decide to shoot you as a common prowler."

"And risk having the sheriff arrest you?" She shook her head. "That won't do much for your reputation. Then there is Maggie to consider," she reminded him. "If she suspects that you are responsible for Adam and

Lone Wolf's injuries you will lose her forever. Be very careful, Sol. You could end up with nothing and no one."

"Thanks to your father's treachery my life is already pure hell," he sneered bitterly. "He stole something from me that I held dear. And if your brother thinks he can take Maggie from me, he is mistaken. It will be over my dead body!"

"Don't put ideas in my head."

"If it comes to that Adam will still lose Maggie," Sol assured her tersely. "She would never want me to be the sacrifice made to marry your brother. I am her *father.*"

"Not much of one, if you ask me," she sniffed.

"I told you to get out," he snapped hatefully. "And don't come back. Prestons won't be welcome in my home ever again."

"I meant what I said, Sol." Julia retreated a few steps, careful not to turn her back on him. She didn't expect him to grab a pistol and turn it on her, but she wasn't going to bet her life on that. "If anyone else suffers injury, or more cattle turn up missing, then you and I are going to settle this feud once and for all."

On that threatening note Julia darted into the hall and strode toward the front door. She paused on the marble steps when the posted guard veered around the side of the house.

"Nice evening, isn't it?" she said conversationally.

The guard's eyes rounded in disbelief. "Where'd you come from?"

"Never mind. Just let her pass," Sol called from behind her. "We have concluded our business and she won't be back."

Julia clung to the protection of the trees beside the

creek as she made her way back home. She wished she
had been able to identify the sniper as Sol's late-night
guest so she could confirm a connection between the
two. But at least she had found out that Sol still had a
few tricks up his sleeve.

She frowned pensively, recalling what Sol had told
his accomplice about finalizing arrangements soon.

She would dearly like to know what that meant.

Lone Wolf knew he'd been drugged when he awoke,
suffering from the same side effects of dry mouth and
fuzzy brain that Adam had described. Julia had obviously tampered with his meals to keep him bedridden.

Scowling, he flung his legs over the edge of the bed
and shot to his feet. The dark room spun around him and
he had to brace his good arm on the end table to maintain his balance.

"Damn that woman," he grumbled.

Lone Wolf dragged in a cathartic breath and willed
the room to stop spinning around him. His arm still hurt
like a son of a bitch and his knees felt unstable. Wearing only his breeches, he wobbled onto the terrace to
inhale a breath of fresh air. He slowed his step when he
glanced into Adam's room and saw Maggie snuggled
up on the bed.

If Sol could see his daughter cuddled up next to
Adam he would have a stroke. *Let him,* Lone Wolf
thought as he tapped lightly on the door.

Maggie sprang away from Adam, her face flaming
with embarrassment. Her gaze dropped to the bandage
on his arm. "Adam told me what happened. What you
did last Saturday was incredibly brave, Lone Wolf."

His brows jackknifed. "What day is this?"

"Wednesday."

"She drugged me for *four* days?" he howled.

Adam grinned in amusement. "Afraid so. I'm sure Julia decided that it was for your own good."

"Are you feeling better after your mandatory bed rest?" Maggie questioned, biting back a smile.

"Not particularly," Lone Wolf grumbled as he panned the room. "Where is Julia?" He had a few choice words— and none of them were very nice—to fling at his wife.

Adam frowned. "I thought she was with you."

When Lone Wolf shook his head Adam shrugged then winced in discomfort. "Maybe she went downstairs to work on the financial ledgers. She has been keeping track of the accounts since Pa died."

"I'll check," Maggie volunteered.

"No, the last thing you need is to be spotted by one of the servants," Lone Wolf warned. "If word gets back to your father he will have a chaperone sticking to you like an extra set of skin."

Maggie sank gracefully into the chair. "That's the last thing I need right now. Papa and I had an argument this afternoon. A shouting match was more like it," she clarified. "He announced that he has made arrangements for me to marry a rancher who lives near Abilene and that I am to abide by his decision."

"What!" Adam crowed.

Maggie nodded. "I swore I would marry no one and certainly not a stranger that he picked out for me." She glanced at Adam. "I should go now. You look tired."

Lone Wolf looked away when Maggie walked over to kiss Adam goodbye. He pretended not to hear the whispered exchange of endearments. Or the sound of breathless kisses.

When Maggie exited the room Lone Wolf followed her across the terrace. "I'll accompany you home."

"No, you need your rest, too," she insisted. "Besides, I've learned to be cautious. I also carry a pistol." She smiled impishly. "Julia taught me to shoot and we spent plenty of evenings lurking around in the dark, seeking adventure."

"Ah yes, my dear wife, the bad influence."

"My father says the same thing about her," Maggie snickered. "But Julia is very unique, as well as my constant source of inspiration. I think you are very fortunate to have her, Lone Wolf."

Fortunate? He wasn't so sure.

"I would do anything for Julia," Maggie insisted. "She is the sister I never had. She has strength of character and she provides support when I need it most. If only my father…" Her voice trailed off and she sighed. "We are headed for a clash of wills, I'm afraid. I'm tempted to defect to the Preston camp, but I fear that will only make matters worse. I love Adam, but my father is still my father."

When Maggie descended the steps, Lone Wolf waited until she disappeared into the shadows before turning away. He could understand why Julia was reluctant to tell Maggie that Sol might be behind the shootings.

Divided loyalty would tear Maggie apart.

Of course, in Lone Wolf's opinion, Maggie was wasting her affection on Sol. The man had no saving graces and he sure as hell didn't deserve a kindhearted daughter like Maggie.

Lurching around, Lone Wolf veered back to his room to swallow down the entire glass of water, wishing he could wash away the unpleasant taste of laudanum. Then he made a quick search of the house and realized Julia was not in residence. An uneasy sensation skittered down his spine. If she had sighted the sniper and raced off to get herself shot he was going to strangle her—provided she survived.

Confound it, he was going to have to shackle that woman to the banister so he could keep a close watch on her.

Back in his room, Lone Wolf paced the floorboards until he saw a silhouette darting across the balcony. He reached for his pistols on the nightstand. When the darkly clad figure breezed into the room he caught a whiff of the familiar fragrance. Scowling, he set aside his weapons.

"Where the hell have you been?" he demanded gruffly.

"Good evening to you, too," she said saucily.

He glared at her. "Answer me, damn it."

"Getting some fresh air."

Julia pulled the cap from her head and shook out that wild mane of red-gold hair, letting it cascade down the middle of her back. He itched to run his fingers through the silky tendrils, but he squelched the forbidden impulse and stared suspiciously at her.

"You were gone a long time. How far did you have to go to find *fresh air?*"

"What are you doing out of bed?" she asked, trying to sidetrack him, no doubt. It wasn't going to work.

"Someone drugged me for several days. I was looking for the culprit." He frowned darkly. "Don't ever do that again."

Julia shed her jacket then draped it over the chair.

"It's been another long, exhausting day. Could we postpone this lecture until tomorrow?"

"No. Where were you?" he persisted.

Julia refused to tell him, because he was in a foul mood—and so was she. She was also bone weary and she felt as if the weight of the world were strapped to her shoulders. She wished she could magically wave her arms and make everything right. Wished Adam was back on his feet and Lone Wolf's arm was functioning at full capacity. His shooting arm, no less, she mused as she stared at the white bandage that stood out in sharp contrast against his bronzed skin.

Although he was still glaring at her, Julia slid her arms around his waist and rested her cheek on the muscled wall of his chest. She didn't know why she found it so easy to initiate physical contact with him after she had kept all other men at arm's length. But she enjoyed touching him, enjoyed snuggling up against him.

She smiled contentedly when he looped his left arm around her shoulder and rested his chin on the crown of her head. They stood there for a long moment, and she savored the security and sense of peace that stole over her.

Although her world kept flipping upside down the burden didn't seem so insurmountable while she was in the protective circle of Lone Wolf's arms.

"You defeat me, woman," he murmured a few moments later. "That isn't a feeling I'm accustomed to or comfortable with."

"Sorry to hear that." Her lips grazed his chest and she inhaled his musky fragrance. "When I'm here with you like this, I feel I've come home. Safe and sound. Nothing bad can touch me here."

She heard his rumbling groan, felt his arm glide up as he tipped her face to his. "I know I'm going to regret this," he murmured.

Then he kissed her in a way that was somewhere between the hard, silencing kiss down by the creek and the gentle merging of lips that had sealed their wedding vows.

Desire rippled through her and she instinctively leaned into him, feeling the change overcome his masculine body, knowing she was responsible for it. Even if it was just a natural male response to close contact with a woman.

Maybe he wasn't responding to her specifically, but it was still encouraging to know that he wasn't completely immune to her.

When his hand skimmed over her breasts, caressing her through the fabric of her shirt, Julia moaned aloud. She reveled in his touch, marveled at the maelstrom of sensations his caresses aroused in her.

I could become hopelessly lost in this man, she thought as she kissed him as thoroughly and deeply as he kissed her. For the first time in her life she wanted to know what passion was about, wanted to share her body with a man.

This man, for *he* alone tempted her beyond measure.

When he eased her down on the bed Julia went willingly. He moved above her, positioning himself intimately between her legs. His powerful body pressed her into the mattress. But it wasn't panic from being restrained that overcame her; it was an amazing sense of right, of burgeoning sensual pleasure. She could feel his hard length pressing against her inner thigh and she brazenly reached down to appease her feminine curiosity by stroking him through the fabric of his breeches.

When his hand covered hers, moving her wandering hand back to his washboard belly, she frowned in disappointment.

"This is not a good idea," he said hoarsely. "First off, my arm hurts something fierce and I can't brace myself on it. And worse, you're *killing* me. We will both be better off if we keep this marriage strictly one of pretense." He huffed out a shaky breath. "Damn it, what in the hell are we doing?"

"I don't know, but I was enjoying it."

He barked a frustrated laugh as he rolled away to stare up at the canopy. "That's not what I need to hear right now."

Julia propped her head on her hand and stared into his shadowed face. "You know something, Vince?"

"I know lots of things. Be more specific."

She chuckled at his dry sense of humor. It was just one more thing about him that fascinated her. In addition to that incredibly masculine body that he was being stingy with.

"I'm not averse to this marriage being more than a name-only proposition," she told him candidly.

"I didn't need to hear that, either," he said with a scowl. "I'm trying to be noble and sensible!"

She grinned impudently. "You don't have to be honorable for my benefit. And I don't see why I can't have you if I want you. After all, I have a license that says I can."

He glanced sideways at her and she noticed the smile that quirked his lips. "Are you purposely trying to drive me crazy or is this just another example of you being you?"

She pulled a face. "You sound like my brother."

"Believe me, my present interest in you is about as far from brotherly as it can get," he declared.

"Good. I don't need another brother."

She leaned over to kiss him and he dodged her kiss.

"Yeah, you do. A house full of brothers to protect you from making an irreversible mistake that you will inevitably regret."

Frustrated, Julia levered herself upright then stared him down. "If you don't want me then just come right out and say so. If you want someone who has more experience with men, I can understand that, but—"

"How much experience do you have?" he interrupted.

"None, and that won't change unless you cooperate. Blast it, I don't see why I can't practice passion on you. Who would have thought it would take an act of congress to get you to teach me—"

He pressed his forefinger to her lips to shush her. "Julia," he said, "I want you like hell blazing. That is a fact. But it is not the point."

She nipped his fingertip with her teeth. "Here we go with the preaching again."

He chuckled and sighed. Her playful nature utterly beguiled him. That was not a good thing when he was trying so hard to remain professional and detached, as he did during every other assignment. This one was getting too personal and that worried him to the extreme.

"You deserve better than a quick tumble in the sheets with a man who has only one good arm," he went on to say. "The other one is still throbbing torturously. Trust me, *not* getting involved is best for both of us."

Damn, was he really turning her down? Yes, he was, because it didn't seem fair to her…

And he couldn't believe he was having this conversation with himself. Yet, here he was, lying beside more woman than he had ever encountered in his thirty-two years of existence and he was telling her no.

What man in his right mind would do that?

He blew out an exasperated breath. "If you feel the same way in a few days, after the emotional furor you've endured dies down, then let me know and we'll talk. Until then, let's try sleeping in the same bed. See how that works out."

She chuckled as she bent over him to press a kiss to his lips before he could avoid her again. A waterfall of silky hair tumbled across his face and chest and he mentally kicked himself for being so sensible and noble. Damn, he wanted her—badly. If he wasn't careful, forbidden desire was going to outmuscle his common sense and all would be lost.

"You are the sweetest man I know, Vince Lone Wolf."

"Sweet?" he snorted. "I've been called a lot of things, most of them too crude to repeat, but never *sweet*."

"Well, you are," she insisted as she rolled off the bed.

He watched her pluck up her nightgown, then duck behind the dressing screen. It wasn't difficult to imagine how she might look naked. The prospect turned him hard and aching all over again. He was still throbbing uncomfortably—his arm and elsewhere—when she eased into bed beside him a moment later.

Don't get used to this. Don't start liking it too much, he warned himself as Julia cushioned her head on his shoulder and draped her arm across his belly.

"By the way, you're still fired as a bodyguard," she whispered against his skin.

"You didn't pay my advance so I'm not quitting until I'm good and ready," he said. "Good-night, Julia."

When she didn't reply he angled his head to see that she had immediately fallen asleep. It was amazing that she could be chatty one moment and conk right out the next.

He wondered where she had been this evening, wondered if her late-night excursion had exhausted her or if the constant rush of adrenaline caused by stumbling from one traumatic incident to the next had finally caught up with her.

Whatever the case, she slumped against him. Her breath caressed his neck, making his craving for her difficult to ignore. He shifted his tender arm into a more comfortable position then closed his eyes. He had never spent the entire night with a woman. Neither had he gone to bed with a woman without sex being his primary objective.

But with Julia everything was completely backward and out of the ordinary.

That didn't really surprise him, because so was she.

Out of the ordinary.

He wondered how long it would take to forget each unique memory of her that was being stored up in his heart. How long would it be before he forgot that she was the last thing he saw when he went to sleep and the first thing he laid eyes on in the morning?

He drifted off before he could satisfactorily calculate the answer to that question.

Chapter Ten

The next morning Lone Wolf woke up alone in bed. He hadn't heard Julia get up—and that bothered him. He was getting soft, he decided as he tested his injured arm and found it as stiff and sore as it had been the previous night. He should camp out on the lawn where it was easier to remember to sleep with one eye open and to keep both ears pricked to the sound of trouble.

Sleeping with Julia disrupted all his natural instincts—save one. And that one could get them both in trouble if he didn't watch out.

Lone Wolf grabbed his shirt, then let it hang open because trying to fasten the buttons one-handed didn't seem worth the effort. Raking his hair away from his face, he headed for Adam's room.

"You look a damn sight better," Lone Wolf observed as he watched Adam eat.

"I feel a damn sight better," Adam said between bites of ham and toast. "Want some breakfast?"

Lone Wolf propped himself against the wall to appraise the additional color that had returned to Adam's face. "I'll pass. Your sister keeps doctoring the food with laudanum and I don't want to risk that again. I'll fix something for myself."

Adam stared warily at his food then set it aside. His gaze landed squarely on the ring finger of Lone Wolf's hand. "Still playing the marriage charade to the hilt, I see."

Lone Wolf shifted awkwardly then decided to tell Adam the truth. He looked well enough to deal with the facts. "Your sister decided that pretense wasn't good enough for her. She made me marry her the day we were in town."

Adam's eyes popped. *"What!"* he crowed.

"You heard me. She wanted a marriage certificate. Something about claiming her trust fund to cover ranch losses and making sure Sol Griffin didn't do some checking to discover the marriage was a hoax." He noticed Adam's disgruntled expression then added, "I know you wouldn't pick me for your sister, but this is the way she wanted it. I don't have to tell you how headstrong she is, do I?"

Adam gave him a steely-eyed look, overprotective older brother to Julia that he was. "Where are you sleeping?"

Lone Wolf looked him straight in the eye and didn't so much as blink. "In her bed. With her. Nothing happened, not that it's your business since we are officially married. As I said, *her* idea, not mine. I had planned to stick with a pretend marriage."

Adam's snort indicated that he didn't believe it.

"Believe it," Lone Wolf insisted.

Adam slumped against the mound of pillows. "Damn it, she's doing it again."

Lone Wolf frowned, befuddled. "Doing what again?"

"Going a little crazy, behaving rashly, just like she did when Pa died." He glanced apologetically at Lone Wolf. "Don't take this the wrong way, and make no mistake that I am immensely grateful that you're here to help, but a marriage is permanent. Not a temporary assignment. What was Julia thinking? You can't just shrug out of it like a winter coat."

"That's what I said, more or less." He cocked a brow. "But have you ever tried to argue with that woman when she has made up her mind?"

Adam sighed audibly. "Yeah, several times."

"Ever win one?"

He shook his blond head then chuckled. "No, not that I recall. Welcome to my world, Lone Wolf."

"So…where is that green-eyed hellion?"

"She rode out with some of the men to check for cut fences and missing cattle. And yes, I objected strenuously. I told her to stay here and keep a low profile. For all the good it did. She's as fearless and daring as ever."

Lone Wolf pushed away from the wall. "Which pasture?"

"Southwest. The one that joins Sol's. That's where some of the rustling incidents have taken place."

Lone Wolf strode off to grab his boots and hardware. He grimaced as he strapped on his double holsters. If it became necessary to start shooting with both pistols blazing his right-hand accuracy was going to be way off the mark.

It better not come to that so soon after the injury, he thought as he surged down the hall to grab a bite to eat on the go. His job would be a hell of a lot easier if Julia would confine herself to the house like a normal woman.

Too bad she had the kind of restless energy and spirit that made a sedentary lifestyle impossible.

Grateful that one of the cowboys offered to saddle his piebald gelding, Lone Wolf mounted up and loped south. He winced at the throb in his arm that pulsed in rhythm with the jarring motion of the horse's gait.

Twenty minutes later he spotted a half-dozen cowboys—and one shiny-haired strawberry blonde.

Lone Wolf sighed in exasperation.

The men were stretching new barbwire across the break in the fence. Julia was working industriously beside the men. Scowling, Lone Wolf walked his horse downhill to join them.

"We lost a few more head last night," Frank Slater, the foreman, told Lone Wolf.

"Any sign of the missing livestock?"

Frank shook his gray head then wiped the sweat from his brow. "The tracks lead west."

Lone Wolf headed toward the gate that sat two hundred yards north. The fact that the fence had been cut when there was a gate nearby indicated the rustlers were spitefully making extra work for the ranch hands. He stared into the distance, curious to know where the cattle had been stashed.

Frank might not have had the time or inclination to pursue the tracks, but Lone Wolf made a living following telltale prints.

He took note that Julia had mounted her horse and was approaching him. "At least put on your hat," he grumbled. "No sense being obvious and presenting yourself as a target."

To his surprise she did as he asked without argument. Did that count as winning a round with Julia? He tossed aside the thought and focused on the trampled grass and prints that turned north about three hundred yards from the broken fence. The tracks indicated that three riders had moved a dozen cattle from the Prestons' pasture. He wondered if the tracks led west to join the Griffin herd grazing in the distance.

But that would be too obvious, he supposed.

A few minutes later he spotted the ashes from a campfire and several smeared prints. "The rustlers must have altered the brands here," he commented. "Your cattle are either pinned up at the railhead in Dodge, ready to be shipped east, or they have been driven to Abilene."

Julia muttered in irritation. "This is a spiteful form of retaliation, no doubt."

He stared curiously at her. "For what?" He got a bad feeling when she avoided looking at him and shifted uneasily in the saddle. "Julia, what did you do?"

"Promise you won't get upset?"

"I'm not promising any such thing. Now what did you do?"

She exhaled dramatically, glanced fleetingly at him then averted her eyes. "I went to Griffin Ranch last night."

"Damn it! I was afraid you were going to say that," he grumbled sourly.

"I wanted to see how Maggie managed to sneak from the house. I watched her climb down from the second story via the sprawling shade tree." She paused briefly then said, "I followed her route so I could confront Sol."

"Damn it, woman!" he exploded. "You shouldn't have gone off alone."

"I am not afraid of Sol, and the likelihood of him attacking me is far less than that of a man," she argued. "Besides, I have been spiriting around in the dark since I was a child and I know how to dodge trouble."

"Maybe so, but I still don't like it," he grumbled.

"When I arrived I overheard Sol talking to another man in his office," Julia reported. "But I couldn't get into position to see who it was. They were discussing some sort of arrangements that are to be finalized shortly. Unfortunately I only caught the tail end of that conversation."

He glared at her good and hard. "Probably the sale of your property because we're all slated to be six feet under by then. Sooner, if you keep pulling stupid stunts."

Her chin elevated a notch. "I returned unscathed, didn't I? And isn't it better to know as many details as possible to counter future attacks?"

"Not if your life is the sacrifice. And what good would it do for you to know the facts if you're dead? You couldn't relay them to Adam or me, now could you?"

She waved off his scowl. "Sol might hire someone to shoot at us, but he's smart enough not to get caught with a smoking gun in his hand and my lifeless body sprawled on the floor in his house," she said reasonably. "Everyone in town knows there has been bad blood between us since the scandal. Sol wouldn't risk any repercussions. It would be the same as signing his own death warrant."

She peered up at him, needing to share her concern about Maggie. Lately he was the first place she came for comfort and support. "Sol has arranged a marriage for Maggie that is scheduled to take place in two months."

"If you'd have stayed home where you belonged last night you'd have heard the news from Maggie," he said irritably.

"She might have been told of the arrangements," Julia countered, "but Sol has finalized the agreement, whether Maggie objects or not. Adam is going to lose her, Lone Wolf."

"He hasn't lost her yet. If we can't link the rustling and bushwhacking to Sol in the next two weeks then we'll make use of our last resort."

"An elopement and secret marriage," Julia guessed. "By then Adam should be up and around and able to defend himself when Sol comes unglued. Which he will. He swore last night that a Preston is never going to wed a Griffin unless it's over his dead body."

"I'd love to arrange that for him," Lone Wolf said bitterly.

She touched his hand, demanding his undivided attention. "I went in through the unlocked door to Sol's bedroom. It's a memorial to his wife. All of Rachel's belongings are still intact, as if he expects her to walk into the room any moment. I swear the man is clinging to the past with both fists."

She gave his hand a consoling squeeze. "I also saw a photograph of a young girl who must be your mother. The heart-shaped locket you described was draped over the corner of the picture frame. I think it's another memory from the past that Sol refuses to release."

"That makes no sense." He frowned. "Sol told me all those years ago that his sister was dead to him. If she chose to live with a savage then she relinquished her birthright and forfeited all contact with her white family."

Julia's mouth dropped open. "Are you saying that he expected her to take her own life rather than to become the wife of a Cheyenne warrior?"

Lone Wolf nodded abruptly. "If he had the slightest compassion for my mother he sure as hell fooled me."

Julia sighed heavily. "I just don't understand that man."

"Who can figure out what runs through a lunatic's mind," he snorted as he veered back to the Prestons' pasture. "We better head to town to see if we can find your cattle before they're long gone. If we're lucky they are penned up at the railhead at Dodge instead of being driven to Abilene."

Lone Wolf rode past stock pens full of bawling cattle then halted when he noticed the fresh brands smeared on the livestock's hips. When he called Julia's attention to the calves she muttered something about branding Sol with the Preston brand.

He was all in favor of seeing his uncle marked for life, but until he had irrefutable proof of Sol's involvement he couldn't file charges.

"Stay here while I find the man in charge," Lone Wolf insisted.

Julia was off her horse in a single bound. "No, I'm coming with you."

"Lost another one," Lone Wolf said under his breath.

Together they strode into the small clapboard office beside the railroad tracks. Despite the gravity of recovering stolen cattle Lone Wolf couldn't help but smile when Julia thrust back her shoulders, tilted her chin and took charge of the situation. She marched up to the manager—who, according to the nameplate on his desk, was John Penders. He didn't glance up from his stack of papers immediately so Julia rapped her knuckles on his desk to demand his attention.

"I am here to notify you that a dozen cattle from Preston Ranch were stolen last night and rebranded. We saw our cattle in stock pen number seven. I want to know who brought them in."

The frizzy-haired man with a thin goatee looked past her to focus on Lone Wolf. Julia knew immediately that the man recognized her new husband. Penders surged to his feet to check out her accusation. Julia noted that Lone Wolf had flashed the man a lethal stare, which he quickly masked behind a neutral expression for her benefit.

She supposed she should be offended that he had used his commanding presence to make sure her request stuck and that she got immediate results, but she didn't mind having him there to back her up. There were many times, she decided, that having a legendary shootist guarding your back was a good thing. This was one of those times.

"Thank you," she murmured as she brushed past Lone Wolf to follow the barrel-bellied manager outside.

"Anytime, Julia," he said as he trailed behind her.

"Are these the cattle that you claim are yours?" John Penders asked, pointing to the black calves.

Julia gestured toward the fresh brand seared over the Lazy P brand. "They are our cattle," she said with absolute certainty. "They were stolen from our pasture last night. Lone Wolf found the abandoned campfire where the brands were changed. He determined that there were three riders involved. I want to know whose name is listed on the bill of sale."

John returned to the office to rifle through the receipts. "A man named Les Mitchum told me that he brought the cattle up the trail from Texas."

"Not unless Texas has annexed Preston Ranch," Lone Wolf snorted. "Describe Les Mitchum to me."

"About your size," John said. "Thick brown hair, beard and mustache. Dark eyes. A scar on his left temple."

"Long canvas coat and broad-brimmed hat?" Julia asked.

John nodded his bushy head. "Yes, ma'am. Mitchum said he or one of his men would be here tomorrow to collect for the cattle. Guess you'll be wanting to take 'em home with you."

"Yes, we hadn't planned to sell those yearlings until this fall," she informed him.

"I'm going to report this incident to Sheriff Danson," Lone Wolf said. "The Prestons have had problems with rustlers too often lately. If you see anything suspicious, such as freshly worked brands, I would appreciate it if you would contact me at the ranch."

"Sure, glad to do it," John replied. "Don't want no trouble with you, Lone Wolf."

"And I don't want any trouble coming in my new wife's direction. She's had enough on her mind since her brother was bushwhacked."

"Wife?" John's eyes rounded and his startled regard bounced from Lone Wolf to Julia, then to their banded left hands.

She should be accustomed to that stunned reaction by now, but it still rankled that folks had difficulty accepting this marriage. Of course, everyone judged Lone Wolf by his formidable reputation and mixed breeding.

She seemed to be the only one who had taken the time to get to know him and discovered that beneath the gruff, rugged exterior was an intriguing and honorable man.

"I'll be around tomorrow to see who comes to collect payment for those stolen cattle," Lone Wolf promised.

While John called to one of the attendants to open the gate to release the calves Julia and Lone Wolf mounted their horses. Lone Wolf was duly impressed by Julia's practiced technique of sweeping back and forth behind the cattle and by her ability to move them in the direction she wanted them to go without sending them charging off at a dead run.

But, since Adam had confided that Julia had thrust herself into ranch duties after their father's death, he shouldn't be surprised that she could herd cattle as efficiently as a man.

Of course, this wasn't the same as chasing wild buffalo cross-country or rounding up herds of skittish mustangs, as Lone Wolf had done while he lived with the Cheyenne. In fact, it was rather tame in comparison. Nonetheless, Julia wasn't one to sit back and watch. She was involved and she seemed to prefer activity.

While they drove the herd to the ranch Lone Wolf scanned the countryside to make sure the pesky sniper never had a clear shot at them. When he spotted three cowboys on guard duty he gave a loud whistle to gain their attention.

"Your men can help you corral the cattle and get them branded properly," Lone Wolf told Julia. "I'm riding back to town to inform the sheriff of the rustling. Then I want to scout out the area. I'll be back after dark."

To his surprise, Julia eased her horse up beside him, leaned out to hook her hand around his neck then kissed him soundly. "Be careful," she murmured. "I want you to come home safe and sound."

While Julia and the cowboys herded the calves to the corral, Lone Wolf sat in the saddle, staring after her. *Come home safe and sound.* He hadn't had a place to call home in two decades.

Home. That had a nice ring to it.

Careful, Lone Wolf, he cautioned himself. *This is still a temporary assignment, married or not. You don't have a home, remember? You've managed just fine without one for years.*

On the wings of that realistic reminder he reined his horse toward town.

While the cowboys reworked the brands on the calves Julia checked on her brother. She blinked in surprise when she walked into his room and found him sitting on the bed.

"Are you sure it isn't too soon for this?" she questioned worriedly. "The last thing you need is a relapse."

Adam nodded his ruffled blond head. "Doc Connor came by to check on me. He said I could sit upright and move around a bit." He stared distastefully at the room. "This severe case of cabin fever is as bad as the wound, if you want the truth."

When Adam rose unsteadily to his feet, Julia rushed over to lend support then assisted him to the nearest chair.

"Damn." He huffed and puffed to catch his breath. "Who would have thought walking across the room would take so much effort." Adam swore again. "I don't like having to leave you to take charge of everything, Jules. It feels like I'm shirking my duties and dropping all the responsibilities around here on you."

"That's what family is for," she assured him. "We take care of each other and we take turns taking charge when necessary. Plus, we have Lone Wolf on our side and he just got through making sure that I had no trouble gathering the stolen cattle that he tracked to the stock pens in Dodge."

She smiled wryly. "The manager was all too eager to cooperate after Lone Wolf gave him The Look."

Adam managed a grin. "I'd like to learn that technique myself. Might come in handy occasionally."

His expression sobered as he settled himself carefully in the chair. "Now, about this marriage, Jules. I sincerely hope you know what you're doing. Pretend marriage is one thing, but *official* is something else. If · you married Lone Wolf just so you could acquire your trust fund to recoup our losses then that is beyond the call of duty. We could have tightened our belts and managed without it."

"Now we won't have to." Julia pulled up another chair and sat down directly across from Adam. "Furthermore, I know what I'm doing," she declared. "An extra benefit of this arrangement is that I don't have to deal with any more pretentious marriage offers that don't interest me."

Adam glowered. "I'd like to resolve that problem for Maggie, too. Damn Sol and his machinations!"

"Not to worry on that count," she insisted with a dismissive flick of her wrist. "Maggie isn't interested in anyone but you. She will pitch a fit if Sol tries to marry her off while you're injured and incapable of objecting.

We will deal with Sol on that matter when the time comes." Julia took a deep breath then said, "There is something you need to know about Lone Wolf."

"Like what?" he grumbled. Obviously he was still brooding about the distasteful prospect of Maggie's upcoming marriage to someone besides him.

"Lone Wolf is Sol's nephew."

Adam's head snapped up then he winced at the abrupt movement. "What the devil are you talking about?"

"Sol's younger sister, Isabella, was captured by the Cheyenne when she was a young woman," Julia reported. "She and her Cheyenne husband were killed in a massacre when Lone Wolf was fourteen. Before she died, Isabella told him to go to Sol for help. But Sol rejected him and sent him away to survive as best he could in the wilds."

She smiled reassuringly at her brother. "My point is that Lone Wolf is not going to allow his first cousin to be carted off to Abilene against her will. He has his own ax to grind with Sol and he wants that devious scoundrel to get exactly what he deserves, just as we do."

Adam blinked rapidly, trying to digest the unexpected information. Then he smiled slyly. "Lone Wolf must be enjoying the fact that he's joined forces against Sol and that you married him. That should infuriate Sol to no end."

Julia bobbed her head. "I think it's time for Maggie to know the truth about Lone Wolf. If she knows her father denied refuge to his sister's orphan son then she might understand that Sol is also capable of plotting against us."

"I'll tell her tonight," Adam said as he absently massaged his chest wound. "They are really cousins? How about that. I think Mags will be pleased. She told me that she enjoyed Lone Wolf's company the night he escorted her home. This information also assures me that he has Maggie's best interests at heart."

"He's a good and decent man, Adam," Julia murmured. "He has been misjudged by those who haven't taken the time to get to know him. I like him. A lot."

Adam quirked his lips. "So I've noticed. You never did give your other suitors a second glance. Not that I minded. I didn't approve of them, either."

He took her hand in his, giving it a fond squeeze. "I just don't want to see you hurt, Jules. I don't know how much you can expect from Lone Wolf. I wouldn't have figured him for the marrying kind, except maybe for this connection to Sol and the vindication that he's probably enjoying. I agree that he deserves a little revenge, but not at your expense."

"I'm not expecting more than Lone Wolf is capable of giving." That was a lie. Julia wanted more than an in-name-only marriage. But she didn't confide that to Adam. He had enough to fret about. "Lone Wolf has made it possible to acquire the trust and he is here to protect us. After our problems are resolved we will decide what to do about our marriage."

When the color drained from Adam's cheeks, Julia urged him back to bed. "I think you have been up long enough."

"Unfortunately you're right." Adam leaned heavily against Julia. "Blasted wound. And damn Sol for the bastard he is. If not for Maggie I would return the favor as soon as I'm able."

Carefully, Julia eased her brother back to bed. He nodded off almost immediately. When she pivoted around, the housekeeper appeared with a heaping tray of food.

"He's out again, I see," Nora Dickerson murmured. "I've been stuffing him full of food every chance I get." She offered the tray to Julia. "You take this and I'll prepare something for Adam when he wakes up."

"Thank you, Nora. I don't know what we would do without you around to keep this place running smoothly."

Nora smiled. "You're like my own children and you know it." Her graying brows swooped down. "But I'm a bit concerned about this sudden marriage of yours and so is Frank Slater. We agree that it's good to have a man of Lone Wolf's caliber here to keep watch over you and Adam. Still…"

Julia waved off her concerns. "It's a match made in heaven."

Nora snickered. "Don't know about that, hon. But I must say that you did find someone who can keep up with you. Don't think those other dandies would have stood a chance." She stared contemplatively at Julia. "It takes a certain kind of man to deal with a spirited woman. Maybe he *is* what you need."

Julia strode off with tray in hand, thinking Nora was probably right. And so was Lone Wolf when he said that while a gentleman might have certain expectations for a wife, he was satisfied letting her be herself.

Which was another reason she felt so comfortable with Lone Wolf. He didn't seem to mind that she was assertive and headstrong. Most of the time anyway. But she could tell there were times when he wished she would stand aside and let him handle situations.

Things might turn out well between them if Lone

Wolf would fall a little bit in love with her, she thought wistfully as she ate her meal. Because the truth was that she thought she might be just a little bit in love with him…and she wasn't even sure exactly when or how that had happened.

Too soon or not, that was how she felt. She hadn't planned on getting so attached to him, but she was. She secretly wished her growing affection for Lone Wolf wasn't one-sided. But she knew he didn't return her affection.

She had to learn to live with that, too.

Chapter Eleven

Two days after the rustling incident Lone Wolf was thumbing through the wanted posters when Sheriff Danson released his overnight "guests" who had been detained for drunken and disorderly behavior on South Side. A suspicious frown furrowed Lone Wolf's brow as he watched the unkempt, scraggly-haired ruffian swagger past him.

Floyd McNeese was a local tough that Lone Wolf had tangled with once or twice at a saloon. The ruffian wasn't beneath taking any job that could keep him in whiskey money. He was the perfect candidate to handle dirty work.

When Floyd exited Lone Wolf turned his attention to the sheriff. "Where was Floyd when you hauled him in?"

Danson plunked down in his chair then propped up his feet on the edge of his desk. "He was firing off his pistol outside Sand Plum Saloon. The two other drunks with him scurried off before I could snag them." He glanced quizzically at Lone Wolf. "Why? You think he might be involved in the rustling you reported?"

Lone Wolf shrugged as he checked the posters. So far he had come across no one by the name of Les Mitchum. "There were three riders herding Preston's stolen cattle. When it comes to *worthless,* McNeese heads up the list and I wouldn't be surprised to discover that he is involved."

"Can't say that I wouldn't put something like that past McNeese," Danson agreed. "But you know how hard it is to pin rustling on men around here. There are herds coming up the trails from Texas most of the year, carrying more brands than anyone can keep up with. Men like McNeese and his cohorts can sort off a few head and drive them to the stock pens. It's hard to gather enough evidence to press charges." He cocked a dark brow. "Find anything on that Mitchum character?"

"Not yet, but there's no guarantee that he doesn't have an alias. Some of the thieves I've tracked down have a list of names as long as their arms. If not for descriptions I'd have a hell of a time sorting out who's who."

Sheriff Danson leaned back in his chair then clasped his hands behind his head. "You know, I can't believe I'm about to say this, but I think you and Julia make a suitable couple."

"Yeah? What makes you think so?" he asked without looking up from the stack of posters.

Danson chuckled. "Pretty though she is, and as many gents in these parts that have proposed to her, she's just…" He paused, searching for an appropriate description.

Lone Wolf smiled wryly. "Headstrong? Unconventional? Daring? Fearless? Feisty?"

Danson nodded and grinned. "Her daddy used to

fret over her something fierce. Used to say that when the Lord passed out spunk and energy that Julia sneaked through the line thrice."

"Amen to that," Lone Wolf seconded.

"Still, I consider you one lucky devil. Life with Julia could never be dull."

"Probably not...." His voice trailed off when a sketch of a man named Will Butler, who had a noticeable scar on the side of his face, nabbed his attention. He turned the poster toward Danson. "Does he look familiar?"

The sheriff shrugged his thick shoulders. "No, can't say that I've seen him around."

"He fits the stockyard manager's description. Wanted in Newton for robbery and murder three years ago. He's never been apprehended. This could be the man who shot Adam."

"Damn, just what we need around here. Another potential threat. As if the cowboys at trail's end don't get liquored up and try to blow the lid off this town often enough."

Lone Wolf tucked the poster into his shirt pocket then headed for the door. "Telegraph the marshal in Newton to find out what you can about Butler. I'll follow McNeese and see where he goes to roost...and who's there to meet him. Then I'll show this poster to John Penders."

"Most likely he'll make a beeline for his favorite watering hole," Danson predicted. "I'll find out what I can about Butler."

Lone Wolf mounted his horse and watched Floyd McNeese stride across the Plaza—which was nothing more than one hundred yards of sand and sagebrush that was bisected by railroad tracks. The division separated the town's unruly South Side from its sedate counterpart.

Lone Wolf was curious to learn what color of horse Floyd rode. Dun? Sorrel? Bay? If Will Butler, alias Les Mitchum, was working with the local toughs, the man might be switching horses during the ambushes. Lone Wolf had every intention of dogging McNeese's footsteps to find out who his cohorts were.

While lightning flared across the night sky and thunder rumbled overhead Julia paced the covered veranda on the front porch. It was nearly midnight. Maggie had come and gone before the storm rolled in, but Lone Wolf wasn't present and accounted for. He'd left before lunch. All sorts of worst-case scenarios were chasing each other around Julia's head.

She kept assuring herself that Lone Wolf was capable of handling wily outlaws and threatening thunderstorms, but that didn't alleviate her mounting concern. First off, Lone Wolf had been wounded and was still recovering. Secondly, they had yet to locate or officially identify the sniper. The elusive scoundrel could be on Lone Wolf's trail at this very moment. Thirdly, Julia had grown accustomed to Lone Wolf's presence and not having him underfoot made her restless and uneasy.

Two weeks ago she had only known the gunfighter by reputation. Now he was an integral part of her life and she wanted to keep it that way.

Julia sighed impatiently and paced some more. She had never met a man who had made such a lasting impression on her. Strange how you could know some folks for years and never develop an attachment. And others just walked in and took up permanent residence in your thoughts immediately.

While lightning streaked through the thunderheads, Julia cast one last anxious glance toward the rolling hills. She was tempted to climb aboard her horse and search for Lone Wolf, but at the same time she felt obliged to check on her brother.

Someone needed to be here in case the sniper decided a stormy night provided the perfect opportunity to sneak in and finish off Adam.

Muttering at Lone Wolf's unexplained absence, Julia entered the house then took the steps two at a time to check on her brother. She tested the lock on the terrace door, brushed her hand across Adam's brow to make certain his fever hadn't risen, and then went to her room.

She plunked down into the chair she had positioned as her lookout post for the second-story balcony. Tired though she was, she resolved to keep the vigil, just in case the sound effects of the storm overrode the approach of an intruder.

Despite her good intentions she nodded off. Her head drooped against her shoulder and her fingers went slack on the pistol she had laid on her lap.

Lone Wolf eased quietly into the bedroom then smiled when lightning flared, spotlighting Julia who was asleep in the chair that faced the balcony. He could have told her that she was wasting her time because he had chased off an intruder a half hour earlier.

Unfortunately, he hadn't been close enough to get off a shot. The sniper had spotted him and thundered off in the downpour.

Sighing tiredly, Lone Wolf peeled off his wet jacket

and shirt then hung them on the hook by the door. Then he lightly tapped Julia on the shoulder to wake her. When she startled, he calmed her.

"Shh, it's just me."

Her breath gushed out in a sigh as she surged from the chair to hug the stuffing out of him. He winced when her hand accidentally clamped over his tender upper arm.

"Where have you been so long? I was worried about you." Her muffled voice vibrated against his bare chest. "What time is it? Why do you smell like cheap perfume and cigar smoke?"

Lone Wolf smiled in amusement. Not only did Julia fall asleep quickly but also she awoke to fire off questions like a Gatling gun, he noted.

"Which one of those questions do you want me to answer first?" he asked as he nuzzled his chin on the top of her curly head and inhaled her alluring scent.

She leaned back to peer up at him. It was all he could do not to kiss her senseless. Damn, he wanted another intoxicating taste of her. In addition, holding her close always caused his sap to rise in two seconds flat. His intense reaction to this woman worried him. Despite his best efforts, it was nearly impossible to remain detached with her.

And certainly, he couldn't remain physically undisturbed when she was within kissing distance.

"First tell me about the cheap perfume," she requested.

"Two saloon girls tried to drape themselves in my lap. After I bought them drinks they left me alone."

"Did they really?" she challenged.

He grinned. "Who's asking? The paying client or the jealous wife?"

She stepped back, then lurched around to stare out at the rain pounding against the terrace. "I'm sorry. I didn't ask for fidelity in this arrangement and that isn't any of my business. So…what have you been doing all the day, and half of the night, that applies to this assignment?"

Did Julia actually dislike the prospect of him being with another woman? he wondered as he heel-and-toed out of his boots. "I've been keeping surveillance on possible rustling suspects. It's time-consuming and it takes you all sorts of places. It almost never happens that you find out what you want to know in the first ten minutes."

Julia pivoted toward him, studying his shadowed profile, wondering if she could depend on him to tell her the truth. Had he eased his needs with another woman and refused to tell her in order to spare her feelings? She found the prospect upsetting because she was not unreceptive to learning what passion was all about. With *him* specifically.

Unfortunately, he had told her not to rush into something she might later regret. Well, for his information she regretted that she hadn't demanded her wifely rights already.

"Did you find out whatever it was that you wanted to know?" she questioned, wishing she had the nerve to ask him what she really wanted to know. Which was, would he ever want this marriage to progress to a more intimate level?

Or was he less than enthused with the prospect because she had no experience whatsoever with men?

"I did find out some interesting information," he reported. "Sheriff Danson kept one of the local thugs overnight in jail. When Floyd McNeese was released I followed him across the Plaza to South Side. After several rounds of drinks and a few hands of poker he mounted his sorrel gelding to meet up with two other ruffians. One of them was riding a dun with three white stockings. The other one was mounted on a bay pony."

"The sniper's horses," Julia muttered.

"Most likely. I stood watch while the three men made camp at an abandoned lean-to used by railroad workers when they were building tracks. I was hoping Les Mitchum, the character that the stockyard manager described to us, might show up."

"Did he?" Julia asked eagerly.

Lone Wolf shook his head. "He never approached the stockyards or the camp, which suggests that the rustling was a spiteful retaliation. Either that or someone alerted the hombres that we were waiting for them to show up to collect the money."

Her shoulders slumped defeatedly.

"But at least I have one lead," he said encouragingly. "According to the wanted poster I picked up in the sheriff's office, then showed to John Penders to confirm the match, Mitchum's real name is Will Butler. Danson received a telegram confirming that the fugitive wanted in Newton for robbery and murder is likely the same man. Oddly enough, Butler has been missing for three years."

"Which is about the same time this feud started and the rustling incidents began." She stared curiously at him. "Did any of the men ride toward Griffin Ranch?"

"No." Lone Wolf sank down on the edge of the bed to place his collection of his sidearms on the nightstand. "Sol didn't show up at their camp for a late-night conference, either. The three thugs proceeded to drink themselves into a stupor then tucked in to wait out the storm."

When he told her about scaring off the sniper earlier, she smiled gratefully. "But we still have no connection between Sol and the rustlers or the sniper." Disheartened, she grabbed her nightgown and headed for the dressing screen.

"No, but I do know where the goons go to roost. Sooner or later they will contact whoever is paying them to rustle your cattle or conspire with the sniper."

"Maybe the rustling incidents aren't even related to Sol's feud with us," she said as she disrobed. "Maybe Adam and I have jumped to the wrong conclusions. Do you think I've been irrationally suspicious?"

Lone Wolf closed his eyes tightly and tried to concentrate on their conversation. He tried not to think about Julia naked. It wasn't easy. It was easier to imagine Julia slowly and seductively peeling off every article of clothing that he could hear rustling behind the dressing screen.

Cursing his vivid imagination and the slow burn sizzling through his body, he determinedly turned his wayward thoughts to her question. "Nothing confirms Sol's connection. The same holds true for Whittaker or Clement. But it would be one hell of a coincidence if the sniper owns three different horses that *just happen* to match the mounts ridden by the local hooligans I've been watching. Someone has gone to extensive effort to set up diversions and smoke screens to keep us from pinpointing the culprit responsible for your problems."

"Lone Wolf?"

"Yeah?" He frowned, puzzled by the uncertainty in

her tone of voice. Julia uncertain? That didn't sound like the daring woman he had come to know. "Is something wrong?"

"Yes." She emerged from the dressing screen and stood at the foot of the bed. "What is it about me that puts you off?"

"What?" He gaped at her, dumbfounded.

"Am I too outspoken? Too assertive? Too independent? Not pretty enough for your tastes?"

"Julia, I don't think this conversation is going—"

"Just answer the blasted question," she interrupted impatiently. "I have been rejecting proposals for years. Then I marry you and you don't seem particularly interested in the things men usually want from women." She sighed audibly. "I really want to know why you find me so easy to resist."

Easy to resist? Hell! Sleeping beside her the past few nights and not succumbing to the nearly overwhelming need to seduce her took every smidgen of willpower and self-restraint he could muster. He deserved a damn medal for his efforts.

When she sank down beside him on the bed, her shoulder brushed against his arm. He groaned inwardly as need and pleasure bombarded him.

"Do you know what I think?" she murmured.

"No, but I'm sure you're going to tell me." He tried not to breathe, for fear he would absorb her enticing scent again and get stirred up worse than he was already.

She ignored his flippant remark and said, "I think you were just looking for an excuse to come home late again. I think you would have preferred it if I had been in bed asleep so you wouldn't have to deal with me."

He was sorry to say that the thought had crossed his

mind a time—or six—while he was hunkered in the underbrush to keep surveillance on the rustling suspects. Call him a coward, but he had hoped to slide into bed without waking Julia.

"You want the truth, I suppose," he grumbled.

"From you? Always."

"Fine. The truth is that it's difficult to sleep beside you and not want you. I told you that before and I meant it. I can't think of anything I don't like about you."

"Then why can't we—?"

"Because I'm wondering the same thing everyone else who sees us together is wondering," he cut in. "Why would you want anything to do with me when you can do so much better?"

He flinched when she bounded to her feet and loomed over him, her eyes blazing with annoyance. "That is the dumbest thing I have ever heard you say!" she huffed.

"Is it? Then you haven't known me long enough. I say stupid things all the damn time."

She swatted his good shoulder. "Stop being caustic. I am attracted to you and you need to accept that."

Lone Wolf stared grimly at her. "What you think you're feeling is just misdirected emotion," he insisted. "I'm here to provide hired muscle. Naturally you're grateful and relieved, but don't confuse those feelings with attraction or desire, Julia. This marriage serves several useful purposes that benefit us both. But there is no need to complicate matters."

She crossed her arms over her chest. "I see. So basically you're saying that if I'm curious about passion then I should experiment with someone else so we can keep this marriage uncomplicated. That sounds *more* complicated to me. But, of course, I'm not an expert in these matters."

The thought of Julia turning to another man to experiment with intimacy put him in a sour mood. "What is wrong with remaining innocent of men?"

"I am married and I want to know and feel passion. With you," she replied in true, straightforward Julia fashion, then stared him down. "It's *time,* Lone Wolf. And you are not winning this argument, because I have made up my mind."

Lone Wolf knew he was in serious trouble when she flung her arms around his neck and kissed him as if she were a drowning victim going down for the last time. He could feel the taut peaks of her breasts boring into his chest and her feminine warmth seeped into him. He forgot to breathe—didn't see any reason why he needed to—when her bent knee brushed against his hard length as she glided her leg suggestively between his thighs.

Her luscious body half covered his, and every nerve and muscle in his oversensitive body leaped to eager attention. The exquisite taste of her, the erotic feel of her shapely contours meshed to his was his undoing. He couldn't remember a time when this feisty, alluring female wasn't in his thoughts. He couldn't think past the hungry need that had been gnawing at him since she came charging into his life.

And for certain he had never won an outright argument with this willful woman.

It didn't look as if he was going to win this one, either.

Lightning flared across the room, spotlighting Julia like an incandescent vision from an erotic fantasy. Lone Wolf was lost, defeated and bewitched. All the sensible reasons he shouldn't consummate this temporary marriage escaped him completely. Nothing seemed to matter as much as claiming Julia as his own and exploring the tantalizing sensations she constantly aroused in him.

"I give up," Lone Wolf murmured when she lifted her head to stare at him with those mesmerizing green eyes. "You win."

His concession brought a smile to her kiss-swollen lips. "You never give up," she contradicted as she brushed her fingertips over his chest. "You just gave in. *Finally.*"

Then she kissed him again, as if he meant something special to her. That was the crowning blow that crumbled his common sense. He grabbed the hem of her nightgown, tugged it up and over her head, and flung it across the room.

Lightning flashed again and he saw her curvaceous body for the first time. His imagination—vivid though it had been—did not do Julia justice. She was absolute feminine perfection and he yearned to memorize every luscious inch of her silky flesh. He wanted to know her enticing body by taste and touch.

To that pleasurable and dedicated end, he took his sweet time nibbling at the curve of her neck. He coasted his hands over the rise of her creamy breasts, then explored the lush planes and contours of her belly, hips and thighs.

"Lone Wolf?" Her breath hitched and he felt her tremble beneath his featherlight kisses and caresses.

"Vince," he corrected huskily as his lips skimmed her breast. Then he flicked at the pebbled crest with his tongue. "For this, we should be on a first-name basis, Julia. This is as intimate and personal as it can get."

When he suckled her nipple then shifted to offer the

same erotic attention to the other breast, he felt her hand glide down his back. Her nails dug into his flesh, the steady pressure assuring him that he was giving her pleasure.

Lone Wolf realized there and then that he couldn't be satisfied unless she experienced every burgeoning need, every fiery sensation that passion had to offer. He suspected it was her insatiable curiosity that provoked her to experiment with desire. And he couldn't live with himself if he disappointed her, failed to satisfy her completely.

This, he realized, was vastly different from his occasional and very impersonal liaisons.

This was Julia and she mattered to him, whether he wished that to be true or not.

"Mmm…I never dreamed there was pleasure such as this," she murmured as wave upon wave of delirious sensations crested over her.

As much as she reveled in Vince's amazingly gentle touch she felt deprived of exploring him. She wanted to return each breathless sensation that he instilled in her. She wanted to claim the same power and control that he held over her body.

The thought of taking without giving back was unacceptable to her. Even if she had no experience with men she had to find a way to please him to the same wondrous degree that he had pleased her.

When this night ended she vowed to have plenty of experience at seducing the one man who tempted her and intrigued her as no other man had. Before he could work his mystifying magic on her body and leave her totally oblivious, Julia pushed his hands away and came to her knees beside him.

"Did I hurt you? Was I too rough with you?" he asked.

The unexpected concern in his raspy voice squeezed her heart. She realized that he *did* care about her in his own limited way. He cared enough to be gentle and she could have kissed him senseless for revealing the fact to her.

But first she was going to make a thorough study of his masculine body. She was going to learn the location of each battle scar that had once brought him pain. She was going to learn every curve and contour of his muscled flesh until she knew his body as well as she did her own. Maybe better.

Purposefully, Julia skimmed her lips down his breastbone, letting her unbound hair caress his shoulders and chest as her kisses drifted over his washboard belly.

"You didn't hurt me," she assured him, her moist breath whispering over his abdomen. "You couldn't. And I have no wish to hurt you, either. But be patient with me. This is my first time trying to please a man and I want to get good at it."

"Aw, damn," he breathed unsteadily. "Might as well fit me for a pine box, woman. You're killing me already."

She chuckled in playful amusement when he groaned in response to her brazen touch. "I can see the front-page headlines. Legendary Gunfighter Brought Down By A Woman."

"Died of pleasure," he said on another tormented moan. "Can't think of a better way to go, though."

Vince sucked in his breath when the feel of her silky hair and warm lips glided over his sensitized skin, igniting wildfires in his blood, leaving him burning out of control. He had never allowed a woman to touch and explore him as freely as Julia. Never wanted anyone to have this much control over him. But Julia made him feel defenseless. Made him *like* feeling defenseless. She left him tumbling helter-skelter in a world of searing heat and addictive pleasure.

His thoughts shattered and his body nearly exploded when she folded her hand around his aching shaft. When she stroked him with thumb and fingertips from base to tip he groaned aloud as flames surged through his bloodstream.

The woman was too bold and inquisitive, he decided as he struggled to prevent hyperventilating. She was turning him wrong side out, triggering mindless sensations at such alarming speed that he swore he couldn't last another minute.

"Enough," he gasped, clutching at her roaming hand.

"But I—"

He curled his hand around her neck, drawing her head back to his. He kissed her. *Devoured her* was more accurate. Her brazen touch provoked so many ravenous sensations that he wasn't as gentle as he knew he should have been. He took her mouth, plunging his tongue into the sweet recesses as thoroughly and deeply as he wanted to sink into her body.

And when he finally felt a small measure of control returning, he vowed that he wouldn't take Julia until she was as hot and hungry for him as he had been the moment before.

He wanted her to feel that same panicky desperation, the same urgent need to meld body, breath and spirit into one shimmering essence.

Despite the twinge in his injured arm, he braced himself up on one hand and caressed her tenderly with the other. A satisfied smile tugged at his lips when she involuntarily arched toward him. He felt her flesh quiver beneath his caress, and the need to be inside her nearly overwhelmed him.

"Vince…ah…" Her voice broke as his lips feathered over her concave belly and his hand skimmed her inner thighs. "This is going to be a contest to see who kills the other one first, isn't it?"

"Last man standing wins," he whispered as he trailed his forefinger over the damp curls between her legs.

He groaned as liquid fire burned his fingertips, urging him to take her. Now. But if this turned out to be the first and last time he was allowed to touch Julia, then he refused to deprive either of them of even one pleasurable sensation. He wanted to taste her completely, to know her as no other man had, to know her as he had known no other woman.

He eased between her legs, opening her body with a gentle nudge of his shoulder. When he flicked at her softest flesh with his tongue and forefinger he felt her answering response arcing through him. He gave her the most intimate of all kisses, tasted the passion he had summoned from her and felt the world shift out of focus as need burgeoned inside him. The wild tremors that racked her body echoed through him as he tasted her again and again.

He heard her cry out his name until her voice and her body shattered around him. He never knew a woman so full of explosive passion, never realized that he could experience so much pleasure in watching a woman unravel beneath his touch. When Julia all but came apart on his lips and fingertips she clawed desperately at him, her breath ragged, her voice a hoarse whimper of erotic torment.

Then he braced himself above her on his good arm and told himself to move deliberately and carefully during this crucial moment. He didn't want to hurt her more than necessary. But she lifted her hand to enfold him, guiding him exactly to her. When she arched against him, all attempts to proceed slowly flitted off like the wind-driven rain that pounded outside.

"I love you," she whispered as he plunged helplessly into her, burying himself deeply inside her, feeling the fragile barrier of innocence give way.

He felt her wince momentarily then relax against him, welcoming him, accepting him. He savored the feel of her body surrounding him, making him a living, breathing part of her.

"I love you," she murmured again as he moved in ancient rhythm, bombarded by one incredible sensation after another.

He didn't believe her, of course, but he was too far gone to tell her that it was only passion speaking, that she really didn't know the difference and wouldn't until the distorting haze of pleasure parted like the clouds of the sweeping thunderstorm. But her words did breathe life into that empty place in his heart, even while he reminded himself that passion was a shimmering mirage that would evaporate with the vanishing heat of the moment.

When Julia grabbed a handful of his long hair and pulled his head down to kiss him frantically Vince responded instinctively. He moved against her, plunging and withdrawing, driven by such overwhelming sensations that the last of his control slipped its leash.

He heard her breath catch and he was afraid that he was hurting her as he rocked hard against her. When he tried to pull away, she clamped her hands on his hips, holding him intimately against her.

"I want all you have to give and I demand nothing less," she whispered against his lips.

As he buried himself to the hilt he reminded himself that in this, as in all else, Julia did nothing halfway. For years he had held his emotions under careful control, but that was impossible when he was with Julia. Taking without giving something back wasn't an option when he was with her like this. And so he offered himself up to her, as they rode out the wild storm of passion in the wondrous circle of each other's arms.

When he heard her choked cry of pleasure and felt her uncontrollable release caressing him intimately he pinwheeled over the edge of oblivion. His breath gushed from his chest and pleasure too profound and intense to describe buffeted him. He clutched Julia tightly to him as one helpless shudder after another pummeled him.

And when the monsoon of immeasurable passion finally passed Vince knew beyond all doubt that whatever he had been doing when he found himself in a woman's arms did not remotely compare to what he experienced with Julia now. She shattered him, reinvented him. She exposed each vulnerability that he had spent two decades building barriers to protect.

The unsettling realization that, in the arms of this one woman, he was completely at her mercy disturbed him greatly. She had come to matter too much. She touched off too many tender emotions inside him.

He had sworn almost twenty years earlier that he

would never let anyone close enough to hurt him, as he had been hurt when he lost his family. He had trained himself to become an invincible warrior who spit in the face of adversity and met every challenge. He had taught himself to disregard every condemning and condescending comment directed at him, because he didn't give a damn what anyone thought.

But he cared what Julia thought, because this green-eyed siren beguiled him. She drew carefully guarded emotion from him as easily as he drew water from a well. And then she had kissed him one last time with such amazing tenderness that his defenses took another direct hit. When she whispered those three sweet-but-tormenting words to him, Vince had tried to harden his heart and his defenses. He refused to believe that she knew what she was saying or how she really felt.

He didn't want to be on hand when Julia came to her senses and realized that it wasn't love but rather temporary passion she felt for him. He could face almost anything—and had—but he couldn't bear to watch her misconstrued affection dissolve into indifference.

And it would eventually, he was sure of it.

He couldn't stay here, dreading that inevitable moment when she realized she didn't love him, after all. He didn't want to be around when she discovered that her driving emotion had been gratitude because he had been here to help her resolve her problems.

Lone Wolf held Julia close to his heart, savoring the pleasure she gave him, until she drifted off to sleep. Then he eased off the bed to gather his clothes.

If there was one irrefutable truth that he had learned in his difficult life it was that there were no fairy tales with happy endings for men like him. If he had any brains left in his head—and, at the moment, he couldn't swear he did—he would get the hell out of Dodge while the getting was good.

No emotional farewells, he vowed. He would just go and he would deal with this assignment at a distance so he could get his priorities straight. His perspective had turned inside out and backward since the night Julia had come barreling into his life, and wanting her in the worst way had begun to dominate his thoughts.

But things were about to change, he assured himself.

Vince Lone Wolf was what he was. A tough, battle-hardened gunfighter hired to apprehend dangerous criminals. He wasn't gentle or sensitive and he wasn't good husband material. He wasn't a valued confidant or friend to anyone, either.

As he strapped on his holsters he glanced back at the bed and felt unwanted emotion hit him like a shotgun blast in the chest. Until this moment he had merely existed, doing what he did best—fight and survive. It was all he knew. If he let himself believe Julia's whispered words of affection it would destroy his ability to function efficiently in his world. It would make him wish for things that could never be.

Lone Wolf slipped the gold band from his finger then laid it on the nightstand. He wasn't waiting for Julia to realize her reckless mistake and toss his belongings on the front lawn to end this mismatched marriage. He had been paid in full for taking this assignment that he should have left alone.

Making love with Julia had cost him far more than he could bear to lose and still contend with his dangerous profession.

This assignment, this woman, could cost him his

heart—and whatever passed for his soul. He had to walk away right now and not look back. It was a simple matter of survival.

Chapter Twelve

The next morning Julia came awake, serenaded by the steady patter of rain. She reached for Lone Wolf and found only the empty space beside her. She raked the wild tumble of hair away from her face, and her breath stalled in her chest when she saw the gold band lying on the nightstand. Her alarmed gaze flew to the corner of the room where Lone Wolf placed his saddlebags each night.

There was nothing but another empty space—the same size as the hole in her heart.

The contentment that had surrounded her when she woke up vanished. The man she hadn't been able to stop herself from falling in love with—the man who had taught her the meaning of incredible passion—had disappeared, leaving behind his ring.

Disheartened and confused, she picked up the gold band. She didn't understand what she had done to provoke Lone Wolf to leave. Had she been a disappointment to him? Had she been too uninhibited? Or too inexperienced to completely satisfy him? Or had her whispered words—ones that he hadn't returned because he didn't share her sentiments—prompted him to leave?

Feelings of inadequacy and uncertainty hounded Julia as she snuggled beneath the quilt to ward off the chill of the rainy morning. She had offered Lone Wolf her heart and her love, and he didn't want either of them. Julia wasn't even sure that he'd been all that sated when she gave him her body.

She wished there was someone she could confide in, someone who could explain what she might have done wrong that had caused Lone Wolf to walk away. He had been the one she turned to for guidance and comfort. Now he was gone.

Why? she cried silently. *Why can't he love me the way I love him?*

Disillusioned and hurt, Julia rolled from bed to grab her robe. She wondered if Lone Wolf had removed himself from her life because he didn't need her affection. And maybe not even her passion.

She suspected he could get that from any woman.

Frustrated, Julia made several trips up and down the steps to heat water and fill the tub. She hoped that a good soaking would lift her spirits, but being alone with her troubled thoughts only made matters worse.

An hour later she dressed in her usual attire of breeches and shirt then checked on Adam. She was relieved to see that the housekeeper had brought him a tray and that he was eating his way through a heaping plate of food.

As for Julia, discovering that her new husband had abandoned her so quickly and easily, and didn't return her affection, spoiled her appetite.

"You look much better this morning," she observed as she put up a bold front and breezed into the room.

"Thanks," Adam replied between bites. "I would like to take a bath and then try ambling down the hall. Can Lone Wolf assist me?"

Julia averted her gaze and fidgeted. "He is already up and gone. I don't know when he'll be back."

He might have walked away from a marriage that didn't suit him and a wife who failed to meet his expectations, but she had no doubt that he wouldn't disregard this assignment until he completed it satisfactorily.

"I'll ask Frank to help you," she offered.

"When Maggie came over last night she said she wouldn't be able to get away for the next two evenings. She also mentioned that her father insisted that she attend Audrey Clement's engagement reception this afternoon."

Julia sighed when the image of Audrey Holier-Than-Thou Clement popped to mind. She had also received an invitation to the party, but she hadn't planned to attend. But if Maggie was going, it would make the stuffy social function bearable. Plus, she could use a distraction from tormenting thoughts of Lone Wolf and the ease with which he had left her behind. In addition, she might find out something that connected Benjamin Clement to the sniper attacks and rustling.

"Perhaps you can tell Mags about her kinship with Lone Wolf," Adam requested. "I planned to do it last night, but we..." His voice trailed off. "It...uh...slipped my mind."

"I'll tell her if I have the chance," Julia promised reluctantly before she spun toward the door. "Frank will be upstairs in a few minutes to help you."

"Thanks, Jules. I'm hoping I can build up my stamina then venture outside within the next few days. I don't like being a burden. You have enough responsibilities heaped on you. We are supposed to be a team."

"Do you see me complaining?"

"No, and that's what worries me," he teased. "If I'm out of commission for too long you'll be running the show. I will never be reinstated as co-owner of the ranch."

Julia turned back to flash her brother an impudent grin. "You're right. That *is* incentive to recover quickly."

At least she had her brother to lean on, she consoled herself on the way out the front door. He would always be there to cheer her up when thoughts of Lone Wolf brought her down. Knowing Lone Wolf was out there somewhere was small comfort. She wanted him here, but he had made it abundantly clear—without voicing the words—that he wasn't coming back, not in the capacity of her husband.

For the past four years she'd wondered if she was capable of love because no one had drawn her interest or inspired her desire. But she had definitely discovered what it felt like to love a man wholeheartedly.

She had also found out how it felt to be rejected.

That she could have done without…because, sure enough, it hurt something fierce.

A steady drizzle pattered in the leaves of the overhanging trees while Lone Wolf stood sentinel on the western boundary of Preston Ranch. He was tempted to storm over to Sol's house and drag a confession of guilt from him.

Beating it out of him had tremendous appeal at the moment.

He wanted Sol to be the guilty party, wanted to complete this investigation and leave. But he had to be thorough and patient to solve this perplexing case.

After the night he had shared with Julia, he felt the panicky urge to run far and fast. He was eager to take any assignment if it would distract him from this tangle of emotions—all of which had Julia's name attached to them.

Damnation, it drove him crazy knowing that she had mistakenly thought she had fallen in love with him. First off, he wasn't lovable. Secondly, he knew the newness of passion had put those words on her tongue. By placing distance between them, Lone Wolf predicted Julia would reassess her misguided affection and realize she was mistaken.

I love you. The bittersweet echo of Julia's voice swept through his mind, as it had a hundred times since he'd crept off the previous night. Lone Wolf ground his teeth and reminded himself that there were certain illusions in this world that a sensible man could not believe in, for fear of destroying himself. He couldn't permit himself to think for even one moment that Julia might actually be in love with him.

If he knew nothing else it was that she was a hell of a lot better off without him and that he didn't deserve her. But idiot that he was, he had yielded to the forbidden temptation of claiming her as his own—if only for one night.

His anguished thoughts trailed off while he surveyed the area through his field glasses, checking for anything or anyone that looked suspicious and out of place. His attention settled on the curly-haired woman who walked from the ranch house and headed toward the barn. Frustration left him scowling as he watched Julia disappear into the shadows of the barn, then reappear as she and Frank Slater returned to the house.

Seeing her, even at a distance, was still too close for his peace of mind.

He wondered how many miles he would have to put between them before he forgot how she made him feel, forgot how it felt to hold her…how it felt to be inside her.

The scintillating thought made him scowl all over again. Lone Wolf stuffed the field glasses in his pocket and reined his horse toward Griffin Ranch. It was high time he focused absolute concentration on the three men who had camped out at the lean-to west of Dodge.

Hopefully, one of the men would show up at the stock pens to collect payment for the stolen cattle. He intended to be on hand in case that happened so he could interrogate the scoundrel. It had to be better than torturing himself with thoughts of a woman who had no place in his life.

And certainly, he had no place in *hers*.

By the time Julia arrived at Audrey's reception at four o'clock that afternoon the skies had cleared. The much-welcomed rain had soaked into the pastures and the fresh scent in the air signaled a hopeful new beginning.

Julia forced herself to think in terms of making a new start in life—one that wouldn't include Lone Wolf. He didn't want her. He didn't need her and she had to accept that.

Resolved to concentrating her efforts on approaching Maggie about her kinship to Lone Wolf, Julia drove the carriage into town. Frank Slater had suggested the three cowboys accompany her since they needed to pick up supplies. Ordinarily she would have thwarted Frank's discreet attempt to provide bodyguards, but she was too depressed to protest.

While the cowboys veered away from Front Street to stop at their favorite watering hole before they purchased supplies, Julia headed toward the Clements' ostentatious home. Honestly, she would rather be whipped than put on her party manners for Audrey and her gaggle of pretentious friends. If not for the chance to see if Benjamin had any suspicious-looking characters lurking about and to visit with Maggie, Julia wouldn't have come at all.

"Julia, so glad you could make it," Audrey's voice was full of false enthusiasm as she flashed the diamond-and-ruby engagement ring that was large enough to choke a horse. "Isn't this ring incredible? Gerald insisted that I have nothing but the best his money could buy. Of course, distinguished politician that he is, he has a dignified image to uphold. So naturally our marriage ceremony will be held in the state capitol next week. All of Papa's friends and Gerald's distinguished associates will be in attendance."

When Audrey purposely flaunted the oversize ring in her face, Julia dutifully praised the sparkling jewels.

"Word around town is that you married some no-account mercenary." Audrey covered her mouth—with her left hand, of course, so the ring could glitter in the light. "Oh dear, that didn't come out right."

Nothing ever came out right when it passed Audrey's lips. This young woman was a glaring example of snobbish western aristocracy at its worst. Her father had pampered and spoiled her and she reeked of self-importance, as he did.

"Let me see *your* ring," Audrey insisted.

A flock of young women, dressed in frilly finery, surged toward Julia. Unashamed, she held up her left hand.

Audrey frowned disapprovingly, as did her prissy friends. "Well, I suppose if that's the best the mercenary can afford it will have to do. Now, what was his name again? Wolf-something or other? Isn't he that rough-looking half-breed that no respectable citizen prefers to associate with?"

Julia held her composure, difficult though it was.

When Audrey shook her head copper-red ringlets danced around her porcelain face. She leaned close to say, "*Really,* Julia, what possessed you to marry some-one so far beneath your station? Unconventional though you are, offers from dignified gentlemen would suit you better."

Julia knew she was being baited, but she still said, "There are none better than Lone Wolf. We suit per-fectly."

"If you wanted to win a gun battle, I suppose that might be true," Audrey replied airily. "But as a hus-band?" She wrinkled her nose distastefully. "I would never let myself become that desperate for a match." She smiled snidely. "Of course, after the embarrassing scandal that has been hanging over your head like a black cloud for the past three years, that might be the best you can do."

Julia wondered if this pretentious debutante had any idea how close she had come to being strangled. Will-fully, Julia resisted the temptation. She pushed onto tiptoe to glance around the beehive coiffure that made Audrey appear a foot taller than she actually was.

"Oh, good, Maggie is here." She veered around the bevy of highfalutin females and breezed off.

Maggie smiled in playful amusement as Julia plopped down beside her on the couch. "Don't you just love to be harassed the moment you come through Audrey's door?"

She watched Audrey swan into the room like a regal princess entering court. "It is always a challenge to survive the torture chamber she sets up at her front door." She quirked a brow at Maggie. "Which method of torment did she apply to you? The shameless scandal between our families or your forbidden infatuation with my brother?"

"Both," Maggie confided. "Audrey has been in rare form since her engagement to the state politician that her father's banking connections landed for her. I've heard there is a business merger involved. In fact, I overheard Benjamin Clement tell Papa that the railroad has spent the past few years arranging for expansion. Property value and right-of-way easements will quadruple when the spur comes our direction. Papa claims he can make a fortune by selling off sites for new businesses along the new route.

"Which direction are the tracks to be laid?" she asked, wondering if this might be the reason Benjamin kept offering to purchase the ranch.

"Southeast. The idea is to bring the railheads closer to the influx of Texas cattle," Maggie reported. "Papa says that real estate prices will escalate when the private information in legislative committees goes public."

Southeast? Julia frowned pensively. If that were true then the railroad would cut across Griffin Ranch and Preston Ranch. Water from their spring-fed stream would be in great demand, too. If new communities sprang up along the rails they would be sitting on a gold mine of financial opportunity....

Suddenly Sol's and Benjamin's interest in acquiring Preston Ranch made perfect sense. They both had the inside track on privileged information. Either of them could have resorted to drastic measures to force a sale. No doubt, both men wanted to get their hands on valuable property before the expansion became public knowledge.

Julia couldn't say for certain if the ambushes were scare tactics or earnest attempts on their lives. The sniper had become overly cautious since Lone Wolf had arrived. Just what was the purpose of the rustling and ambushes? The machinations of a feuding neighbor? Or was something else actually going on here? Personal gain and social distinction from land sales could be the motive. Was she missing other valuable clues?

The need to inform Maggie of Lone Wolf's identity warred with her eagerness to do some investigating of her own. She also needed to confide her suspicions about Sol's possible involvement in the bushwhackings. Difficult though it would be for Maggie to hear, she had to realize that if Sol was heartless enough to deny refuge to his distraught nephew then he was capable of hiring a henchman to frighten and maim his neighbors in hopes of acquiring their valuable property. With the Prestons out of the way, Sol could become one of the most influential and wealthiest men in the state.

No doubt, that would go a long way in appeasing the humiliation Sol had suffered because of the scandal.

Julia bounded from the sofa to fetch two cups of punch from the dining room. Then she returned to hand one to Maggie.

For all she knew the business arrangement she had overheard Sol mention to his unidentified guest was the acquisition of Preston Ranch. And then again, Benjamin Clement might be the one responsible. At this point, Julia wouldn't put anything past either man.

Maggie frowned worriedly as Julia handed her the glass of punch. "Is something wrong? You look grim." Alarm flared in her eyes. "Is it Adam? Did he suffer a setback? Dear God—"

Julia flung up her hand. "Adam is doing exceptionally well. In fact, he was ambulating along the upstairs hall when I left the house."

Maggie half collapsed in relief.

"What I need to tell you is—"

Audrey appeared in front of them. "I can't believe the two of you are still speaking after that shameless affair your parents had," she taunted.

"Go sharpen your tongue on someone else," Julia said, shooing the annoying pest away. "Maggie and I are engaged in serious conversation."

Audrey recoiled in offended dignity. "I don't know why I bothered to invite either of you to my party."

"Of course you do," Julia said without missing a beat. "You wanted a scapegoat and whipping boy. Unfortunately Maggie and I have never had any interest in your spiteful games. We find them as trite and boring as you are."

Audrey's angry expression caused her face to pucker like a sun-dried prune. "I will have you thrown out. Papa wields a lot of power around here, you know. He will have you blacklisted from every social function," she threatened vindictively.

"Don't be too quick to offend me, Audrey. My new

husband won't take your threats lightly." Julia smiled impishly, and said, "He happens to be very protective of me and, believe me, you wouldn't want to square off against a man of his exceptional combat skills. Wouldn't it be a pity if you met your demise before you can marry State Senator Russell?"

While Audrey stood there in her frilly gown of ice-blue satin and lace, her jaw scraping her chest and her eyes popping, Julia thrust the cup of punch at her, then pulled Maggie to her feet.

"I think I shall go tell Lone Wolf right this minute that you have been a rude, condescending hostess."

Audrey sputtered and gasped in outrage while Julia and Maggie sailed toward the foyer.

"Nothing like burning bridges behind you," Maggie murmured as they walked onto the porch.

"Oh dear, did I step too far over the line?" Julia asked in mock concern.

"Considering the harassment Audrey the Terrible has been dishing out since we were schoolgirls? *No.* That witch was years overdue for a dressing-down." She grinned brightly. "I'm delighted that I was here to see it happen."

Julia gestured for Maggie to join her in the buggy. A drive around the block would provide the privacy needed to impart the information, she decided. She wondered fleetingly why *she* was the one who had gotten stuck with this unpleasant task.

Well, here goes, she thought as she took a steadying breath. "Maggie, what I wanted to tell you, before Audrey interrupted us, is that you are related to the man I married."

There, she had said it. The truth was out in the open at last.

Chapter Thirteen

Maggie stared at her, nonplussed. "What are you talking about?"

"There is a very good reason your grandfather and Vince Lone Wolf bear the same given name," Julia stated. "It is not a coincidence."

Maggie's delicate brows shot up like exclamation marks. "Are you telling me that Lone Wolf is my half brother?" she crowed in amazement.

"No, he's your first cousin. Your Aunt Isabella, who was captured by the Cheyenne, was Lone Wolf's mother."

"That is impossible!" Maggie denied heatedly. "Papa said his sister succumbed to smallpox. Lone Wolf is mistaken."

Julia shook her head and smiled compassionately. "No, he isn't. I'm sure you have seen the gold locket that hangs on the edge of the picture frame in Sol's room."

Maggie nodded jerkily. "Of course, but—"

"Isabella and her Cheyenne husband were killed in

a massacre when Lone Wolf was a young teenager. Before she died, she gave him the locket and told him to take it to Sol as proof of his identity," Julia said as gently as she knew how.

Maggie gaped at her, confused and bewildered.

Now for the difficult part, Julia mused. "Orphaned, grieving and desperate, Lone Wolf made the long journey from Indian Territory to reach your ranch and asked for refuge. Sol wanted nothing to do with Lone Wolf. He even called him the spawn of a savage and ordered him never to contact him or your mother or you, because he refused to claim kinship with a half-breed."

"My father turned away his own nephew when he was alone and desperate?" Her voice rose sharply. "He wouldn't do that!"

Julia reached over to grasp Maggie's clenched fist. "Mags, you are my dearest friend. Surely you understand how difficult it is for me to confide this to you, because it contradicts your beliefs in your father. I cringe just thinking that the telling is causing you anguish."

"There has to be some reasonable explanation," Maggie erupted, near hysterics. Her nails bit into Julia's hand, the outward manifestation of her inner turmoil and mounting frustration. Wild-eyed, she insisted, "None of this makes sense. Papa must have thought Lone Wolf was trying to manipulate and deceive him!"

"Whatever the reason, Lone Wolf had to survive by himself in the wilds. He was deprived of the affection, protection and the security of a home that we've enjoyed for years."

"I don't believe it," Maggie blurted out, shaking her head in denial, fighting the onslaught of tears. "Dear God…"

"But despite what happened in the past. Or *why*," Julia continued, "you and Lone Wolf are family. He told me himself that he was pleased to see how lovely and charming his cousin turned out to be."

Maggie swiped at the tears that slid down her cheeks. "You are mistaken about Papa," she muttered angrily. "I cannot believe that you think Papa could be so cruel!"

Now for the most difficult part of all, Julia thought as she watched shock, disbelief and denial cloud Maggie's expression. Julia didn't want to have to lay all her suspicions about Sol on the line, but Maggie had been kept in the dark far too long already. Julia prayed frantically that getting her fears and concerns out in the open wouldn't come at the cost of Maggie's treasured friendship.

"Adam and I have been reluctant to tell you that evidence indicates your father might be behind the rustling. The tracks from our stolen cattle trailed across your property. The sniper who shot at Adam, and also winged Lone Wolf, was hiding in the trees on your side of the fence."

Maggie lurched back as if she had been slapped, and she very nearly catapulted herself off the seat. Her shaking hands clamped on the railing to anchor herself. Her eyes shot wide open and furious outrage flamed her cheeks.

"Papa would never ambush Adam to keep us separated!" she insisted hotly. "You are being deliberately cruel and hateful to say such things and I refuse to listen to another word of these vicious lies! He *wouldn't*—"

"He sent you to Saint Louis to keep you and Adam apart, didn't he?" Julia interrupted softly but firmly.

"He told Adam to keep his distance from you. Or else…
That was an ultimatum and a threat, Maggie."

Maggie's face drained of all color and she shook her
head fiercely. "No, I don't believe it!" she cried in dismay.

"The sniper that I saw in the copse of trees is about
Lone Wolf's size and stature," Julia reported. "He has
brown hair, dark beard, mustache and a scar on his temple. He goes by the name Les Mitchum or Will Butler.
Have you seen anyone matching that description approach your father?"

"No! And this can't be true! I am not listening to any
more of your crazed speculations!" Maggie railed as she
gathered herself on the seat, preparing to leap to the
street. "You are no friend of mine if you believe that my
father tried to kill Adam. Papa has his flaws, but he
would *never* do that! I swear, Julia, you're being as
cruel as Audrey!"

Julia reined the horse to a halt when Maggie bailed
out. She sighed in frustration as Maggie stormed off,
flashing her one mutinous glower after another. "As
difficult as it is for you to hear, it has been tormenting
me, knowing that we would have to confide our suspicions to you eventually," she said as she drove alongside her infuriated friend. "You are like a sister to me,
Mags, and it hurts me knowing I've hurt you."

"Go away and leave me be!" Maggie spouted angrily. She jerked up the front hem of her fashionable
gown and took off at a dead run to reach her own buggy.
"Don't come near me again! I have nothing to say to
you *ever!*"

Julia didn't call out to Maggie again, didn't try to
stop her wild flight. She knew Maggie needed time to

sort out the riptide of emotions that pulled her in two directions at once. Julia felt as if she had been as cruel as Sol had been to Lone Wolf. She doubted, however, that Sol was feeling the guilt and regret that was eating *her* alive at the moment.

Better that Maggie is furious with you than with Adam, Julia thought as she reversed direction. At least Adam didn't have to see the look of horrified shock and disbelief on Maggie's face. That would have tormented him to no end—and he was barely back on his own feet as it was.

"I really have to hand it to you, Jules," she said to herself. "First you put off Lone Wolf and send him running away from you. Then you give Audrey what she's had coming for years, and in front of her snobbish friends, no less. Then to top off a really lousy day you emotionally devastate the one true friend you have in the world."

Ordinarily Julia didn't waste time with self-pity because it was counterproductive. But today she indulged herself. She had lost the man she loved because of her numerous failures and flaws. She had lost her best friend, which would ultimately torment her own brother. Plus, Audrey and the other socialites she had offended would make sure her name was dragged through every mud hole in town—at least twice.

She looked skyward, wondering what else could possibly go wrong today. She didn't send the question winging heavenward—for fear that it might sound like a challenge. Considering the day she'd had already, she didn't want to push her luck.

Impatient and annoyed, Lone Wolf strode down Front Street toward the sheriff's office. He had spent the afternoon waiting for at least one of the three rustler suspects to show up at the stock pens. He'd wasted his time, so he rode out to the place where the men had holed up. They were still passed out, making it impossible to glean information. The elusive sniper hadn't shown up, either. Where the hell was the man? How did he know to avoid the camp or stock pens?

There was something about this case that didn't feel right to Lone Wolf. Damned if he could figure out what it was though. Of course, this assignment was more complicated than usual because too many of his thoughts—and all of his emotions—kept getting tangled up with mental images of Julia.

Common sense told him to keep his distance from her and focus on this case. But his heart kept telling him that she was the best thing that had ever happened to him and he should enjoy their temporary marriage as long as it lasted. He should take advantage of the fact that she fancied herself in love with him instead of discouraging her.

His conflicting thoughts trailed off when he saw Maggie Griffin racing her buggy down the street at a dangerously fast clip. The expression on her face alerted him that something was terribly wrong. Concerned, he stepped off the boardwalk to hail her.

When he realized several passersby were staring reproachfully at him for approaching Maggie, he stopped dead in his tracks.

To his surprise Maggie stamped on the brake and skidded to a halt beside him. When she noticed the attention they were drawing she tilted her chin to a defiant angle that reminded him of Julia.

"Get in, Lone Wolf," she insisted as she patted the empty space beside her. "I need to speak with you."

"Are you sure? You might not want to deal with the inevitable gossip," he cautioned.

She stared at him for a long moment then glanced at the people watching them curiously. Muttering something about folks minding their own business, she scooted sideways to allow him plenty of room to climb aboard.

She made a production of handing the reins to him, too.

"Take us somewhere so we can speak privately."

With all eyes focused on them, Lone Wolf veered northeast toward the sand and gypsum bluff where Boot Hill was located. From there you could see approaching riders from a mile away.

"You didn't have to stop," he said a moment later. "When I saw you coming down the street and noticed the tormented look on your face I forgot my place. You should have driven past me without a second glance."

To Lone Wolf's complete dismay Maggie's composure crumpled. An unexplained sob burst from her lips as she covered her face with her hands. Lone Wolf had only one experience at consoling a distressed female. He still wasn't very good at it. Nevertheless he reached over to pat Maggie's quaking shoulders.

"I don't know what's wrong, but if you tell me what it is I'll try to fix it for you," he offered.

Her blue eyes, swimming with tears, lifted to him. "I've done a terrible thing," she wailed loudly.

Lone Wolf wrapped a comforting arm around her. "I don't think you're capable of terrible things. I know dozens of rotten people, but you aren't one of them."

She sniffled then stared at him for such a long, intense moment that he squirmed on the seat. "You have my father's eyes and the same shape of forehead. Why didn't I notice that before?"

He pulled away. Oh hell. She knew. That was why she was so upset that she could barely stem her tears. She didn't want to claim kinship to him, either.

"I refused to believe my father would be so heartless as to turn away a desperate boy," she said, her voice cracking with barely controlled emotion. "But he did, didn't he?" Her teary gaze locked on him. "I want to hear it from you, Lone Wolf. Did you bring your mother's locket to him? The locket Papa keeps in his bedroom beside Aunt Isabella's picture?"

Lone Wolf expelled a sigh. For years he had dreamed of approaching his first cousin and telling her what a cruel bastard her father was, wishing he could turn her against Sol as retribution for his hurtful rejection. But he had gotten to know Maggie, like her and he didn't want to hurt her.

"Answer me," she demanded when he didn't reply immediately.

"Yes," he admitted. "I brought the locket to Sol at my mother's insistence, after my parents were killed. But Sol sent me away."

That was putting it mildly. Sol had *shouted* him off the ranch and cursed his very existence.

"I am not after part of your inheritance," he was quick to assure her. "I only wanted to get to know you." He smiled faintly. "You're all the family I have, Maggie."

To his astonishment she flung her arms around his neck and buried her face against his shoulder. Then she bawled her head off. He had the feeling that, like Julia, Maggie was venting the emotional turmoil that had been roiling inside her since Adam's life-threatening injury.

Dealing with Julia had made it easier for him to console his cousin. He patted her soothingly on the back while she soaked his shirt with tears. She sobbed and wailed for several minutes before she managed to pull herself together. Finally she uprighted herself and wiped her red-rimmed eyes.

"I am going to confront my father with this."

"No," he advised. "You and Sol are already at odds because of his plans to marry you to someone besides Adam."

"Are you also convinced that Papa is behind the bushwackings?" She stared pointedly at his mending arm.

"Sol has his share of motive and opportunity. But all I have is circumstantial evidence. Until the sniper or rustlers make contact with their employer all I have is conjecture. But your father holds a grudge against the Prestons and that's public knowledge. I think you have to prepare yourself for the possibility that your father might be involved."

Maggie crumpled on the seat and hauled in several deep breaths. Then she nodded. "Now that I've dealt with my outrage and disbelief I realize how difficult it must have been for Julia to confide her suspicions. I feel horribly guilty for lashing out at her. I didn't want to believe Papa deceived me and that he could be that cruel to you and to Adam."

Lone Wolf winced. So it had been Julia rather than Adam who had been stuck with the unenviable task. He knew it must have been incredibly hard for Julia.

And he hadn't been there to help her.

Hell, *he* should have been the one to tell Maggie.

"I was hateful to Jules," Maggie murmured regretfully. "She probably thinks I despise her. I can't sneak over tonight to see Adam or to apologize to Jules. Papa wants me to finalize the last-minute arrangements for the party tomorrow night. He plans to introduce me to my unwanted fiancé," she added disdainfully.

Lone Wolf smiled wryly. "Telling Adam about the soiree held in honor of your unwanted engagement would be almost as difficult as Julia telling you about her suspicions." He cocked a brow. "You didn't bother to tell Adam, did you?"

Maggie grimaced. "I lost my nerve. Of course, I'm not as courageous as Jules." She clutched Lone Wolf's hand and stared pleadingly at him. "You have to tell Jules that I didn't mean what I said. She'd already clashed with Audrey Clement earlier and had to endure the snide comments about your marriage."

"Hell," Lone Wolf grumbled.

He suspected Julia had been ostracized because of his reputation. Damn, the woman really had had a bad day. He had made it worse by abandoning her without a word of explanation.

But sooner or later she would realize that he was only the place she came to for consolation…and a night of reckless passion.

The memory of their night together tried to muscle into his thoughts. Willfully he forced the erotic visions aside.

"Will you tell Jules how sorry I am that I refused to believe her?" Maggie implored. "I realize how hard it was for her, how hard *I* was on her. As difficult as it was, I know that I prefer to hear the information from my best friend."

Although Lone Wolf had vowed to keep his distance

from Julia he couldn't deny Maggie's request. "I'll tell her, but you have to promise not to confront Sol with what you know. You're going to have to put up a bold front, Maggie, and make the best of tomorrow night's party. Can you do that?"

She nodded. "When I think of all Julia has had to do and how strong she has had to be through the crisis with Adam, plus this feud with my father, I am amazed that she has held up so well."

Maggie chuckled unexpectedly. "Telling off Audrey this afternoon was an excellent release for her frustration, no doubt. Watching Julia give Audrey and her snooty friends what they had coming was worth the trip to town."

"Wish I'd been there," Lone Wolf murmured.

"You definitely missed something," Maggie guaranteed. "Audrey would have run crying to Benjamin if he hadn't left for a business meeting."

The comment put Lone Wolf on immediate alert. "Did you see who was with Benjamin?"

"Yes, some scrawny little man, but I only saw his departing back as he veered around the side of the house."

Lone Wolf frowned pensively as Maggie dragged in a restorative breath then gestured toward town. "I think I'm ready to go home now. And thank you for being here to help me pull myself back together."

"Always happy to assist my favorite cousin," he said with a wink and a grin.

She smiled at his playful remark. "You are my favorite cousin as well. Our second and third cousins, who I was forced to live with in Saint Louis, reminded me of Audrey Clement. You wouldn't like them, either." Her expression sobered as she clutched his hand. "I want you to know that I do not share my father's sentiments.

If there is anything I can do for you, anything at all, all you have to do is ask."

Humbled by her generosity and sincerity, Lone Wolf murmured a heartfelt thank-you.

During the ride, Lone Wolf resigned himself to the fact that he was going to have to return to Preston Ranch—and face Julia, who probably wanted nothing to do with him after he had left her.

For a man rumored to have nerves of steel, he felt incredibly jittery about the prospect of seeing Julia again.

Coward, he chastised himself as he stepped down from the buggy on the outskirts of town. While he watched Maggie drive away, he wondered if he should confront Julia nonchalantly and act as if nothing had happened. Or should he blurt out an apology the moment he saw her? Or maybe he should let her rake him over the coals and vent her exasperation first.

That would probably be the best approach, he decided as he hiked down the street. Although his life had been one dangerous foray after another for years on end, he was beginning to think that dodging bullets and confronting gun-toting outlaws was easier than dealing with the erupting emotions he'd faced during this assignment.

At dead center of his inner turmoil was his fascination with the green-eyed hellion who had become his wife—in every sense of the word. Grumbling, he strode down the boardwalk at a fast clip, wishing he could outrun the emotions Julia triggered inside him—and knowing he never would.

After her difficult conversation with Maggie, Julia met up with the hired hands and sent them on their way home without her. Then she veered into the general store to make several personal purchases for Adam and herself. She exited a half hour later—and accidentally collided with Lone Wolf.

Her breath came out in a whoosh and she dropped her packages in her effort to latch onto the supporting beam so she wouldn't land in an unceremonious heap at his feet.

Her wounded dignity could not have survived that.

When Lone Wolf snaked out his hand to steady her Julia reflexively recoiled. His touch evoked too many bittersweet memories and she was in no mood to revisit them after the difficult day she'd had. Heavens, she was having trouble holding her composure as it was! Her pride would take a mortifying beating if she fell to pieces in front of him.

"Are you all right?" Lone Wolf asked as he hunkered down to gather up the scattered packages.

No, I'm not all right! You broke my heart and I don't understand why you walked away and left your wedding band behind, she thought in tormented frustration. But to him she said, "I'm fine. Never better." *Liar,* her conscience said.

Her focus settled on his face momentarily, then moved away. She noticed that he was no more anxious to make eye contact than she was.

Her attention dropped to the bare ring finger on his left hand and her heart gave another painful lurch. Her pulse pounded in her ears and tears threatened to betray her as she watched him stack up the packages, then surge to his feet.

"I'm sorry. I didn't mean to plow into you," he murmured. "I didn't see you coming. I'll carry these packages for you."

"No," she refused, scooping them from his arms—and going to noticeable extremes to keep from touching him in the process. "I can manage on my own, thank you very much."

Lone Wolf recalled that there was something he was supposed to tell Julia, but for the life of him he couldn't remember what it was. Running into her—literally and unexpectedly—had caught him so far off guard that it took all his concentration to pretend to be emotionally detached.

Plus, seeing her decked out in that alluring yellow gown that displayed the luscious curves he had become intimately acquainted with the previous night distracted him to no end. He felt more awkward and uncomfortable than he ever had in his whole life.

"Have you interrogated the rustlers yet?" she asked as she stared at the air over his left shoulder.

"No," he replied, his attention on *her* left shoulder. He didn't think he could look directly at her if he hoped to retain his train of thought and project an air of nonchalance.

"I gave up waiting for those hooligans to sober up. I'm on my way to Danson's office to request arrest warrants. I plan to question the suspects after they've been locked up overnight and can't get their hands on more whiskey."

Julia shifted uneasily from one foot to the other. So did he. "Julia," he said with a gusty sigh. "About last night—"

"You made your feelings known without saying anything at all last night. You *left*," she cut in sharply. "Obviously you didn't like where you were…or whom you were with."

Nothing could have been further from the truth, but telling her so would make matters worse. Lone Wolf raked his fingers through his hair then sighed audibly. "I was… I think…" He swore under his breath, unsure what to say to make Julia understand that he was unnecessarily complicating her life and that she was better off without him. "I—"

"I should be going," she interrupted. "I have other errands to run before I go home. I'm sure you have better things to do than chitchat with me."

Julia clutched the packages to her chest and looked the other way. She had never felt so uncomfortable and ill at ease around Lone Wolf before. But the fact that he had left her in the middle of the night—without taking his wedding ring with him—changed everything between them.

Now she was at a loss as to how to relate to him. She wanted to rant and rave at him for leaving her and their marriage behind. But she refused to make a scene on Front Street. She and Lone Wolf were drawing more than their fair share of attention—as usual. No need to make things worse.

When she tried to veer around him, he sidestepped to block her path. Reluctantly she lifted her face to his and got lost in the mesmerizing depths of his hazel eyes. Feelings of rejection swamped and buffeted her. Her heart turned over in her chest and a silent sob clogged her throat when her unrequited love for him hit her right where she lived.

"Julia, I never meant… I didn't—"

"*Goodbye*, Lone Wolf," she cut him off at the pass. "There is nothing left for us to say to each other. We are wasting each other's time. Now if you'll excuse me."

Julia swerved around him, refusing to wait for him to say whatever it was he thought he was obliged to say. Another moment and she would have humiliated herself by succumbing to the tears that were swimming in her eyes. Choking back a sob, she scurried down the boardwalk. She didn't look back, either. Truly, there was nothing more to say.

Skidding to a halt, Julia dumped the packages into the carriage, then dragged in a cathartic breath. Squaring her shoulders and tilting her chin, she pelted down the street. All the while she cursed the image of Lone Wolf's ruggedly handsome face floating in her mind's eye. She hoped he was happy now that he had walked away from her for good.

Muffling a sniff, Julia headed toward Thomas Whittaker's law office to sign the necessary papers so she could take possession of her trust fund. She quickened her step, hoping to arrive before Thomas closed up for the evening.

Although thoughts of her conversation with Lone Wolf kept getting in her way, Julia recalled something Maggie had said at the party. She wanted to ask Thomas's opinion. The prospect of railway expansion crossing Preston property and providing right-of-way and building-site sales would certainly improve ranch profits, she mused pensively. It might also explain Benjamin and Sol's eagerness to claim the land.

Surely Thomas had heard the rumors that something was afoot with the railroad companies. His half brother was State Senator Gerald Russell, after all. He might be able to offer advice on possible land-site sales if real estate investors approached her. Between that prospect and the money in her trust fund she shouldn't have trouble covering ranch expenses.

Julia's thoughts trailed off when she heard muffled voices in the alley. She glanced sideways to see Harvey Fowler involved in an angry debate with the man she immediately recognized as the sniper. Her first impulse was to reverse direction and dart down the street to alert Lone Wolf. But when the tall, burly henchman backhanded Harvey and sent him sprawling in the dirt, the need to protect Harvey from another painful blow overcame her.

Julia fished her pistol from her reticule, hoping to catch the sniper unaware. Unfortunately, Harvey saw her coming and spoiled her surprise attack.

"Get outta here, Julia!" he called as he wiped his bloody mouth with the back of his hand.

Will Butler—or Les Mitchum and whatever else he called himself—whirled around and simultaneously slid one of his pistols from his holster. Julia cursed under her breath when she found herself squared off against the snarling ruffian. Unease riveted her when she reminded herself that this was the sharpshooter who had wounded Adam and Lone Wolf at long range—with alarming accuracy. Now he was holding a well-used six-shooter and all she had was a piddly, single-shot derringer.

"Well, well," Will Butler smirked. "You saved us a lot of trouble by showing up here, didn't you?"

"Us?" Julia's disappointed gaze darted to Harvey. He was in on the two ambushes? Damn him!

Harvey bolted to his feet and clawed at his sidearm. "No! Leave her alone! I told you that I wouldn't—"

Julia grimaced when Butler, keeping one pistol trained on her, snatched up the second firearm to use as a club. When Harvey moved in too close, Butler slammed the pistol into his face. Julia heard the crunch of bone and knew the brutal blow had broken Harvey's nose. A pained groan tumbled from his lips as his legs folded beneath him and he wilted in the dirt.

"Mouthy brat," Butler growled as he stalked boldly toward Julia, his steely eyes trained on her trigger finger.

Julia had never shot at a man before and her momentary hesitation cost her dearly. The gunman lashed out with his boot heel, knocking the pistol from her hand. Julia reflexively grabbed her stinging wrist and smashed fingers. Preservation instinct had her whirling toward the street.

She was pretty sure she could sprint back to the boardwalk and flag down Lone Wolf before Butler caught up with her—or shot her down. Whichever came first. But she hadn't counted on tripping on the hem of her own gown and stumbling into a graceless sprawl. She opened her mouth to scream Lone Wolf's name, but the butt of Butler's pistol cracked against the back of her skull.

Shards of white light glittered before her eyes.

That was the last thing she saw before blinding pain exploded in her head and the world turned pitch-black.

Chapter Fourteen

Lone Wolf paced around the sheriff's office, impatiently waiting for Danson to return with the arrest warrants the judge had issued. Lone Wolf preferred not to be alone right now. He wanted a distraction to help him forget how poorly he had handled his unexpected encounter with Julia.

Tongue-tied idiot that he had suddenly become, he hadn't apologized for walking out on her last night. Neither had he conveyed Maggie's apology. Which meant he would have to ride out to the ranch—and hope he conducted himself better in Julia's presence this evening than he had this afternoon.

Or maybe he could take the coward's way out and ask Adam to relay the messages to his sister. That would save him from facing Julia again and trying to pretend he wasn't enormously affected by her.

"Sorry for the delay," Danson said as he rushed into the office. "The judge was in conference."

"Who's on trial?" Lone Wolf asked as he accepted the bench warrants Danson handed to him.

"No one. It was something about legal land descriptions and railroad right-of-ways that Whittaker was handling for Benjamin Clement and Sol Griffin. They were in the judge's chambers with some scrawny little man I didn't know."

Lone Wolf frowned warily. This mysterious little man kept cropping up in conversations lately. Who the hell was he? He also wondered if the legal ramifications discussed in the judge's chambers had any bearing on this puzzling case.

"Do you think you can get information out of those alleged rustlers if they're stuck in my jail overnight?"

"It's the only place guaranteed to sober them up," Lone Wolf said, distracted. "I need answers and I need them now."

"I'll help you haul their unconscious carcasses to town," Danson volunteered as he strode outside to fetch the wagon.

Lone Wolf sank down on the buckboard. He was anxious to arrest the suspects so they could dry out. Then he needed to return to Preston Ranch to deliver Maggie's apology, as well as his own, to Julia. He was *not* looking forward to that. The awkward encounter this afternoon had been a disaster.

Julia regained consciousness to find herself blindfolded, bound, gagged and stuffed in a musty storeroom. She didn't know exactly where she was, but she knew Harvey Fowler was bound up in the same fashion beside her because she could feel him shudder and moan groggily.

When she heard distant voices she strained to make out the words, but they were indecipherable. She tensed apprehensively when she heard footsteps approach.

"A damn shame this daredevil had to poke her nose where it didn't belong," Will Butler said as he hovered over her. "So much for relying strictly on scare tactics, eh, boss?"

Julia heard the shuffling of another pair of feet, but whoever the man was, he didn't voice one word to divulge his identity. But it was a man, she deduced, because she didn't hear the swish of petticoats and skirts.

"You just *had* to be difficult, didn't you?" Butler grumbled at her. "First you married that bounty hunter to make things more complicated. Then you gave the sheriff a detailed description of me so I had to lie low. Now here you are, cluttering up the storeroom and forcing our hand again."

Julia cursed into her gag, wishing Butler and his mysterious employer could hear the damning epithets that wished them as deep in hell as a buzzard could fly in a week.

"If not for Harvey's sudden streak of loyalty to you this *accident* you're about to have might not have been necessary."

Julia muttered another oath to Butler's name. She was annoyed that she was going to die without knowing exactly who was behind the bushwhackings and why. For the money, she supposed. It was always about greed, power and influence, wasn't it? But who wanted her land badly enough to resort to injuries and now murder—*hers,* to be specific.

"Time for you and Harvey to take a ride in your buggy," Butler declared. "Don't go away, darlin', I'll be right back." His taunting laughter echoed around the room. "Since it's dark outside we won't have to worry about anyone recognizing you."

She heard the door creak open before Butler added, "Buggy accidents are a damn fine way to dispose of uncooperative folks and unwanted complications, aren't they, boss? Worked well enough three years ago, didn't it?"

His footsteps faded and Julia swallowed hard. Sickening dread pooled in the pit of her belly. She had the inescapable feeling that *her* upcoming buggy accident was as precisely planned as her father's had been. Julia wondered if Rachel Griffin had been at the wrong place at the wrong time, or if she had been marked for death, too.

Of course, none of these speculations would do her any good, Julia mused fatalistically. Dead women told no tales.

Damnation, she would give almost anything to know who was pacing the storeroom, waiting for Butler to return with her buggy. She strained her ears and tried to pick up a telltale clue that identified the mastermind. But there was nothing except muffled footfalls stirring up dust and an occasional clicking sound she couldn't identify, especially when the prospect of her upcoming death kept sidetracking her.

Was Sol lurking nearby? Had he discovered that Rachel and Julia's father were having an affair? Had he *arranged* the carriage wreck to punish them for their infidelity?

She heard the jingle of harnesses and the rattle of the buggy outside the door, then Butler strode inside.

"It's a shame you won't be around to see how efficiently we remove the threat of that pesky husband you latched onto in such a rush," Butler taunted. "I—"

Harvey's muffled groan and desperate struggles in-

terrupted whatever Will Butler intended to say—much
to Julia's dismay.

She wasn't sure how Butler and his boss planned to
deal with Lone Wolf, but she predicted the scheming
bastards had concocted some fiendish plan to get rid of
him, too. Although she was aggravated at Lone Wolf because he didn't love her, she didn't want to drag him
down in this quagmire. She preferred that he remained
safe and unharmed.

Without another word Butler walked over to grab
Harvey's bound feet and drag him toward the back exit
of the storeroom. Then he clamped hold of Julia's upper
arms and tried to haul her across the floor in like manner.

Julia squirmed for release, lashing out to knock Butler off his feet, if only to enjoy a measure of spiteful satisfaction before she met her maker. She heard him
squawk then kerplop on the floor. A cloud of foul curses
filled the room while she rolled toward the fresh air that
gushed through the open doorway.

"Come back here, you troublesome bitch! I'll be
glad to be rid of you," Butler snarled as he jerked her
upright. "Don't worry, boss, I'll take care of her brother,
just as planned, after I'm finished with her."

To Julia's outraged fury, Butler draped her over his
shoulder. She bucked and kicked him with her bound
feet, and then lurched sideways, trying to throw him off
balance before he tossed her into the storage rack
behind the buggy seat. She felt her purse—minus her
pistol—being tossed against her shoulder. No doubt, the
kidnappers didn't want incriminating evidence lying
around.

Harvey was obviously still too dazed to put up a

fight when Butler snatched him up from the storeroom. Julia heard Harvey's moan when Butler dropped him atop her like a feed sack. She gasped for breath when Harvey's body slumped motionlessly upon her.

It was after dark when Lone Wolf swung down from his piebald pony. He stared anxiously at the Prestons' spacious ranch house and wondered how the thought of encountering Julia again could cause so many contradicting emotions inside him.

The damnable truth was that he *missed* her like crazy. Yet, he was apprehensive about the upcoming encounter and wondered what kind of reception to expect from her this time.

Since Julia hadn't tossed his belongings on the lawn he took that as a good sign. What belongings? he asked himself as he mounted the front steps. He didn't leave his saddlebags behind when he left each morning. She didn't have the chance to show her displeasure by hurling his clothes on the lawn.

Lone Wolf mentally rehearsed what he intended to say to Julia, then hauled in a bracing breath. "Might as well get this over with," he mumbled as he strode through the foyer, then nodded a greeting to Nora Dickerson, the housekeeper.

Lone Wolf halted at the head of the steps when he saw Adam in the upstairs hall. "Glad to see you're up and moving."

Adam braced his arm against the wall for support. "I'm up but I'm not moving very fast yet." He stared quizzically at Lone Wolf. "Did you track the rustlers to Sol's place?"

Lone Wolf shook his head. "No. But by tomorrow I

should have the information from the rustling suspects that the sheriff and I hauled to jail."

Adam glanced past Lone Wolf's broad shoulders. "Where's Jules? I thought she'd be home from Audrey's party hours ago. Did you see her while you were in town?"

"Yes." *Unfortunately,* he thought with an inward grimace. "She mentioned that she had other errands to run after she made some purchases at the general store."

Lone Wolf pivoted when he heard footsteps on the stairs. He wasn't sure if he was relieved or disappointed to see that it wasn't Julia but rather Nora who approached. He stepped down to help her with a heaping tray of food.

"Figured you and Adam might as well eat while it's hot," Nora waddled over to check Adam for fever. "I thought Julia would be back by now. The cowboys that Frank sent along with her returned two hours ago."

Lone Wolf hurriedly finished his meal, then praised Nora's culinary talents. He didn't exaggerate when he told her nothing tasted quite as good as it did when *she* cooked it.

Nora beamed with delight. "Well, aren't you just the nicest man to say so."

Right, he was a real peach, he thought with self-deprecation. Last night he had run scared from the alien feelings Julia evoked in him and from her whispered confession that he knew she couldn't possibly mean. This afternoon his unease had left him too rattled to remember what he wanted to tell her when they ran into each other in town.

And what was taking her so long to get home? he wondered impatiently. It was half past dark. The thought of her tramping around alone triggered his protective instincts. Of course, she would bristle at being cautioned about prowling at night since she claimed she'd been doing it for years.

Lone Wolf doubted that lecturing her on that subject would be a good idea right now—all things considered.

Restless, Lone Wolf paced the floor while Adam finished eating. When Nora left he helped Adam disrobe for bed.

"I've had about enough of being an invalid," Adam complained while Lone Wolf removed his shirt. "I feel helpless and useless. Knowing Sol plans to marry off Maggie isn't doing a damn thing for my disposition, either."

Lone Wolf suspected Adam's mood would deteriorate rapidly if he knew Maggie's unwanted fiancé would arrive tomorrow.

When Adam nodded off, Lone Wolf strode into the bedroom suite he shared with Julia. One look at the bed caused a myriad of forbidden memories to bombard him. He remembered—all too vividly—the intense pleasure and dangerous emotions he had experienced while he held her in his arms.

Damnation, even if he lived to be one hundred he would never forget the incredible night of passion they had shared. It had been the most intimate and satisfying encounter of his life, much as he was afraid to admit it.

He spotted the gold band that lay on the nightstand near his side of the bed. He didn't know what possessed him, but he walked over to pick it up, then slid it back on his finger—where it felt like it belonged.

And hell's bells, he was going crazy waiting for Julia

to show up so he could tell her…*what?* He had no idea. He just knew that nothing had been the same, because he felt empty and alone after he had left her in the middle of the night and then watched her rush away from him this afternoon.

Lone Wolf wheeled around and strode into the hall. Julia's lengthy absence made him edgy and he decided to track her down. He whipped open the front door in time to see a young lad slide off his horse. Wariness furrowed his brow when he saw the note in the boy's hand.

"I was told to give this to you," the boy said. "You are Lone Wolf, aren't you? I've seen you in town a few times."

"Who sent you here?" he demanded hurriedly.

"A man who's tall like you," the boy said. "Brown beard, mustache and scar. He gave me four bits to deliver the note."

Cold fury blazed through Lone Wolf's veins as he read the missive from the sniper: *I will exchange your wife's life for the signed deed to Preston Ranch. Sol*

Lurching around, Lone Wolf took the steps two at a time. He gave Adam a nudge to rouse him, then he thrust the note at him. Adam snarled maliciously after he read the missive. When he tried to push upright Lone Wolf forestalled him.

"This has *trap* written all over it," he cautioned. "If Julia is being held hostage and I go after her, then you will be here alone. The sniper gave a young boy the message to deliver and I expect he's out there waiting to pick me off. Then he'll come for you since you're vulnerable. I'll send Frank and some reinforcements upstairs to stand guard."

"But I can't let you ride off to become a sitting duck—"

"Don't argue," Lone Wolf snapped brusquely. "This is what I do, Adam. I'm accustomed to dealing with devious, cunning criminals and I can smell trouble brewing here. If you aren't sprawled out in bed like live bait it might set off a chain reaction that gets Julia killed."

He didn't mention the grim prospect that it might be too late to save Julia. The awful thought churned in his gut like an indigestible meal. He hadn't experienced such unnerving sensations since the massacre had left him a grieving orphan.

He retrieved Adam's pistols, then tucked them beneath the quilt. "Frank and his men can station themselves in the dark corners of the room and have a clear view of both doors."

"How are you going to—?"

Lone Wolf didn't waste time with details. He blazed down the steps then ducked out the back door. Immersing himself in the shadows, he rushed to the barn. He saddled an unfamiliar horse so it wouldn't be easy for the sniper to recognize him. Then he jogged to the bunkhouse to alert Frank Slater.

After the cowboys armed themselves to the teeth and skulked off to protect Adam, Lone Wolf mounted up. Instead of riding directly toward Griffin Ranch, he clung to the underbrush of the meandering stream. When he reached the back of Sol's house thirty minutes later he followed the same route Julia had told him that Maggie used when she sneaked off. He waited until the guard circled around the house before darting to the oversize shade tree to make his ascent to the balcony.

Anger and anticipation mounting, he picked his way along the tree limbs to reach the second story. He had only seen Sol Griffin at a distance the past few years, but this time the heartless bastard would meet him face-to-face. Sol wouldn't be dealing with a bereaved orphan who had come begging for help, either. Lone Wolf was now the fearless warrior that Sol had forced him to become. Sol was going to deal with the bottled resentment and fury that accompanied Lone Wolf when he came to this ranch to rescue Julia.

If Sol Griffin had harmed one hair on Julia's head then he was as good as dead, Lone Wolf vowed resolutely. No sooner had the thought leaped to mind than the repercussions Maggie might face slammed into him. He fully understood the inner conflict Julia and Adam battled because of the ongoing feud with Sol. Their affection for Maggie prevented them from all-out retaliation against Sol's attacks on the ranch.

"Damn that conniving bastard," Lone Wolf muttered as he hopped agilely onto the balcony. Well fine. So he couldn't kill the son of a bitch outright for trying to wipe out the Prestons. But he was going to make Sol dreadfully sorry for the pain and frustration he'd caused his neighbors…and his unwanted nephew.

While Will Butler veered the buggy off the beaten path, Julia's mind raced. She was desperate to foil Butler's dastardly scheme. She could list several selfish reasons she didn't want to end up dead, but the need to survive and learn the identity of the mastermind who had arranged her father's and Rachel's deaths provided plenty of incentive.

Julia burrowed her head against Harvey's shoulder to inch her blindfold upward until it toppled sideways. Urgency assailed her when she noticed Butler was skirting the towering cliffs that overlooked the creek.

Think, damn it! Julia scolded herself. She had to gain control of the buggy before Butler sent it plummeting over the ledge to shatter on the stream bank.

Julia groped to locate her reticule. Although there wasn't much inside it that might serve as a makeshift weapon she could use the chain strap to choke Butler— if she could wrest her hands free. Frantically she struggled with the rope that manacled her wrists behind her back. A few moments later she wriggled one hand free.

She glanced hopefully at Harvey, thinking this would be the perfect time for him to wake up so they could combine forces—but he didn't budge.

Clutching the reticule in her fists, Julia drew her legs beneath her. In one swift motion she shot to her feet to hook the chain around Butler's throat. She gave the chain a quick twist to keep it taut then dropped back atop of Harvey before Butler could make a grab for her.

Vile curses erupted from Butler's curled lips as he clawed at the tight chain. When it didn't budge he grabbed his pistol. Julia swerved sideways, using her bound feet to dislodge the weapon before he could turn it on her. Then she braced her feet on the back of the seat and yanked as hard as she could on the chain. Butler writhed and sputtered, while still trying to maintain control of the speeding carriage.

The buggy hit a deep rut, launching Butler sideways. He gasped frantically for breath and his arms flailed wildly in an effort to relieve the chokehold Julia had on him. She yelped in terror when the buggy swerved perilously close to the crumbling edge of the cliff.

Although Butler had blacked out, she was reluctant to release her grasp on him and lunge over the buggy seat to grab the reins that had fallen to the floorboards.

If Butler regained consciousness and attacked her, all would be lost.

Damned if I do and damned if I don't, Julia thought as the back wheel of the carriage dropped over the edge.

Her instinct for preservation finally prompted her to fling herself over Butler's slumped body to reach the reins.

But it was too late. The wooden tongue of the buggy shattered. The horse's wild scream pierced the night air. It floundered, scrabbled to maintain its footing against the weight of the upended buggy. Another shrill whinny split the air as the frightened steed staggered ever closer to the ledge.

Julia screamed in horror when the off-balance carriage slammed against the stone cliff, jarring her loose from the seat and catapulting her through the air.

She hoped the sniper didn't survive this fall to finish off her brother and Lone Wolf—

That was her last thought before she collided with the rock-strewn hillside. Pain exploded through her body. Darkness swallowed her up…and the world became deathly silent.…

Chapter Fifteen

Lone Wolf eased soundlessly inside the bedroom to see that Sol's shrines to his departed wife and to his sister were exactly as Julia had described them. Desperate though he was to locate Julia his footsteps halted to study the photograph of his mother. Impulsively he plucked up the keepsake locket and tucked it into his pocket.

Unresolved anger and resentment burned in his belly as he moved silently across the room then stepped into the hall. Maggie's loud voice and Sol's angry retort wafted up to him. He would have preferred that Maggie be upstairs, away from the inevitable clash between uncle and nephew. She didn't need to be on hand to watch him twist Sol's arm a dozen different ways to find out where he had stashed Julia.

"You can hold this blasted soiree to announce my engagement if you want," he heard Maggie snap at Sol. "But I am *not* marrying a man I haven't met and certainly don't love!"

"This is best for you and I have the final say in the

matter," Sol growled back. "You will never marry Adam Preston, not after what his father did to this family!"

"Was what he did to you any worse than what you did to your own nephew when he came here, desperate for help?"

"Well hell," Lone Wolf muttered as he stationed himself behind the door to the study. He'd hoped Maggie would keep her newfound knowledge to herself—until after this situation had been resolved. Unfortunately, she'd blurted out the accusation in a fit of temper and Sol erupted like Old Faithful.

"*He* told you that?" Sol blared. "He is purposely trying to turn you against your own father."

"Is it true?" Maggie demanded relentlessly.

Lone Wolf didn't wait for the inevitable denial. He stepped into clear view. "Tell her the truth, Uncle Sol," he insisted as he studied, at close range, the older version of the man whose image had tormented him for almost two decades.

A host of bitter feelings rose from their shallow graves while Lone Wolf glared at the tall, rangy rancher. The fierce impact of anger roiled inside him as he watched Sol's gray brows rise on his forehead.

When Sol lurched toward his desk—intent on grabbing a firearm, no doubt—Lone Wolf's pistol cleared leather in nothing flat. Despite the strain in his right arm, he took extreme satisfaction in holding Sol at gunpoint.

"You can't imagine how much I'd like you to go for your gun, Sol," he said with a deadly hiss. "Surely you realize that the first dozen men who drew down on me represented *you*. That made protecting myself a lot easier."

"Get out of my sight," Sol demanded.

"I'd love to accommodate you, Uncle, but I'm not leaving here without Julia."

Sol smirked. "She's not here. After she sneaked in here last week I told her never to set foot in my house again."

"I don't believe you," Lone Wolf growled. "Where is she? I'll tear this place upside down to find her, so save yourself the trouble of cleaning up after me."

Sol glowered at him. "I don't give a damn whether you believe me or not. But she *isn't* here."

Lone Wolf reached into his shirt pocket, then tossed the note at Sol's feet. "Needless to say that I didn't bring the deed with me."

Eyeing Lone Wolf warily, Sol picked up the folded paper. He read the note, then tossed it aside. "I didn't write this. I'm not holding Julia for ransom and I didn't order you to bring the deed to Preston land, though I'd like to have it."

Lone Wolf's deep-seated resentment prevented him from believing the denial.

Maggie raced toward her father. "Papa, if you are holding Julia I demand that you release her at once!"

Lone Wolf scowled when Maggie crossed his line of fire. He swore inventively when Sol took advantage of Maggie's interference to dart behind his desk. Lone Wolf went after him—taking the shortest route over the top of the desk to kick away the pistol Sol had hurriedly fished from the drawer.

When the weapon went flying from his fist Sol bellowed in pained fury. He bolted up to backhand Lone Wolf across the cheek, sending him lurching back a step.

"Stop it! Both of you!" Maggie screeched as she stepped between them.

"Get back, damn it," Sol snapped at his daughter.

He threw a punch at Lone Wolf, who shifted so quickly that the blow barely grazed his chin. Lone Wolf took supreme pleasure in doubling his left fist and reaching around Maggie to clobber Sol in the jaw. The older man's head snapped backward. He stumbled against the table that held the lantern.

When the glass globe shattered, kerosene and flames danced across the wooden floor. Swearing, Sol scrambled to his feet. He jerked off his jacket to frantically pound out the fire.

"You would love to burn this place down around me, wouldn't you?" he muttered furiously.

Lone Wolf didn't reply, just grabbed the afghan that was draped on the back of the couch and fought the fire. He would have liked to torch the place and watch it burn around Sol, but he didn't want Maggie's birthplace to go up in flames.

At least he had gotten off one good punch to rattle Sol's brain, he consoled himself as he smothered the fire. It had felt good. Great, in fact. It went a long way in appeasing the frustrated emotion he had been carrying around with him since the fateful day Sol had rejected him.

Lone Wolf stalked over to grab Sol by the collar of his shirt then lifted him right off the floor. "Where is she?"

"I haven't seen her," Sol spat, writhing for release.

"Papa, did you hire the sniper to ambush Adam and Lone Wolf?" Maggie questioned. "And you better tell me the God's truth. Did you shoot Adam to warn him away from me?"

"Of course not," Sol denied vehemently.

Lone Wolf didn't believe him, but Maggie looked as if she desperately wanted to. No doubt, Sol was counting on years of devotion from his daughter to see him through.

A sudden commotion at the front door prompted Lone Wolf to reach for his pistol. He clamped his arm around Sol's throat so he couldn't escape. Using Sol as his shield of armor he spun toward the unidentified sound.

His breath gushed from his chest when he saw one of Sol's cowhands assisting a battered Julia inside.

"Oh, my God!" Maggie chirped. "Jules, what happened?"

Lone Wolf jerked Sol sideways then stuffed the pistol barrel against his forehead. "Give me one excuse to blow your head off, you son of a bitch, and I'll take it. If you reach for that discarded weapon it will be the last thing you do."

Something in his expression must have alerted Sol that he was dead serious because the color drained from his face. His Adam's apple bobbed as he nodded his tousled head.

When Lone Wolf hurried toward Julia, Maggie retrieved the pistol to make sure Sol didn't change his mind. Her alarmed stare was still on Julia's tattered clothes and battered face—as was Lone Wolf's. A deep gash slashed across Julia's forehead and blood soaked the sleeve of her gown. He could only imagine what other injuries she had sustained that weren't as visible but every bit as painful.

Lone Wolf cast Sol another murderous glance, vowing to extract a pound of his flesh later for putting Julia through a terrifying ordeal. When she wobbled unsteadily on her feet, he scooped her into his arms and held her protectively to him.

"I found her a mile from the house while I was checking for stray cattle," the cowboy reported. "She was unconscious, but she came to a moment ago when I lifted her from my horse."

"Sweet mercy, Jules," Maggie gasped in concern. "Who did this to you?"

Lone Wolf swore foully when Julia tried to open her eyes. The left one was swollen shut and her bottom lip was split. He had no explanation for why her torn clothes were damp, but he didn't need to be a licensed physician to know that her left arm was badly sprained—or maybe even broken. She was holding it gingerly against her ribs, as if it was causing her severe pain. He also noticed the rope burns on her wrists and ankles.

The thought of the mistreatment she had obviously suffered filled him with outrage.

"Ride into town to fetch Doc Connor," Lone Wolf ordered the cowhand. "See if you can locate the sheriff, too." He glanced back at Maggie. "Get some water and bandages." To Sol he said, "Bring me a bottle of whiskey."

Everyone scattered to do his bidding—even Sol, much to Lone Wolf's surprise.

Julia licked her split lip and peered up at him with a one-eyed squint. "So glad I got here before you and Sol ended up killing each other," she murmured.

"Considering the way you look, it's a wonder you got here at all," he said as he gently laid Julia on the couch.

"Why are you here, Lone Wolf?" she questioned.

"Butler sent a boy to your ranch with a note, claiming Sol was holding you for ransom in exchange for the deed."

She frowned as she shifted uncomfortably on the sofa. When Lone Wolf heard her sharp intake of breath, he wondered if she had broken a few ribs. He pressed his fingertips gently against her side. She made a terrible face and her breath hitched. Bruised or broken, he wasn't sure which. When he lifted the ragged hem of her gown he saw the bloody scrapes and scratches that covered her legs.

"What in the hell happened to you, sweetheart?" he demanded.

He wanted to retaliate against whoever had abused her, to make him suffer as she had suffered. Never in his life had he wanted to take someone else's pain and bear it as his own, but he would have gladly done it for Julia. Seeing her hurt was killing him one excruciating inch at a time.

In addition, shame and guilt bombarded him. He had left Julia vulnerable and unprotected. *This was his fault!*

Her focus took in Sol, who had returned with a whiskey bottle and a glass. "The same thing that happened to me also happened to Papa and Rachel," she said, watching Sol carefully. "You wouldn't know anything about that, would you?"

"What?" Sol staggered back as if he'd been gut-punched. "What the blazes are you talking about?"

"Their buggy wreck was no accident." Julia levered herself up on an elbow, grimaced then added, "Neither was this disaster." She peered up at Lone Wolf. "The sniper died without giving up his employer's name." She stared suspiciously at Sol. "I'm not sure about Harvey Fowler's condition. Please ride out to the wreckage to check on him."

"Butler and Fowler were in cahoots?" Lone Wolf choked out.

"We need to help Harvey if we can," Julia murmured before she took a sip of the whiskey Sol held to her lips. She sputtered and wheezed to catch her breath. "Ride two miles north of the bend of the creek. The buggy went over the cliff. Bring Butler's hat and long canvas coat back with you."

"You went over the cliff?" Lone Wolf howled in shock.

Fear pummeled him when her eyes rolled back in her head and she slumped motionlessly on the couch. Panic seized him as he leaned down to make sure she was still breathing. He nearly collapsed in relief when he felt her breath stirring faintly against his cheek.

"I am not responsible for this!" Sol repeated emphatically. "I know you have no reason to trust me, but I swear to God that I don't know anything about Julia's ordeal. I didn't know anything about the attempt on Adam's life, or yours, either, until I heard the news in town."

Lone Wolf stared him down.

"It's true that I didn't want Maggie to associate with the Prestons because of the embarrassing scandal surrounding Rachel's death," Sol went on, "but this isn't my doing!"

Lone Wolf was reluctant to believe Sol. He could be staging this act to spare his life. When Sol got down on his knees to blot Julia's numerous scratches with the damp cloth Maggie provided, making a show of concern for her, Lone Wolf's opinion wavered momentarily. He contemplated Sol's seemingly shocked reaction to Julia's announcement that her father and Rachel's deaths weren't accidental.

Guilty or innocent? He couldn't say for certain.

He wished he had all the facts and could make sense of tonight's fiasco. He needed more details, but Julia had blacked out.

She didn't respond when he tried to jostle her awake.

And that worried the hell out of him, especially when he discovered the oversize knot on the back of her skull.

"I'll take care of her until the doctor arrives," Maggie assured him as she brushed another cloth lightly over Julia's skinned forehead. "You'd best check on Harvey and the sniper as she requested."

The very last thing Lone Wolf wanted to do was leave Julia until he knew that she wasn't suffering serious internal injury and would survive the hellish ordeal. But he reminded himself that Julia probably preferred not to have him underfoot. Which was probably why she had specifically delegated the task to him. Even though she was dazed and in pain she hadn't forgotten that she was angry and disappointed in him for abandoning her last night and for not being close at hand when disaster struck this evening.

Hell, *he* was angry and disappointed in himself, so why shouldn't she be? He'd let her down. He hadn't been there to prevent her from being a victim of abduction. When she needed him most he had failed her. And that tormented him.

Lone Wolf left the house, guilt ridden and befuddled by Julia's request to retrieve Butler's hat and jacket. He didn't have a clue what she might possibly want with the garments.

He didn't want to leave her at all, but if it made her feel better to know the fate of that foolish brat named Harvey—who had somehow gotten mixed up with Butler—Lone Wolf would honor her wishes.

Then he was going to strangle the kid for getting involved in whatever the hell was going on around here.

Damn it, seeing Julia, who was usually so full of lively spirit, lying there motionless and unresponsive, had nearly done him in. He understood how she'd felt when Adam had ordered her to ride to Lone Wolf's camp for assistance.

Wondering if Julia would be alive when he returned was enough to drive him a lot closer to loco than he already was.

Fifteen minutes later Lone Wolf located the scattered wreckage strewn down the side of the steep cliff. He swore foully, astonished that Julia had survived the fall.

He saw the silhouette of the horse grazing on the cliff. A moment later he spotted Butler lying facedown in the shallows of the creek. His brows shot up when he noticed the gold chain from Julia's purse wrapped around Butler's neck. He didn't know if Butler had drowned, strangled or suffered fatal injury from the fall. But it was too bad the one man who could identify the mastermind was dead.

He glanced sideways to see two lengths of rope lying in the mud beside Butler. Near as he could figure Julia had been bound, but had somehow managed to encircle the purse chain around Butler's neck. Lone Wolf had to give Julia high marks for ingenuity. She had managed to save herself from disaster. From the look of things she had made her way down to Butler's body in the stream to confiscate his knife so she could cut herself loose.

Which explained why her clothes were damp.

Damn it, you *should have been there to spare her from this nightmare,* came the harsh voice inside his head once again. *You failed her when she needed you most.*

Knowing he might have prevented the misery and terror that Julia had suffered caused his heart to twist inside his chest. Cursing himself up one side and down the other, Lone Wolf did as Julia requested by confiscating Butler's garments. Then he lurched around to follow the scattered debris up the slope.

He found Harvey sprawled halfway uphill. The kid was bleeding and unconscious. He was also bound, blindfolded and gagged, as Julia must have been when she was abducted. Lone Wolf tried to puzzle out the connection between Will Butler and Harvey Fowler. He wasn't sure if the kid was a victim or one of the culprits who had served his purpose and was slated to be silenced permanently.

Who the devil had ordered this execution? That was the million-dollar question and he was anxious to find the answer.

Squatting down on his haunches, Lone Wolf pressed his fingertips to Harvey's throat. The kid's pulse was weak and erratic and Lone Wolf was hesitant to speculate on Harvey's chances of survival. Nevertheless, he cut the kid loose, scooped him up and carried him to his horse.

He swung up behind Harvey to hold him in place, then headed toward Sol's house. Careful not to jar Harvey more than necessary—and wondering why he bothered since the kid was probably embroiled in this deadly scheme—he walked the horse south to Sol's ranch.

Lone Wolf planned to move Julia to her own home as soon as Doc Connor gave his permission. He didn't want to be beholden to Sol. Funny, he had waited years to confront Sol face-to-face. He had even wrangled a marriage to Julia, as an added provocation to infuriate his uncle. But none of the old hurt and resentment held a candle to the revenge Lone Wolf intended to heap on whoever had tried to dispose of Julia.

Never in his life had he wanted to destroy someone as much as he wanted to get his hands on the mastermind who had tried to murder Julia.

To compound his helpless fury, his own awful feelings refused to let up on him.

Carrying an excessive load of guilt and anger, he toted Harvey's unconscious body back to the house. Then he hurried upstairs to make certain Julia was still among the living.

Chapter Sixteen

Julia was jolted awake by the offensive smelling salts Doc Connor waved under her nose. Grimacing, she glanced past the physician to note that she had been carried into one of the Griffins' guest rooms. Maggie, Sol and Lone Wolf stood at the foot of the bed, staring at her in concern.

When she tried to lever herself off her bruised hip every muscle and joint in her body protested. She collapsed on the pillow with a pained groan.

"Stay where you are, sweetheart," Lone Wolf cautioned as he veered around the edge of the bed to sink down beside her.

Why was he calling her sweetheart? Obviously he was trying to keep up appearances, she decided. Either that or she was near death and he was being especially nice to her before she flew off to the pearly gates.

"Well, young lady, you are extremely fortunate to be alive after the spill you took," Doc Connor said. He gestured to the array of bandages that covered her body. "You got banged up pretty good. Your arm isn't broken, but it's severely sprained. You'll need to wear a sling to protect it."

He nodded toward her head. "I sewed up that gash on your forehead, as well as the one on your thigh. But I can't do much about the knot on the back of your skull. As for your eye, the swelling should go down in a few days."

When the physician tried to give her a spoonful of laudanum she clamped her mouth shut tightly and stared at him in defiance. She knew what effect the medication had had on Adam and Lone Wolf, because she had crammed it down their throats to keep them in bed. She didn't have time to be sedated. There was a murderer on the loose. If she didn't figure out who he was and locate him tonight he would know something had gone wrong and attempt to flee.

Come hell or high water, Julia intended to be involved in tracking down the culprit and enjoy the supreme satisfaction of watching him be marched off to jail.

"You'll feel better if you take this," the doctor cajoled with a smile. "Come on, Julia, open up."

"No," she refused, careful to remain closed lipped while she spoke. "There's something I have to do and it won't wait."

"Whatever it is I'll take care of it for you," Lone Wolf promised faithfully.

"Is Harvey still alive?" she asked, favoring the tender side of her mouth.

"Yes," Lone Wolf reported. "He's banged up worse than you are, but he survived the wreck."

"Besides all his bodily injuries, Harvey has a serious concussion that will keep him bedridden for a couple of weeks," the doctor inserted. "He's still unconscious. He wasn't able to tell Lone Wolf anything."

Well, so much for learning what Harvey knew about the cunning culprit, Julia thought in disappointment. "Did you bring back Butler's clothes?" she asked Lone Wolf.

He nodded. "*Now* will you tell me what the blazes happened out there?" he demanded in an impatient tone. "I don't want the condensed version, either. I want details. And then I'm going to figure out who did this to you and pay him back—in spades!"

The fierce expression that puckered his bronzed face made Julia feel ten times better. Even if Lone Wolf didn't love her, he obviously cared enough about her to want her would-be murderer apprehended and punished.

Too bad she didn't know for sure who it was.

She cut Sol a contemplative glance.

After she sipped from the glass Lone Wolf held to her lips, she explained the events leading up to the buggy wreck that had claimed the life of the one man who knew for certain who was behind the three-year-old murders and the recent ambushes.

She glanced suspiciously at Sol again, noting that he acted as surprised by the evening events as everyone else in the room. But still… "Who was in your study last week before I confronted you?" she demanded out of the blue.

"Albert Richmond," Sol replied. "Why do you ask?"

She waved off the question with her good arm. "This is important. Describe him to me."

"Short, thin. Curly hair and thick glasses. Benjamin Clement put me in contact with him because he had privileged information about the railroad's upcoming expansion."

Lone Wolf jerked up his head and frowned. "Was Richmond on hand for the conference in the judge's chambers this afternoon?"

Sol nodded as he paced back and forth at the end of the bed. "Albert Richmond is State Senator Gerald Russell's political consultant. Benjamin introduced us."

"The same Gerald Russell who is going to marry Benjamin Clement's daughter," Julia mused aloud. "The very same Benjamin who recently made another offer to buy our ranch."

Lone Wolf glared at Sol. "Was Whittaker verifying legal land descriptions so you and Benjamin would be able to sell real estate to the railroad and prospective businesses when the expansion is publicly announced?"

"Yes." Sol shifted awkwardly. "I was told to keep the information under my hat and to have my property surveyed and updated so that when the railroad company contacted me about land sales the transfers could be made without a hitch."

"And only those with inside information, provided by the state senator's assistant, would profit," Lone Wolf presumed.

While Lone Wolf fired questions at Sol about Albert Richmond, the advisor who worked with Benjamin's future son-in-law, Julia watched Sol pace nervously at the foot of the bed. Her thoughts whirled, transporting her back to that mysterious storeroom where she'd been bound and blindfolded.

Sol's pacing triggered a half-forgotten memory. She remembered hearing the footsteps of the unidentified mastermind moving back and forth across the creaking floors in the storeroom. Step, step, step…pause… click…pause…snap…

A shiver of remembered unease trickled down her spine as the sounds drifted across her mind. Step, step, step…pause…click…pause…snap…

"Oh, my God!" Julia croaked when she suddenly realized where she must have been and what had caused the *click* and *snap* sounds she heard in between the impatient pacing.

Lone Wolf was hovering over her in a heartbeat, studying the stricken expression on her bruised face. "What's wrong?"

"I think I figured out where I was stashed after Butler knocked me unconscious in the alley." She swallowed visibly as she peered up at him with her one-eyed squint. "Do you remember the day Benjamin showed up to offer to buy the ranch? The same day Whittaker came to check on Adam?"

He nodded impatiently. "Yeah, what about it?"

"Remember when we announced our marriage and Whittaker paced back and forth, as if he were posing questions to a witness on the stand? Remember his nervous habit of checking his timepiece? *That's* the sound I heard while I was blindfolded! The pacing. The opening and shutting of the fancy gold watch he always carries."

"Whittaker?" Lone Wolf erupted furiously. "He ordered your death? Your *lawyer?*"

Julia nodded then requested another drink. Lone Wolf's fingers were clenched so tightly around the glass that it was a wonder it didn't shatter in his fist. Damn, but he would like to get his hands on that weasely attorney!

"Whittaker *has* to be involved," Julia insisted.

"Which is why he also was taking such pains today to make sure the legal description to Preston Ranch was accurate," Sol presumed. "If you and Adam were out of his way, and he could dispose of Lone Wolf, then he could quickly purchase the land transactions and turn a staggering profit."

"I suspect that I was slated to be murdered after Butler disposed of Julia," Lone Wolf said. "The note I received might have been an invitation to my own bushwhacking, one that, in turn, left Adam vulnerable to another attack."

"Either that or you and I were supposed to kill each other because of that note," Sol speculated.

"Whittaker tried to get rid of us, just as he orchestrated Papa and Rachel's deaths," Julia presumed. "He wanted the Prestons and Griffins to be at odds so we would blame each other for the problems we've faced. Slowly but surely he maneuvered into position to acquire the property that the railroads surveyed for expansion. His half brother, Gerald Russell, must have supplied him with information when the railroad company ran their requests for additional spurs through the state senate committee."

"When we didn't resort to bushwhackings to dispose of each other and rustling to provoke more ill feelings, Whittaker arranged them to stir up trouble," Sol muttered.

Lone Wolf didn't understand all the whys and whatfors of Whittaker's obsessive greed for money and power, but he *did* want to repay the bastard who was responsible for leaving Julia bruised and battered—and damn lucky to be alive.

When Sol spat a curse that consigned Whittaker to

a place where the hottest climates prevailed, Lone Wolf seconded the notion.

His vindictive thoughts trailed off when Julia levered herself up on an elbow then tried to sit up. "Oh no, you don't," he said sternly. "You are down for the count." He glanced over his shoulder for reinforcement. "Tell her, Doc."

"You need to rest," the physician chimed in.

"I will be all too eager to rest and recuperate as soon as I pay Whittaker a visit and make sure he is the one responsible for this nightmare," Julia negotiated.

"Absolutely not," Lone Wolf objected. "I'll handle this."

Plus, he didn't want any witnesses when he used his time-honored techniques of extracting facts and details from a closemouthed criminal. To his dismay, Julia ignored his protest and swung her legs over the edge of the bed. Now why wasn't he surprised that she ignored his order to stay put?

"Mags, may I borrow a pair of breeches and a shirt?" Julia requested.

"She doesn't own any," Sol said on Maggie's behalf.

"Yes, I do," Maggie contradicted. "I'll fetch them."

"Maggie, would you also be so kind as to ride over to Preston Ranch to tell Adam what happened so the guards can stand down?" Lone Wolf called after his cousin.

"Of course," Maggie agreed quickly. Then her gaze swung to Julia. "I want you to know that I am dreadfully sorry for getting upset with you this afternoon. Forgive me?"

Julia smiled. "Certainly. I'm sorry I upset you."

"Maggie is *not* riding to your ranch," Sol spoke up, "especially not at this late hour."

Lone Wolf loomed over his uncle. Julia could feel the tension arcing across the room. She knew hard feelings still simmered between the two men. Sol was no longer dealing with a vulnerable, bereaved child. Now Sol faced more man than he had ever encountered and he didn't stand a chance against him.

"Maggie is needed for this particular errand," Lone Wolf declared as he used his advantageous height to stare down Sol. "If *you* ride over there, Adam will start shooting because he doesn't know that it might be Whittaker, not you, who had him ambushed." He smiled insolently. "But if you're in an all-fired rush to get yourself killed then be my guest."

Sol scowled. "Fine, I'll ride into town with you."

"With *us*," Julia corrected as she accepted the garments Maggie handed to her.

Lone Wolf stared into her battered face, noted the familiar tilt of her chin, the determination in her eyes— at least in the one that still functioned properly. He sighed in defeat. *"Us."* He had lost another argument and he tried to remember if he had ever won one. He didn't think so.

He glanced back at Sol. "Since your cowhand was unable to locate the sheriff when he went for the doctor you can track down Danson and let him know what happened." He paused deliberately then said. "As for the other business between us, we will continue the discussion later."

Muttering, Sol pivoted on his heels then strode off to have the horses and a buggy readied for the jaunt to town.

Maggie smiled gratefully at Lone Wolf as she breezed past him on her way out the door. "My thanks to you and Julia for providing me with an excuse so I can check on Adam."

"You're welcome, cousin," he said softly.

Doc Connor said, "Julia, this really isn't a good idea. You have had more than enough excitement for one day."

"Not nearly enough," she contradicted. "Just imagine how much better I'm going to feel if I'm on hand to see Whittaker incriminate himself and watch him placed under arrest."

The physician studied the determined tilt of her scraped chin and the gleam in her squint. Then, like Lone Wolf, he caved in. "All right, but do not exert yourself unnecessarily. I still don't like it," he felt compelled to add.

"I wish you could perform surgery to remove her stubborn streak," Lone Wolf murmured as the doctor strode past him.

Doc Connor chuckled as he plucked up his leather bag. "That would indeed make life easier on all of us," he agreed on his way out the door.

"I should tie you down and make you stay here," Lone Wolf grumbled when he and Julia were finally alone in the room.

"Don't try it or your ears will be burning all the way to town and back." She winced when she tried to unfasten the buttons on the back of her tattered gown. Her tender arm and strained muscles made the simple task impossible.

"Let me help," he offered as he stepped up behind her.

Julia's breath hitched when Lone Wolf's fingertips moved over the buttons, exposing her chemise. When she glanced over her shoulder at him, his eyes were focused so intently on her that she got lost in them.

For that space of a few moments their eyes locked. Every whimsical wish she had conjured up swirled through her mind.

This was her prince, she thought. Not Prince Charming, of course, because Lone Wolf was too rugged, hard-edged and tough to be the picture of gentlemanly refinement.

Which was fine with her, because she loved him just as he was. He was everything she wanted from the man of her dreams.

The thought of never seeing Lone Wolf again had tormented her when she had plunged off the edge of the ravine and tumbled pell-mell downhill. She had wanted one more chance to tell him how she felt about him, but she knew that was the last thing he wanted to hear from her. *Then* or *now*.

"Julia, it scared the living hell out of me when you turned up missing," he murmured as he carefully eased the gown down to her waist then helped her into her borrowed shirt.

"I was more than a mite concerned myself," she replied, her voice on the unsteady side—due in whole to the powerful effect his nearness had on her. "I—"

Her voice fizzled out when she noticed he'd slipped the wedding band back on his ring finger. What did that imply?

Before she allowed herself to read something into it, she remembered Whittaker had baited Lone Wolf with a note to confront Sol. Wearing the ring was likely a goading reminder to Sol that someone around here thought he was good enough to marry and claim as family. Lone Wolf had told her that had been part of his incentive for a pretend marriage.

She winced uncomfortably when Lone Wolf drew her to her feet, then tossed aside her ripped dress. She grimaced when she elevated her knee to don the breeches he held up for her.

"All scuffed up the way you are, you actually look as if you belong in my world," Lone Wolf said as he gently eased the breeches up her legs and hips.

He cursed himself soundly for becoming aroused by the sight of Julia's luscious body. It didn't matter what condition she was in—she affected him intensely.

There was no getting around it, he thought defeatedly. No matter how bad this green-eyed hoyden looked—and she definitely didn't look good at the moment—she still beguiled him. She *always* aroused him, and he predicted she always would.

Of course, learning that she'd squared off against Butler in the alley to spare Harvey's life still made him crazy. And certainly, hearing the details of her ordeal tormented him to no end. But she was alive and in one piece—more or less.

He thanked white and Indian deities alike that she had been spared and that he didn't have her death on his conscience. He didn't even want to imagine a world without Julia's vibrant presence in it somewhere.

After she picked up the hat and long coat that had belonged to Butler she took a tentative step forward. Lone Wolf saw her grimace, though she bravely tried to conceal her pain. Reflexively he scooped her up in his arms.

"I'm fine," she said unconvincingly.

"Of course, you are." He headed for the door. "I'm just saving you a few extra steps."

Lone Wolf noted that Julia didn't object too strenuously when he carried her through the hall and down the staircase. Despite the twinge in his mending arm, he toted her outside to sit her carefully in the buggy Sol had readied for them.

He was glad that Sol had elected to ride horseback, giving Julia plenty of room on the seat to make herself comfortable. Either Sol was being courteous or he refused to share the conveyance with his unwanted nephew—not that Lone Wolf cared a whit about reconciling with his uncle, of course.

He had everything he needed. Whether Sol liked it or not—and he was sure he didn't—Lone Wolf had befriended Maggie. That was enough of a family connection to satisfy him. Plus, he had retrieved the keepsake locket that Sol had swiped from him all those years ago.

His craving for revenge and need for vindication didn't seem as important as it once had, he realized in amazement.

When Julia pulled the wide-brimmed hat and ankle-length canvas coat onto her lap, Lone Wolf was puzzled. "I have yet to figure out what you plan to do with these trophies of your triumphant battle against Will Butler."

"It occurred to me earlier that whoever is responsible for the murder attempts is expecting Butler to come walking through the storeroom door to report in." He watched a smile curve the side of Julia's mouth that wasn't split. "Imagine my satisfaction and Whittaker's surprise when he realizes you have arrived on the scene."

Lone Wolf shook his head and laughed—it felt good to laugh after battling intense fear, guilt and frustration for so many hours. "Ah, yes, I remember that every witness who described Butler said that he was about my size. So…you intend to give Whittaker a little rope and see if he will hang himself, hmm?"

She nodded. And injured though she was, that intelligent mind of hers was still churning, he noted. After her traumatic personal experience, and the senseless loss of her father, she harbored the same craving for revenge against Whittaker that Lone Wolf had directed toward Sol. Lone Wolf agreed that Julia had every right to expect justice and vindication.

In addition, he suspected that Whittaker had embezzled money from the Prestons while he "managed" their business affairs. He wouldn't be surprised to learn the trust funds were stashed in bank accounts with Whittaker's name on them. Which would explain why Whittaker had tried to strike Julia and him so quickly after he learned of their marriage. Whittaker would have been exposed for extortion before he could remove the people who stood between him and the property that was about to quadruple in value.

The thought of the extremes to which Whittaker had gone to line his pockets—and what he had tried to do tonight—made Lone Wolf furious. He was going to derive excessive pleasure in hauling that scheming son of a bitch to jail.

With Lone Wolf's assistance, Julia inched down gingerly from the buggy. She watched him shrug on Butler's canvas coat then tuck his long hair under the wide-brimmed hat. She predicted that Whittaker wouldn't realize who had arrived until it was too late. The thought made her smile.

She was going to be here to witness the look of shock

on Whittaker's face when he realized she had survived and that the legendary bounty hunter had come for him.

"Sol, go find the sheriff," Lone Wolf requested quietly.

Sol dismounted. "I'll find him later. Whittaker killed my wife and betrayed me as well as the Prestons. I think I'm entitled to see him receive his just desserts."

Julia could tell that Lone Wolf didn't want Sol underfoot, but Sol refused to budge. Grumbling, Lone Wolf opened the back door and stepped into the darkened storeroom.

She and Sol slipped in quietly behind him.

"Whittaker, I'm back," Lone Wolf called out, disguising his voice.

Julia heard the scrape of a chair in the outer office. The now-familiar footfalls echoed across the wood floor. She also heard the click and snap of Whittaker's pocket watch—the nervous habit that had given him away.

From her position beside the bookcases, she noted that Lone Wolf had stationed himself so that the lighting from the office didn't fall on his face. Whittaker couldn't tell who he was until he chose to identify himself.

"Did everything go as planned?" Whittaker asked as he leaned negligently against the doorjamb.

"Without a hitch," Lone Wolf mumbled.

"And you finished off Adam, after Lone Wolf took the bait of the note that sent him over to confront Griffin?"

"Yeah," Lone Wolf murmured. "Worked like a charm."

"Good. When I start the rumor that Griffin killed Adam to end the long feud and Julia perished in an accident, the whole town will be in an uproar. I'll discreetly have the Prestons' property switched to my name." He glanced over at the dark silhouette that remained in the shadows of the storeroom. "Did you swing by to see if that bounty hunter made short shrift of Griffin for supposedly kidnapping Julia?"

When his companion nodded, Whittaker snickered. "When that surly half-breed stands trial for killing Griffin I'll pull the necessary strings to make sure he hangs."

"There's just one flaw in your plan," Lone Wolf said.

Whittaker smirked arrogantly. "You don't think I can pull this off? Think again, Butler. Didn't I make John Preston and Rachel Griffin disappear and stir up a feud that has satisfactorily explained the rustling, ambushes and the motivation for tonight's murders? All I had to do was be shrewd and patient. It's like a chess game, Butler. You simply wait until the time is right to make your next move."

Whittaker gestured toward the back exit. "I want you to hightail it back to Griffin's ranch to plant some evidence that will thoroughly convince the sheriff that Lone Wolf *did* kill Sol in cold-blooded murder. And if Sol isn't dead already, make sure he is before you leave. I don't want Sol to throw a wrench in my plans now that everything is in place."

Whittaker wheeled toward his office to retrieve the stack of money from the desk drawer to pay his henchman. "You did remember to cut the ropes off the dead bodies after the buggy crash, didn't you? That is *not* the place I want damaging evidence lying around."

Julia tensed in anticipation when Lone Wolf swaggered forward to accept payment for his supposed services. When he tilted his face to the light, Julia heard Whittaker's shocked gasp.

She silently cheered when Lone Wolf doubled his fist and plowed it into the corrupt attorney's jaw. The forceful blow launched Whittaker off his feet and sent him halfway across the office. With a thud and a crash he slammed into his desk.

Julia surged past Lone Wolf, intent on letting this bastard know that she had survived and that she would be in court to testify against him.

Sol was one step behind her, vibrating with fury.

Whittaker wiped the blood from his lip as he stared goggle-eyed at her and Sol. "Where's Butler?" he wheezed.

"Dead," Lone Wolf said coldly.

Julia saw Whittaker go for the pistol that he must have kept stashed in the top drawer of his desk. The cocky fool obviously thought he could dispose of the witnesses by himself. Either that or he was so desperate that he was going to try to take a hostage.

For a split second she found herself frozen to the spot, staring openmouthed at Whittaker, amazed at his reckless daring.

"Duck, damn it!" Lone Wolf roared from behind her.

Chapter Seventeen

Lone Wolf's loud command jolted Julia from her paralyzed daze. She dropped onto her bruised knees, just as Whittaker whipped the pistol barrel into firing position. As she rolled across the floor she saw Lone Wolf launch himself forward to shove Sol sideways the instant before Whittaker fired.

The bullet plugged into the woodwork—where Sol's head had been a moment earlier.

Julia cursed herself soundly for glancing back to check on Sol and Lone Wolf, who had skidded across the floor. Unfortunately, her distraction provided Whittaker time to lunge at her. She winced when he stuffed his smoking gun barrel under her chin. She heard Lone Wolf mutter several pithy oaths as Whittaker clutched her to him like body armor.

"Make one move toward me and she's dead," Whittaker sneered as he forced Julia to her feet by applying enough pressure to her injured arm to make her cooperate.

The icy expression in Lone Wolf's eyes indicated

that he'd reverted to that hard bounty hunter she'd first met. A man would be taking his life into his hands if he pitted himself against such a formidable warrior. Only a man as desperate and panicky as Whittaker would take that risk.

Julia discarded the thought as Whittaker inched toward the dark storeroom, leaving Lone Wolf crouched to pounce.

"Don't even think about it, half-breed. If you try to stop me from leaving, you'll watch her die." He rammed the pistol deeper into her throat to make his point.

"You can't run far enough, fast enough," Lone Wolf snarled, watching Whittaker intently. "I'll make it my mission to hunt you down and torture you, Cheyenne style."

Julia mentally geared up to break the stalemate. While Whittaker focused on the dangerous threat Lone Wolf presented, she slumped lifelessly against him. Whittaker was caught off guard—and off balance—when Julia shoved the pistol away from her neck and collapsed on the floor, leaving Whittaker an open target for Lone Wolf.

Amazed, she watched Lone Wolf's two Peacemakers clear leather in a blur of speed. His first slug hit Whittaker's shooting hand, causing the gun to topple over his bloody fist. The second shot plugged into Whittaker's elbow. The third rapid-fire shot slammed into the lawyer's shoulder.

It immediately dawned on Julia that Lone Wolf was using this murdering scoundrel for target practice and that he easily could have made Whittaker's heart a bull's eye.

"The only reason you're still alive, with one good

hand left, is so you can sign your confession of guilt," Lone Wolf growled ominously while he held the attorney at gunpoint. "But I'm flexible. If you want to be dead I'll be more than happy to accommodate you." There was venom dripping from his voice when he added, "But don't think I'll let you die a quick and painless death, you conniving son of a bitch."

Whimpering like the cowardly bastard he was, Whittaker wilted onto the floor, cradling his right arm against his ribs. While he sat there bleeding all over himself, Julia hauled herself to her feet to loom over him. She spit on his face. "I hope you burn in hell for what you did to my father and Rachel," she growled at him. She raised her leg as if to kick him. "And this is for—"

Her voice dried up when Lone Wolf snaked his arm around her waist and towed her gently backward. "That's enough."

"No, it isn't," she muttered spitefully, still glaring poison darts at the attorney. "*You* shot him three times. *I* should be able to kick him in the gut for good measure."

"I know, sweetheart, but life isn't always fair. Sometimes you don't get to do everything you want." He stared down at Whittaker. "But more importantly, this murderer isn't going to get what *he* wants—which is your money and your property. He is, however, going to get exactly what he deserves under the laws that he has manipulated for his own selfish purposes. If that isn't justice I don't know what is."

While Whittaker whimpered, Lone Wolf looked over his shoulder. "Sol, are you going to track down the sheriff and fetch the doctor or do I have to do that myself, too?"

"You saved my life?" Sol bleated as he climbed to his feet. His astounded gaze locked with Lone Wolf's. *"Why?"*

"Momentary lapse of judgment." He turned his attention back to Whittaker to guard against any last-ditch efforts to escape. "You have a new lease on life, Sol. Don't foul it up by making unreasonable demands on Maggie. She is the only nice thing I have to say about you." He gestured his head toward the office door. "Now get going. I wouldn't want Whittaker to bleed to death before Doc Connor can patch him up and the sheriff hauls him to jail."

After Sol scurried through the front door Julia glanced wryly at Lone Wolf—or tried to. He figured with one eye swollen shut and a split lip it was difficult for her to pull off that particular facial expression effectively.

"Was sparing Sol your good deed for the year?" she asked.

"It was reflex. He was in the path of the bullet and I knocked him out of the way," he said with a shrug. "But I shouldn't have bothered, because I didn't do Adam any favors. Maggie's fiancé is supposed to be here tomorrow night to finalize the arranged marriage."

"What?" Julia erupted at the news. "Sol can't possibly go through with that wedding. Everything has changed now."

"Except maybe Sol's mind," Lone Wolf contended.

Pelting footsteps indicated that Sol had located Sheriff Danson. But then, the report of pistols on the north side of town, where firearms were prohibited, had probably spread like wildfire to reach the sheriff—wherever he had been.

Lone Wolf smiled when he noticed Danson's shirt wasn't buttoned properly and one side of the bottom hem was hanging outside the waistband of his breeches. It was a good bet that Danson had been enjoying the company of a woman and had been interrupted.

Sheriff Danson huffed and puffed for breath as he burst into the office. His stunned gaze landed on Whittaker then leaped to Julia's bruised face. "What the devil happened?"

"They attacked me and they are trying to blame me for—" Whittaker blurted out.

"Shut up!" Julia and Lone Wolf snapped simultaneously.

Sol and Doc Connor showed up a moment later.

"Sol can explain what happened," Lone Wolf insisted as he guided Julia toward the storeroom. "Julia needs a meal and bed rest. After the hell she's been through I intend to see that she gets both. I'll be in tomorrow to interrogate Whittaker."

He glared pointedly at the lawyer. "I intend to get all the facts. You are being charged with two murders and several assassination attempts." He glanced at the sheriff. "You might as well add embezzlement to the list because I'm sure we'll find that he's guilty of that, too."

A few minutes later Lone Wolf carefully situated Julia in the buggy and headed home. "I'm sorry I wasn't on hand when you needed me tonight," he murmured gruffly as her bruised body sagged against his shoulder.

When she didn't reply, he noted that she had fallen asleep in exhaustion. He had worked up the nerve to apologize and she hadn't heard a word he'd said. Lone Wolf slowed the horse's pace to a walk so she could catch a nap—and he could recover from the unnerving jolt of fear that had seized him while he watched Whit-taker hold a gun to her throat. That had scared the be-jesus out of him.

Lone Wolf inhaled a restorative breath as he stared down at Julia. He predicted that when the rush of adren-aline wore off and she remembered the hurt and anger he'd caused by abandoning her, she wouldn't want to see him again. He had hurt her feelings and he had let her down. She would dwell on that unforgivable fact after she got past tonight's traumatic incident.

But even if she chose not to speak to him again, Lone Wolf vowed to handle all necessary duties until the Prestons were back on their feet. Then he would re-move himself from Julia's life, because she and Adam could manage the ranch without his assistance or inter-ference.

Damn but he was going to miss this woman, he thought as he studied her beguiling moonlit features— bruised and swollen though they were at the moment. For a brief moment in his tumbleweed existence, he'd had a temporary home. He had become acquainted with his cousin, Maggie, and he had married a woman who had been through so much turmoil that she had even fancied herself in love with him.

But things would change when Julia finally came to her senses and her life was back to normal again. After she realized that he had only been an emotional crutch and that she no longer needed to lean on him, she would toss his saddlebags on the front lawn—Cheyenne style.

When she sent him on his way he had to make damn sure that his heart was still intact. Otherwise, he wasn't going to be worth a damn to anyone. He couldn't afford to become distracted by thoughts of the unattainable Julia.

That would get him shot in a hurry.

Of course, he was pretty sure that it would take dying to get Julia off his mind for good.

Julia awoke to the warmth of sunshine streaming into her room and the warble of birds in the distance. She could feel every bump, scrape and bruise she had sustained during the painful fall down the slope. Her mouth felt as dry as Death Valley and it demanded tremendous effort to formulate thought.

She suddenly remembered the side effects Adam and Lone Wolf had described after she had given them regular doses of laudanum to make certain they remained in bed to recuperate.

She frowned suspiciously as she stared up at the ceiling. The fact that the swelling had gone down enough for her to see out of both eyes indicated that she had been sedated for more than one night. When she turned sideways she saw Adam lounging in the chair. He looked remarkably well—which was another surefire clue that someone had had a heavy hand in administering sleeping potions to her.

"Welcome to the infirmary," Adam teased.

"Water," she wheezed.

He grabbed the glass on the nightstand then handed it to her. "Don't you just hate it when someone knocks you out with sedatives for days on end? And for your own good no less."

Julia gulped water like a dehydrated camel. "What day is this?" she croaked, barely recognizing her own voice. It sounded as if it had rusted from lack of use.

"Tuesday," he reported. "You've missed a lot of excitement the past few days." He stared meaningfully at her numerous injuries. "But then, I've heard that you had plenty of excitement before you landed in bed and Lone Wolf decided to give you several doses of your own medicine."

Julia levered herself up against the pillows and frowned at her grinning brother. "Are you going to tell me what's been going on or simply badger me?"

"Aren't we in a delightful mood this morning?"

She glowered irritably at him. "No, we are not."

"Well, I am, because I'm not the one being kept in the dark for a change."

"Catch me up," she demanded impatiently.

He snickered at her grouchy expression. "The best news of all is that when Maggie's fiancé showed up for the engagement party that everyone neglected to mention to me—" he frowned in annoyance "—Maggie refused the offer."

"Sol didn't object or intervene?" Julia questioned.

Adam shook his sandy-blond head. "Amazingly enough, no. But Maggie insisted that Lone Wolf attend the party, so maybe he threatened Sol within an inch of his life."

Knowing Lone Wolf was still in the area went a long way in making Julia feel better. He had obviously dropped by to check on her—and had given her another dose of sedative. She wondered if he would stop in to say his official farewell before he accepted another assignment that took him miles away.

She definitely needed to pay him for his services, she reminded herself. It was the perfect excuse to see him one last time before he walked away and left her brokenhearted.

Aching emptiness threatened to consume her when

she realized she was about to lose Lone Wolf forever. Lord, she was going to miss that man like nobody's business.

Adam shifted in his chair then smiled in satisfaction. "Lone Wolf drove me over to Griffin Ranch last night."

Julia cocked a curious brow. "You were *invited?*"

"No," Adam chuckled. "Lone Wolf claimed that from his own experiences that if you waited for an invitation you would never get to go anywhere. He says you should just go and dare folks to deny you."

It outraged her beyond words that Lone Wolf rarely found himself a welcomed guest anywhere. "The story of his life, I suspect," Julia murmured.

Life wasn't fair. She could attest to that. She was about to lose the man she loved because she was too unconventional, wasn't woman enough to captivate him. Or perhaps it was because no woman could hold on to Lone Wolf permanently. Maybe he had accepted his life for what it was and didn't want to make any drastic changes. She, however, would eagerly make a place for him in her life…

"Dear God," Julia breathed when the epiphany hit her right between the eyes.

Adam came to attention beside her. "What's wrong, Jules? Are you having a relapse? Should I summon the doctor?"

"No, I'm fine." She smiled for her brother's benefit.

Julia suddenly found herself unbearably restless. She drew back the quilts to ease from bed. She flinched when she saw the blue, green and black bruises that extended from her knees to her ankles. She doubted the bruises stopped at her knees. They probably extended all the way up to her neck.

She tugged modestly at her nightgown. Who, she wondered, had undressed her and put her to bed? Lone Wolf? Sweet mercy, the sight of her battered body had undoubtedly repulsed him.

"I'm not sure you should be up and moving around yet," Adam cautioned as she paced gingerly from wall to wall. "No offense, Jules, but you still look like hell."

"If you're trying to cheer me up you're going about it backward." She switched direction then said, "You were about to tell me about your visit to Griffin Ranch."

Adam flashed a blinding smile. "I proposed to Maggie."

"And Lone Wolf went along to hold a gun to Sol's head while you popped the question?" she teased.

"That was our last resort. Surprisingly, Sol didn't object. He seems to have buried the hatchet after Lone Wolf got Thomas Whittaker to confess to his numerous crimes."

Julia halted in her tracks. Her intense gaze zeroed in on Adam. "And?" she prodded anxiously.

"He found out that Whittaker had tried to persuade Pa to sell out to him when news of railroad expansion was being whispered about. Pa refused and got suspicious. When Pa asked for an accounting of funds Whittaker had to cover his tracks. He sent a message to Pa that fateful night three years ago. The note said Rachel needed a ride home because her carriage had broken down and Sol was unavailable to help her. Whittaker sent Will Butler to force them off the edge of the ravine." Adam scowled bitterly. "It doesn't seem fair that Pa was killed trying to do *his* good deed by driving Rachel home after she did *her* good deed of delivering her friend's baby."

"I agree wholeheartedly," she murmured. "We lost Papa because of Whittaker's obsessive greed for power and wealth. No doubt, he couldn't be satisfied until he became as influential and successful as his half brother." She smiled sadly, "At least we know that Papa and Rachel weren't having an affair. But because of Whittaker's selfish machinations we were deprived of our father's presence in our lives and three years of close friendship with the Griffins."

The sound of swishing skirts drew Julia's attention. She smiled when Maggie walked in, bearing a tray of steaming food.

"Good to see that you're up and around again." Maggie deposited the tray on the table. Then she bent to press a greeting kiss to Adam's lips.

Julia's heart twisted in her chest as she watched them stare at each other as if they were the only two people in the room. Why couldn't Lone Wolf stare at her like that, feel that way about her? Why couldn't he want her as desperately as Maggie and Adam wanted each other? Why didn't he want to spend the rest of his life with her?

Stop feeling sorry for yourself and be happy for them, she chastised. *They have been in love forever. They have been friends since childhood and they were* destined *to be together.*

Obviously you and Lone Wolf were not.

"I suppose Adam told you the good news." Maggie beamed. "As soon as he feels up to it we are getting married." She smiled devotedly at Adam. "We decided on the simple, no-delay approach that you and Lone Wolf used." She handed Adam a slice of toast, and then faced Julia. "Sit down and eat. You need to regain your strength so you can be on hand to witness our wedding."

Julia returned to bed, propped herself up on a stack of pillows and took the plate Maggie offered her. She felt like a fifth wheel while Maggie and Adam discussed their wedding plans and spoke of moving her belongings to Preston Ranch.

"Oh, before I forget." Maggie turned her attention to Julia. "Audrey Clement is back on the marriage mart. Her father called off the engagement to Gerald Russell because of the scandal and murder charges brought against his half brother, Thomas Whittaker."

"Poor Audrey." Julia couldn't work up much sympathy for the spiteful chit.

"According to Papa, the state senator's chance of reelection dropped off drastically when news began circulating that he had passed along privileged information about the railroad's expansion plans to Whittaker. Come to find out, Russell was due a percentage of the profit they planned to make on the sale of right-of-ways and business lots that Whittaker expected to have while in control of our ranches."

Julia thought it was apropos that both men were going to get what they deserved for gathering confidential information and using it to make themselves extremely wealthy at the Prestons' and Griffins' expense.

"I don't know how Lone Wolf does it." Adam shook his head in amazement. "But he manages to get all the facts during his interrogation sessions."

Julia smiled to herself. Whatever methods Lone Wolf applied to glean facts from criminals seemed to work wonders. And she was glad of it. She wouldn't have wanted the state senator and his conniving half brother to get off scot-free.

Maggie surged to her feet then gently urged Adam

up from the chair. "After I see that Adam is resting comfortably, I'll have a warm soaking bath prepared for you, Jules."

Julia smiled gratefully. A hot relaxing bath was exactly what she needed to ease the soreness in her battered body. "Thank you, Mags. I'm going to enjoy having you around again. We've missed you these past few years."

Julia hoped having Maggie around constantly would fill the void of loneliness that Julia would endure when Lone Wolf walked out of her life.

Although Julia was thrilled that Adam and Maggie could publicly announce their engagement and Sol was back to being neighborly again, thoughts of Lone Wolf still tormented her. She remembered the epiphany that had struck her while she was talking to Adam. She called herself every kind of fool for presuming Lone Wolf would want to fit into her world.

But that wasn't necessarily so. She was trying to write the perfect ending to her personal fairy tale by expecting Lone Wolf to fall madly in love with her and take up residence in her suite at the house. They would become one big happy family with Adam and Maggie living in the opposite wing and sharing the duties and responsibilities at the ranch.

Lone Wolf had his own life and ambitions, she reminded herself. Even if he did love her—which, of course, he didn't because he would have said so if he did—he wasn't like the fortune hunters who pursued her. He wouldn't leap at the chance to move in to take advantage of the potential wealth she had to offer.

If Lone Wolf did love her and asked her to come along with him, where would she stay while he was off ridding the world of cutthroats? In a tent by a nameless stream in a nameless valley on the prairie? Was she willing to pull up stakes, leave her family behind and make whatever sacrifice necessary to be with him?

Julia hated to admit that, although she did love challenge and adventure, the prospect of facing the kind of danger Lone Wolf endured constantly held no appeal.

"Hopeless," she muttered as two cowboys arrived to fill the tub with hot water. She was destined to become a spinster, the doting aunt to Maggie and Adam's children. She would immerse herself in the workings of the ranch to occupy her time and her thoughts, just as she had after her father's death, she decided.

When the tub was full and she was alone, Julia peeled off her nightgown—and confirmed that she was one big unappealing bruise. She sank into the warm water and expelled a contented sigh. The bath soothed her aching body, but it did nothing whatsoever for her splintered soul.

She wished she could magically wave her arms and make Lone Wolf fall in love with her. She wished he would agree to live here and make theirs a real marriage, not a convenient arrangement. She wished she could conjure up a potion that would make Lone Wolf stare at her with the same heartfelt devotion she witnessed in her brother's eyes, in his smile.

Despite all the good that had come of having Lone Wolf resolve the situation at the ranch, Julia needed more. Greedy, that's what she had become. She wasn't much better than Thomas Whittaker, who had plotted, murdered and schemed to acquire valuable property.

Well, she wasn't *that* bad, she reassured herself. All she wanted was the love of the one man who held her heart.

That wasn't asking so much, was it?

It was asking the impossible, Julia thought as she sank beneath the water's surface to soak her head—which was *exactly* what she needed to do if she hoped to eradicate all these unattainable hopes and dreams.

Chapter Eighteen

"Stop doing that," Sol snapped as he clutched at his chest and glared at Lone Wolf, who had materialized from the dark corner of Sol's office. "Announce yourself before you show up unexpectedly." He frowned accusingly. "Are you purposely trying to startle me into heart failure?"

Lone Wolf shrugged noncommittally as he detached himself from the shadows. "Old habit. When you spend half your life tracking outlaws you learn not to go tramping around like an elephant. Stealth has kept me alive and kicking for years."

He stared curiously at Sol. "Why did you send for me? It's late and I want to check on Julia."

For four consecutive nights Lone Wolf had entered Julia's suite to watch her sleep. During the days, he'd gradually seen to it that her life returned to normal. He'd tracked down the bank accounts that Whittaker had opened in various towns to stash her and Adam's sizable trust funds—in his own name.

Lone Wolf had been shocked speechless when he

discovered the astronomical amounts of money the Prestons had inherited from their maternal grandfather. It put to shame the fees and bounties he had saved up the past twelve years.

He cast aside his wandering thoughts and watched Sol wear a rut in the expensive Belgian carpet that graced the middle of his study. "If you invited me here to watch you pace I have more important things to do."

Sol halted in his tracks then wheeled to face him. The grim expression on his face put Lone Wolf's senses on full alert. "I want to…er…thank you for saving my life during the confrontation with Whittaker."

"You already thanked me that night," Lone Wolf said stiffly. "But you're welcome."

"Why did you do it?" Sol's pale blue eyes riveted intently on him.

Lone Wolf propped a shoulder against the wall and crossed his arms over his chest. "I told you. I did it because of Maggie."

Sol gestured toward a chair. "Please sit down."

"No thanks. I prefer to stand, because I'm not planning to be here very long."

While it was true that his long-held resentment for Sol Griffin had begun to dim in intensity, he wasn't going to permit himself to like this man. Reconciliation was out of the question, even if Sol was feeling grateful and appreciative because Lone Wolf had spared him from an oncoming bullet.

"There are things you need to know," Sol burst out, then resumed his nervous pacing. "I don't expect you to understand, but you need to know nonetheless."

"Fine. Tell me," he said impatiently. "But be quick

about it. Being here brings back too many unpleasant memories."

Sol nodded his salt-and-pepper-gray head, accepting Lone Wolf's hostility as justified. "When I lost my sister in that raid I also lost my parents," he confided without glancing in Lone Wolf's direction. "I watched them die, just as Maggie tells me that you had to watch your parents die at the Battle of the Washita."

"The whites can call it what they wish, but it was not a battle. It was a bloody massacre," Lone Wolf muttered bitterly. "Having lost your own parents, you should have sympathized with me when I came to you for help. You should have understood the depth of grief I had suffered."

Sol jerked up his head to stare intently at Lone Wolf's rigid expression. "I understood, but I also hated your father's people for what they had done, even though I was aware that my parents had taken a great risk when they settled on this land that the Cheyenne had claimed." His face puckered in a self-deprecating scowl. "But I hated myself even more because I was supposed to get Isabella to safety in the root cellar when the raiders approached."

Sol's breath gushed out, his shoulders sagged and a tortured grimace settled on his aging features. "I was responsible for Izzie. She was my little sister and I froze."

Lone Wolf noticed Sol's shamed look. There was no question that his uncle thought he had disgraced himself. It was written all over his face.

"I saw one of the warriors charging forward on his horse to snatch up Izzie. I didn't intervene so she could dash to safety," he confessed. "I stayed hidden to protect myself."

Lone Wolf saw his uncle's composure crumple, saw humiliating tears glisten in his eyes. He realized that Sol perceived himself as a coward who had placed his own survival above his sister's.

Of course, Lone Wolf couldn't bring himself to offer an ounce of sympathy, but he did understand that not every man was trained to be self-sacrificing. Also, not every man was an accomplished shootist and fighter, as Lone Wolf had had to become to survive.

His consolation came in knowing that Sol Griffin's shame, regret and guilt had haunted him for almost two decades.

"Your people destroyed my family and turned me into a grieving wretch and a humiliated coward," Sol said after a moment. "I was glad when the government forced the Cheyenne to live on the Indian reservation. Even so, I requested that the army search for Izzie. Years later they reported that they had found a young woman who met her description. I was told that she had perished with the other casualties during Colonel Chivington's unprovoked siege during the Sand Creek Massacre in Colorado."

Now Lone Wolf understood what Sol had meant when he had said that his sister was dead to him. He had emotionally buried her years before Lone Wolf had arrived with the locket. Unknowingly, Lone Wolf had resurrected Sol's shame, guilt and grief.

"When you showed up at my doorstep, a gangly, filthy Cheyenne brat, carrying Izzie's locket and claiming she had sent you to me after she had died, it was like losing her and my parents all over again," Sol said unevenly. "All my inadequacies and anguish rose from their shallow graves to swallow me alive." He turned away abruptly, as if too mortified to face his nephew.

Sol threw up his hands in a gesture of helpless futility then stared through the window at the darkness. "Since you have obviously never been a shameless coward who failed in your obligations and responsibilities you don't understand that bringing you into the family fold was the same as publicizing my failures to my wife and infant daughter. I was a proud fool and you paid for my shame and vanity."

If Sol was confiding his feelings, in hopes that Lone Wolf would forgive and forget so he could feel better about himself, then he was wasting his breath.

"I kept thinking that if not for your very existence Izzie might have sneaked away from the Cheyenne and made her way back to the ranch where she belonged," Sol went on to say. "But her loyalty and devotion was obviously to you. She died so you could survive, as I should have died to save her in the first place." He sighed audibly, his gray head downcast. "Izzie turned out to be much braver than I was."

Lone Wolf fought against the tug of sympathy for a man whose life had been turned upside down once again when a half-breed claiming to be his nephew had arrived unexpectedly, looking like a scroungy mongrel in search of refuge.

"I'm so terribly sorry," Sol choked out, still unable to face Lone Wolf. "I committed a horrible injustice against you and I regret it. You're my blood kin. You needed a home and I turned you away. You should've let me die in Whittaker's office. Maggie would've found solace with Adam. The heartache of losing my wife, after three years of believing that she'd betrayed me with John Preston, would have ended."

"That would have been the easy way out for you,"

Lone Wolf muttered. "You didn't make it easy for me. It was pure hell living alone on the frontier like a wild animal, avoiding civilization for fear I would be rejected as harshly as you rejected me. If not for my Cheyenne training I would be long dead. Much to your delight, I'm sure."

Sol sighed heavily. "I have to carry the blame for your hatred on my conscience as well. Believe me, every time I've seen you at a distance the past decade, I've felt the knife twisting in my gut. I knew you settled in this area as a reminder of my shame and cowardice."

"Too bad I didn't know I had gotten to you so effectively," Lone Wolf said. "I might have felt better."

Sol finally pivoted to face him. A faint smile surfaced on his lips. "You have a bit of your mother's dry wit. She used to drive me crazy with it when we were children. Little barbs. Small jabs delivered with just enough sarcasm to annoy the hell out of me. But she was my little sister and I loved her.... I'll never forgive myself for failing her when she needed me most."

The comment reminded Lone Wolf of what Adam had said about feeling guilty that he was bedridden and leaving Julia to bear the burden at the ranch. He supposed older brothers were taught to look after their little sisters. It had become ingrained in their minds as part of their family obligation.

Lone Wolf remembered how guilty he had felt when he had not been there to protect Julia during her darkest hour. He regretted that he couldn't prevent Butler from absconding with her and putting her through that hellish buggy crash.

Damn it, he did not want to sympathize with Sol.

But he did. And giving ground was like pulling teeth.

"I spoke with my attorney today," Sol continued. "Half of this ranch has been transferred to your name, because half of it rightfully belonged to Izzie…and now to her heir."

Lone Wolf couldn't have been more stunned if Sol had suddenly plowed a fist into his underbelly. His mouth dropped open.

"You're surprised that I have a generous or sentimental bone in my body?" Sol laughed humorlessly. "Believe me, if there is one thing I've learned in life it's that prosperity and prestige don't soothe wounds that run soul deep. I would give all I have to have Izzie and Rachel back. Which is why I couldn't object to letting Adam propose to Maggie. It was unfair to punish the poor young man for sins that his father had *not* committed against me."

He stared regretfully at Lone Wolf. "I have already done that to you, just because Cheyenne blood runs in your veins."

When Lone Wolf felt himself going soft, he pushed away from the wall and came to rigid attention. "I don't want your property, Sol." With feet apart, he crossed his arms over his chest and stared down Sol. "Your sympathy and generosity are about two decades too late. No thanks."

"Better late than never," Sol contended.

"Better *never* than *too late* to help a kid who had nowhere to turn," Lone Wolf said bitterly. "What's done is done."

Sol sighed. "I have to live with that shameful mistake, but if I decide to do a good deed that is years too late in coming, then I will damn well do it. There is nothing you can do about it." He struck the identical unyielding pose—arms crossed over his chest, his feet apart. Sol stared right back at Lone Wolf. "I anticipated your refusal so I added a stipulation to the transfer of property. You can't sell the land or give it away without my permission."

"Ah yes, strings attached. Why am I not surprised?" Lone Wolf said.

"You can only benefit from the profits," Sol went on to say. "The profits will increase substantially when the railroad line comes through and I sell off lots on our *undivided* property."

For the first time Sol approached him then halted an arm's length away. It was as close as they had ever been—well, except for the fisticuffs they had engaged in the night Lone Wolf had stormed in here, believing Sol had taken Julia hostage. To Lone Wolf's amazement Sol extended his hand in a peace-treaty gesture.

Lone Wolf stared at Sol's offered hand. He wasn't sure he was over his animosity. Wasn't sure he *wanted* to be over his animosity just yet. The bitterness had been a part of him for years and it seemed unnatural to give it up.

"This doesn't mean that I have to like you, does it?"

Sol broke into a grin, his hand still hovering in midair. "No, that would make you the better man, now wouldn't it? That would mean that you rose above the bad blood and resentment that has been between us, wouldn't it? This way I get to feel better about myself because I'll know that I have come to like and admire you a hell of a lot more than you appreciate and tolerate me."

Lone Wolf reached out to shake his uncle's hand,

forced into it by the dare, no less. "Damn, Sol, you're sneaky and manipulative."

"Ah yes, two more of my flaws. Thank you so much for bringing them to my attention."

Something very peculiar occurred while Lone Wolf's hand was clasped around Sol's. Years of grudging resentment and justified dislike seemed to drain out of him. It felt strange to relinquish the driving force that had sustained him and motivated him for years on end.

He didn't like discovering that Sol wasn't inherently cruel and heartless. He didn't like learning that he could actually tolerate his uncle's presence for more than a few brief moments. He didn't like feeling appreciative that he had been granted the inheritance from his mother.

For years Lone Wolf had prided himself on knowing that everything he had made of himself he had accomplished on his own. *Without* help from another living soul. He was a self-made man in every sense of the word.

"Just because we've buried the hatchets somewhere besides in each other's backs doesn't mean I have to show up here for Sunday dinner when I'm in this neck of the woods, does it?" Lone Wolf asked.

Sol chuckled. "I suppose not. That would be too much to ask of you. But I was hoping that sometime in the future you could stop by and tell me about Izzie. I want to know what her life was like." His expression turned sincere. "Did she enjoy any happiness with the Cheyenne? Did she spend her life despising me for failing her in her greatest hour of need?"

"She loved my father and he loved her deeply," Lone Wolf confided. "I don't think she would have left him, even if the army had found our secluded camp in the Colorado mountains during those early years and tried to take her home.

"When we were forced to move to the reservation, she disguised herself so she wouldn't be discovered. I think perhaps she shared the same deep devotion for my father that you must have shared with your wife."

Sol nodded as his hand dropped away. "I'm glad to know that she was happy. I was afraid that she lived with fear and suffered brutality as a captive."

"That is not the way of the Cheyenne," Lone Wolf declared. "Women hold greater power and prestige in our culture than they do in white society. Captive though she was in the beginning, she was admired and respected for her wit and wisdom."

When Lone Wolf spun around to take his leave, Sol called after him. "You're all I have left of Izzie. I want you to be happy, too."

Lone Wolf wondered how he was supposed to be happy when he felt responsible for Julia's pain and misery.

An hour later Lone Wolf crept silently into Julia's suite to shed his clothes. As had become his habit since she was injured, he eased carefully into bed beside her. He leaned over to press a tender kiss to the silky curve of her neck.

The conflicting turmoil caused by his encounter with Sol receded into the farthest corner of his mind as he inhaled Julia's tantalizing scent. He closed his eyes, knowing he couldn't keep sneaking in here like a thief in the night to hold her possessively against him. He was procrastinating, making it more difficult to walk away from her forever.

When Julia sighed in her sleep and shifted her hip against his groin, desire throbbed heavily inside him. He wanted her, but he refused to torment himself more than he already had. Sleeping with her was the only pleasure he would allow himself.

It's time to leave Julia behind, came the quiet but relentless voice of reason. He had to leave soon, he thought as he drifted off to sleep. Maybe not tomorrow or the day after, but soon. When he had put Julia's life back in order and completed this assignment, he would have no more excuses to stay. This mismatched marriage had to come to an end.

Lone Wolf knew that.

He was just having trouble convincing his heart.

One week after the ordeal with Whittaker and Butler, Julia resumed her usual activities. She had to force herself to manufacture cheerful smiles for Adam, who had been walking on a cloud since his engagement. Truth was that she missed seeing Lone Wolf terribly and she didn't know if he was even in the state.

Julia had awakened every morning during her recovery, swearing that she had felt Lone Wolf's comforting presence beside her in bed.

Now if that wasn't an indication of a woman lost in whimsical fantasies she didn't know what was.

Weary from a long day of dreaming up activities to keep herself occupied and distracted, Julia bathed then climbed into bed. She dozed off almost immediately— which she had been doing a lot lately. Sometimes she suspected that someone was still sneaking small doses of sedative into her evening meals and drinks to make sure she got plenty of rest.

Two hours later Julia awoke to an unidentified sound. She lay perfectly still when she saw the shadow of a man moving across her room toward her bed. Lone Wolf? she thought, bewildered.

Was this the reason she could swear she could feel his presence at night? Had he actually been sleeping beside her, if only to keep up appearances and reassure her brother?

When he slid silently into bed beside her she didn't say a word, didn't let on that she was awake.

A minute passed. Then another.

"You're awake this time, aren't you?" he whispered.

"How could you tell? I was lying perfectly still."

He chortled softly. "That's how I knew. Every other night you have shifted in your sleep, even while you were sedated."

"And thank you so much for that," she grumbled. "I guess I had it coming after I did the same thing to you."

"Sure 'nuff." He waited a beat then said. "I tracked down every last dollar of your and Adam's trust that Whittaker had stashed in scattered accounts with his name on them. You'll have to testify at his trial next week. I don't know if I'll be back by then to offer my testimony. But rest assured that he isn't going to get off, Julia. There is too much damning evidence against him."

"Won't be back?" Julia repeated. "Where are you going?"

This was it, she realized in dismay. She knew without asking that this would be the last night Lone Wolf spent in her bed. This was his way of saying goodbye.

That last ray of hope withered inside her. She wasn't going to be able to keep Lone Wolf, no matter how much she wanted him. And she definitely wanted him.

"I'm headed to Colorado," he informed her. "The bank robbers still haven't been apprehended. They hit another bank in Denver and took to the hills—"

Julia levered herself onto his bare chest and impulsively kissed him for all she was worth. Even if he didn't love her, even if she was shamelessly inadequate as a lover, she vowed to find a way to pleasure him so that she wouldn't become a forgotten memory. She couldn't bear that thought. He was *not* leaving here with a lukewarm reaction to their first sexual encounter.

Maybe she hadn't satisfied him as completely as he had satisfied her, but she was going to be as inventive and provocative as she knew how.

When he hooked his arm around her waist—to gather her closer or push her away, she didn't know which—she removed his arm from her hip.

"Julia—"

"I want you," she interrupted before he could reject her. "I want to find a way to give you the same incredible pleasure you gave me."

Her hands drifted over his broad chest to encircle his nipples. Then she glided her fingertips over his washboard belly. She heard his guttural groan and decided that he liked what she was doing to him well enough.

And if he thought she was backing away before she knew every inch of his brawny body by taste, by heart, then he had misjudged her.

Maybe she was too bold and uninhibited. And maybe that did put him off. But instinctively she knew this was her last night with Lone Wolf and she wanted it all, for this fleeting moment out of time.

And she made up her mind that she was going to have it.

To that dedicated purpose she skimmed her open mouth over his chest and nipped playfully at him with her teeth. She smiled in satisfaction when he moaned again. Her hand drifted lower, noting that he was naked. And he was sexually aroused.

At least he hadn't become completely immune to her fumbling caresses, she thought, encouraged.

She cupped him in her hand, then shifted above him to take him into her mouth. She kissed and caressed him as intimately as he had kissed and caressed her. His gasp and hiss, and the feel of his hand gliding up and down her back in an answering caress, pleased her to no end. When she flicked at him with her tongue his hand clenched on her hip, assuring her that he was enjoying her touch as much as she delighted in learning every texture and contour of his masculine body.

"Julia…stop…" he said with a panted breath.

"No, I'm enjoying this too much. You don't mind, do you?"

She heard a chuckle rumbling in his chest. "If you keep that up I won't have a *mind* left."

She smiled against his hard flesh then moved her hand experimentally down his shaft. She felt him tremble, heard him groan again. And again. She decided she wasn't completely inept at satisfying a man. Had she been granted more time—like the next fifty years or so—she might get really good at it.

Unfortunately, all she had was tonight and she wasn't going to waste one precious moment of it.

She touched him everywhere at once and sketched every inch of his hair-roughened flesh. She memorized every lean powerful muscle and tendon. She savored the feel of his sinewy body beneath her hands. She stroked his thighs, his hips and his belly as her mouth moved provocatively over his arousal.

"You're killing me, woman," he said on a shaky groan.

"In a good way?" she whispered against his rigid flesh.

"Mmm…" was all he said, so she figured she was getting the hang of pleasing him.

She practiced her newfound skills over again, hoping that the featherlike touch of her hands and lips was as arousing to him as it had been when he had treated her to his erotic caresses.

"Jul—" His voice fizzled out when another sizzling sensation riveted his body.

The woman was driving him insane with her intimate kisses and caresses. He wondered if she had the slightest idea how much self-restraint it required to lie there, body on fire, while she made a slow, thorough study of him. She seemed intent on proving something to herself—or to him—he wasn't sure which. But if she kept this up much longer he was going to explode from internal combustion.

He reached for her, trying to bring her face back to his, needing to devour those hot, moist lips that had been making a feast of him. But she shifted elusively away and nudged him toward the edge of the bed. When she knelt on the floor between his legs he looked down to see that frothy reddish-gold head moving deliberately toward him again.

He felt like throwing back his head and baying at the moon the moment her lips closed around him. She tasted and stroked him repeatedly, and he couldn't find the strength or the will to stop her. She left him feeling weak and helpless. She left him burning from the inside out and kept him panting for breath. He clenched his teeth and called upon what little willpower he could muster when she tortured him again.

And here he had thought their first encounter had brought him to his knees and emptied his mind of everything except the pleasure of loving Julia.

He had the unmistakable feeling that each time with Julia would be more devastating than the time before because she held nothing back. She wasn't afraid of intimacy, wasn't afraid to explore the heights and depths of mindless passion. She was bold and sensual and altogether irresistible.

His thoughts spun like a pinwheel when she stood up to cup his face in her hands. And when she kissed him as if she were dying and he was providing her last breath he could taste his passion for her on her lips. That was the devastating blow that crumpled his self-control.

He devoured her, clamped his arms around her waist and brought her down so that she was straddling his hips. He surged toward her, needing desperately to be inside her right that very moment.

When he found her hot and welcoming, he pressed into her then guided her legs around his waist. His hands glided over the swells of her breasts and he savored the taste and feel of her silky skin against his fingertips and lips.

"Am I getting better at this?" she whispered as she moved above him, holding him in the most exquisite manner imaginable. "Good enough to bring you back to me from time to time?"

It suddenly dawned on him that she wasn't as confident of her ability in passion as he thought. How could she not know that she had seduced him so completely that he was literally shaking with the need for her? How could she not know that her touch set off riveting sensations that rumbled through him like a volcano on the brink of eruption?

"You are incredible," he rasped as his body involuntarily lifted toward hers, craving the deepest penetration, reveling in the feel of her softest flesh closing around him like liquid fire.

"You're just saying that to be nice," she murmured as she locked her arms tightly around his shoulders and rocked rhythmically against him as they rushed blindly toward completion. "But *I love you* and I will go on loving you—"

Her voice disintegrated into a shattered gasp and he felt the sweet tremors of her release caress him intimately. His body responded simultaneously. Sensation upon inexpressible sensation cascaded over him. He rolled sideways, taking Julia with him so that he was above her, driving deeper and deeper while she clung urgently to him. His pulse roared in his ears as the crescendo of passion built then exploded inside him.

Gasping desperately for breath, he felt wild, mind-shattering release roiling through him. He strained against her, then shuddered helplessly in the encompassing circle of her silky arms.

And then she said those three words again. "I love you, Lone Wolf. I will always love you, no matter where you—"

Lone Wolf dropped a kiss to her lips to shush her. He wanted to believe but was afraid to. Afraid to let himself hope, to dream. Maybe in three months he would return, just to see if she still thought there was something lovable and memorable about him.

Certainly he had never had an endearing or lasting effect on anyone else, so why should Julia be any different?

This was just an illusion, he told himself sensibly. Julia had been through too much turmoil to know her own mind and own heart. She needed time to regain her perspective.

Surely three months would be long enough for her to decide if she really meant what she said or if the newness of passion was speaking for her.

"You're leaving anyway, aren't you?" she murmured when he broke the kiss.

"Yes. You'll thank me for it later," he insisted.

She sniffed caustically. "Thank you for breaking my heart? I doubt that."

When he rolled away she turned her back on him. He thought he heard a quiet sob, but then she commenced muttering to herself so he couldn't tell for sure.

Lone Wolf got to his feet to retrieve his clothes. He dressed quickly then glanced back at the bed to see that Julia had pushed up against the headboard and was watching him.

He fastened his shirt and struggled to project an air of detached professionalism. "I didn't press charges against Harvey Fowler, even though he admitted that he was with Butler the morning we had to dodge bullets down by the creek. He is willing to testify against Whittaker." He strapped his double holster around his hips. "I did what you hired me to do. Now your life is back in order."

"Then why do I feel as if my world is falling apart around me?" she murmured unevenly.

He sighed. "You might not realize it yet, Julia, but I'm just the place you came for comfort and protection."

"Is that what you think?" she challenged hotly. "That I don't know what I feel?"

"You have convinced yourself that you should love me because we've been as close as two people can get," he said frankly. "But passion doesn't always equate with love, Julia. It's mostly about appeasing natural urges."

"So if I seek out another man and invite him to my bed you think I will feel the same way about *him?*"

Lone Wolf winced. The prospect of Julia touching another man as intimately as she had touched him—and vice versa—cut all the way to the quick. Nevertheless he said, "Probably. It's—"

He jerked back reflexively when the pillow she launched at him hit him in the face before he saw it coming and had time to react.

"Vince Lone Wolf, you may be law and order's answer to western justice, but I swear you are an absolute idiot!" she growled at him. "I want *you.* No other man will do, but you're either too blind or too stupid—or both—to believe it."

Her voice hitched then she sucked in an audible breath. "Or maybe the truth is that *I'm* just the convenient place *you* came for satisfaction. It would be inconvenient for you to believe that I love you. You don't want to believe that I love you, do you?"

"That's not—" he began.

"Leave," she cut in angrily. "You don't want to love me back. That's plain enough. And maybe you're right. Maybe you have been as convenient for me as I was for you and I simply haven't had time to figure it out yet. Maybe in a week or two I'll change my mind. You certainly seem to think that will turn out to be the case."

Lone Wolf watched her flounce on the bed, disregarding him as if he weren't there. He took his cue. He did Julia the greatest favor a man could do for a woman who was too damn good for him. He put on his boots and he left.

As he rode off into the darkness, he assured himself that when Julia got over being mad—after her bruised feminine pride had time to heal—she would thank him for not taking advantage of her mistaken feelings for him.

Leaving Julia behind was the most difficult thing he had ever done. There were things he would never be able to say to her, feelings and sensations he knew he would never experience again because he only felt them when he was with her.

He was going to miss being a part of a family, too. For a time, his presence had been accepted and welcomed and his opinions had mattered. Now he was back in his isolated world—and he had never felt so lonely and empty in his entire life.

Chapter Nineteen

Six weeks after Lone Wolf rode away, Adam stood on the front porch of the ranch house beside his new wife. He watched his sister race her horse over the rolling hills like a restless spirit. Eventually she circled back to the barn.

"How long do you think Jules's daredevil phase is going to last this time?" Maggie asked worriedly.

"Until he comes back," Adam prophesied.

"Is he even in the state?" Maggie questioned.

"No. Last time I spoke to Sheriff Danson he said that after Lone Wolf captured the men who robbed the bank in Newton he signed on with the Rocky Mountain Detective Agency in Denver," Adam reported. "Now he's on an extensive manhunt for Colorado's most-wanted outlaw gang that has been preying on miners."

Maggie's shoulders slumped and she sighed in dismay. "Jules is eating her heart out for that man. I'm afraid this reckless streak is going to get her seriously hurt." She stared somberly at Adam. "Perhaps we could telegraph Lone Wolf so he'll know how much Jules misses him. He *is* planning to return, isn't he?"

Adam slipped his arm around Maggie's waist and pulled her close. "I hope so. I know I couldn't stand being away from you indefinitely. I missed you like crazy while you were in Saint Louis."

"Oh, Adam, I missed you, too, and I love you so much!" Maggie impulsively flung her arms around his neck and kissed him with all the love and affection that bubbled inside her.

And that was how Julia found her brother and new sister-in-law when she approached the house. Seeing them so happy and so hopelessly devoted to each other was a daily reminder of how lost and miserable she was.

Watching them stare hungrily at each other across the dining table three times a day made matters even worse. Having these lovebirds underfoot when she was so lonely and restless was almost more than she could bear.

Plus, Adam and Maggie were so attuned to each other that they couldn't see how much she was hurting.

How was it possible to be so pleased to see her brother fully recovered and happily married—and still want to rail at him for being so content when she was anything but?

"Will you two please try to restrain yourselves," Julia muttered as she hiked up the front steps.

Adam and Maggie were so deeply involved in their kiss and wandering caresses that they hadn't seen Julia coming—as usual. They sprang away from each other like scalded cats.

"Jules." Adam's voice was a little on the unsteady side. "Glad to see you're back from your ride…and in one piece."

"Do you think it's wise of you to keep breaking in those horses that Frank has barely trained to accept a saddle and bridle?" Maggie frowned at her in concern. "I'm afraid you're going to get bucked off and reinjure your arm."

It would have been rude to snap at Maggie and tell her to mind her own business, because her tone of voice was so full of concern and long-held affection. Nonetheless, Julia felt like barking and snarling at everyone these days. Didn't either of these lovebirds understand that tackling challenging tasks that demanded her full attention was all that kept her from going insane?

Julia missed Lone Wolf to such extremes that it was like suffering withdrawal from a fierce addiction. Her intense need for him struck at irregular intervals, provoking her to lash out at anyone within striking distance.

At the moment she almost hated Lone Wolf for what she had become because her love for him left her hurting and frustrated. She was trying to get over him—she really was—but all these heartbroken feelings inside her refused to subside. She had come to the conclusion that there wasn't a cure for what ailed her.

He had done this to her, she thought resentfully. *He* made her envious of her own brother's happiness. *He* made her jealous of Maggie's good fortune and her loving marriage. And that made her feel ashamed and petty.

He had also made her so desperate to outrun her tortuous yearnings and conflicting feelings that she had resorted to spending her time trying to break the bucking broncs—which occasionally launched her right out of the saddle and left her skidding across the ground.

Of course, she couldn't confide that to Adam or Maggie or Frank, for fear they would gang up on her and refuse to let her engage in activities that helped keep her sane—sort of.

"Julia? Are you all right?" Maggie prompted when she didn't comment immediately.

Julia shook her head and struggled to find her place in the conversation. Oh yes, the cantankerous horses, she reminded herself. "I enjoy breaking the horses to bridle and bit," she said with more enthusiasm than she actually felt.

"It looks a little too dangerous to me." Maggie squeezed Julia's hand affectionately. "I wish you would be more careful. I worry about you."

"I'm fine," she said brightly then sailed through the front door.

"You are *not* fine, Jules," Adam said with brotherly candor as he dogged her footsteps. "You haven't been fine since Lone Wolf left. When do you expect him back?"

Never, she replied silently—and felt her heart lurch painfully in her chest.

"Has he contacted you while he's been on assignment in Colorado?" Maggie asked curiously.

Colorado? Is that where he is? Nice of him to let me know. "No, I'm sure he's very busy." *Much too busy to care that I'm missing him to the extreme.*

She glanced over her shoulder to see Adam and Maggie, arm in arm, staring sympathetically at her. She just couldn't take another night of watching them making eyes at each other over supper. "Please tell Nora that I'll take my meal in my room after I bathe. It's been a long, exhausting day and I'm ready to relax."

"Julia, I'm worried about you," Adam called out as she hurried up the stairs.

"There is nothing to worry about," she tossed over her shoulder. "See you both in the morning."

Julia closed her bedroom door, stared at the empty room she had once shared with Lone Wolf and cursed the image that floated across her mind's eye—for about the millionth time. Damn him! He had struck off for unfamiliar territory to hunt criminals and she was stuck here battling all the bittersweet memories they had made together. She wanted to strangle him for that. There wasn't a place in this house—on this ranch or even in town—that his memory didn't haunt her constantly.

Well, she hoped he was happy, because she was as miserable as she could get. He had been gone more than six weeks and the aching loneliness in her heart hadn't eased off yet.

Would it ever? she wondered in exasperation.

Julia reversed direction to fetch hot water for her bath. Maybe a few trips up and down the steps, toting heavy buckets, would distract her so she could enjoy a few moments of mental relief.

Right there and then Julia made a pact with herself never to fall in love again. It hurt too much. It made her so lonesome she could barely stand herself—or anyone else for that matter.

"Whoever said that it was better to have loved and lost than never loved at all was obviously an idiot," Julia grumbled to herself as she stamped downstairs for the third time. "Why would anyone purposely bring this much pain on herself?"

She drew a determined breath as she carried heated water up the steps. She was *not* going to be in love with Lone Wolf anymore, she decided resolutely. She wasn't going to pine away for him for another second. She would refuse to let his memory color every thought. She was going to stop missing him every waking hour of every day. Starting now.

He isn't coming back. Ever. She needed to accept that fact and stop holding on to the whimsical fantasy that she would wake up one morning and he would magically appear to smile adoringly down at her.

By the time Julia filled the tub and sank into the steaming water she had convinced herself not to waste another ounce of emotion on Lone Wolf—or any other man. It was high time that she got on with her life. As the soothing water began to relax her, she assured herself that tomorrow was going to be the first day of the rest of her life. It would be a better day because she willed it to be so.

"Damn, that was close," Lone Wolf muttered as he sprawled on the ground—and not a second too soon. The bullet that sailed over his head had only missed him by an inch—maybe less.

Here he was in the Colorado mountains, wedged between two boulders, letting this outlaw gang take potshots at him, just because the three detectives he was presently working with thought their plan of attack was better than his.

Well, it wasn't.

To hell with this, Lone Wolf thought as he recoiled to avoid the splatter of rock particles caused by a ricocheting bullet. He was tired of being shot at, sick of living on trail rations. He was fed up with ridding the world of desperadoes and putting his life on the line all the damn time. Let somebody else take all the risks for

a change. He had served his time to protect society—
in spades.

This was his last assignment, he decided as he came
to his knees to survey the towering pile of rocks where
the outlaw gang had holed up. Forcing aside thoughts
of Julia—which distracted him all the livelong day and
night—he appraised the situation logically. Then he
sprang from one boulder to the next like a mountain
goat so he could get the drop on the desperadoes.

No more trying to cooperate with these detectives, he
mused as he flattened himself against the face of stone to
avoid another barrage of oncoming bullets. His forte was
working alone, utilizing the battle strategies he had
learned from the Cheyenne. He had made an exception
on this assignment because he thought that working in
tandem with the other lawmen would alleviate his loneliness.

Turned out that he couldn't have been more wrong.
He had discovered that he could be just as miserable in
a crowd. As soon as he wrapped up this case he was
moving on—alone.

"Lone Wolf, what in the hell—?"

He heard Jake Henning—one of the detectives—
muttering at him in confusion. Lone Wolf sprawled beneath a scrub bush to conceal himself, then mentally
prepared himself to become a one-man posse. Jaw
clenched, a scowl on his lips, he grabbed both pistols
and began systematically firing at the shooting arms of
the four outlaws—the same way he had disarmed and
disabled Thomas Whittaker two months earlier.

When the smoke cleared and the gunfire ceased, the
renegades were writhing on the ground, cradling their
injured arms. After reloading, Lone Wolf held the men

at gunpoint while his compatriots scrambled up the hillside to provide reinforcement, in case he needed it—which he didn't.

"Damn, Lone Wolf, that was the most amazing exhibition of marksmanship I've ever seen," Jake Henning praised. He strode over to collect the outlaws' discarded weapons. "You didn't need us at all, did you? Never did, not to track the outlaws up here or to pin them down. We probably slowed you down."

Lone Wolf didn't deny it. It was the truth, but it didn't matter. All he cared about was wrapping up this mission and leaving these bandits in the custody of the detectives.

He had come face-to-face with the irrefutable truth while he was clinging to that mountain by his fingernails and dodging bullets. And the truth was that he couldn't stand being away from Julia any longer. He was heading back to Dodge City where he should have stayed in the first place.

He had suffered through two months of sheer torture while her memory tormented him. He had tried to be noble and do the right thing by giving her plenty of time and space so she could regain her perspective after the trauma she had endured. But misery and loneliness wore on him every hour of every day. He had reached a breaking point and he was willing to accept her misguided love and savor the chance to be with her for as long as she would have him.

And if he had been gone too long and she had realized that it wasn't love but rather gratitude she felt for him… Well, it would probably kill him. But even if her attitude toward him had changed dramatically he still needed to see her again.

Not seeing her was driving him crazy.

"Where ya goin', Lone Wolf?" Jake asked. "Aren't you hanging around to take credit and collect the bounty on these outlaws? This is *your* coup. We all know it."

"The money is yours. I'm headed to Kansas," he called over his shoulder as he jogged toward his pinto. "Nice knowing you."

Lone Wolf mounted up and reined east, leaving the silhouette of the towering mountains behind him. It was the first time in weeks that he anticipated the dawn of a new day.

He just hoped he hadn't waited too long to contact Julia. If there was one time in his life that he wished he could count on good luck to smile down on him, this was it. If Julia wouldn't take him back he didn't know what he was going to do, but he had discovered the hard way that he no longer functioned worth a damn without Julia.

Unease and uncertainty overcame him as he trotted toward the Kansas border. What the hell was he going to do if Julia didn't want him anymore?

That question ate away at him during his long ride to Dodge City. By the time he reached the boundary of Preston Ranch the suspense was killing him and he almost lost his nerve.

His troubled thoughts scattered when he saw Julia, her red-gold hair flying behind her, thundering over the rolling hills at dusk. He nearly choked on his breath when her horse reared up abruptly and she was forced to hook her arms around the skittish animal's neck to hold her seat.

His gaze narrowed disapprovingly when he saw the horse buck twice. To Julia's credit, though, she didn't fall off. But it did take her a few moments to regain control of her unruly mount because it ducked its head and raced off hell-for-leather.

Apparently Julia was up to her daredevil antics again, he mused sourly. Someone needed to get that woman under control before she killed herself. Undoubtedly her brother wasn't up to the task.

It looked as if the duty would fall to him—*if* Julia would even speak to him after his ten-week absence.

While Julia trotted the misbehaving horse toward the barn Lone Wolf reined toward the spring-fed creek to bathe and shave off the two weeks' growth of whiskers. He intended to look as presentable as possible when he approached Julia. He wasn't much of a prize, but he could look halfway respectable and civilized when he tried.

If there was ever a time in his life that he wanted to make a good impression it was now, he realized as he peeled off his clothes then waded into the creek.

Two hours later, freshly bathed, rested and clean shaven, Lone Wolf dismounted near the front door of the Prestons' ranch house. He glanced toward the barn to see Harvey Fowler wave tentatively at him. The kid had become less hostile after Lone Wolf had pulled a few strings to ensure he didn't wind up serving a life sentence alongside Thomas Whittaker.

Although Harvey admitted that he had been involved in the ambush near the creek and had taken a shot at Lone Wolf, the kid had tried to protect Julia the night she was kidnapped. For that effort, which had almost gotten him killed, Lone Wolf had been lenient enough to give the kid a second chance.

Apparently Julia had taken pity on her former schoolmate and hired him to make sure he stayed out of trouble.

Discarding thoughts of Harvey, Lone Wolf pivoted back toward the front door again. "Now or never," he said to himself as he moved apprehensively up the steps.

The door swung open before he could raise his arm to knock. Lone Wolf blinked in surprise when Nora Dickerson glared at him and said, "'Bout time you got back here. I don't know why you thought *we* could keep that girl under control."

"Nice to see you again, too," he said as he walked past the disgruntled housekeeper.

Nora smiled apologetically. "Sorry. It's just that things have been a little tense around here without you."

Lone Wolf crossed the tiled vestibule then glanced to his left. He was curious when Adam and Maggie sprang off the sofa and made a beeline toward him.

"You better have a damn good excuse for being gone so long and leaving us in charge of that hellion," Adam grumbled as he halted at the parlor door.

Even Maggie didn't offer him a welcoming smile. He thought he could count on his cousin for that, at least.

"I love Julia dearly," Maggie said, "but she is completely out of control and I swear she is on a collision course with self-destruction. You are the only one who can handle her effectively."

Maggie seemed to have a lot more confidence in his ability to handle Julia than he did.

Her arm shot toward the staircase. "*Do* something with your wife, *please.*"

Lone Wolf mounted the steps, assailed by the pleasurable realization that he had been expected to return to the ranch and that everyone was annoyed with him for taking so long to get here. It was as if they wanted him here, accepted him as part of the family.

Well, wasn't that something? He belonged somewhere. He had a family again—even if he wasn't sure he still had a wife.

"You might want to watch what you say to Julia and how you say it," Adam called up to him. "She's as testy and touchy as a person can possibly get. If you look at her the wrong way she'll bite your head off. I know this from experience."

The warning did nothing to reassure Lone Wolf, who had no idea what kind of reception to expect after his lengthy absence. Then he reminded himself that he had squared off against the most ruthless desperadoes in the West and had emerged victorious.

So what does that *have to do with* this, *hotshot?* he asked himself sardonically. Just because he was handy with various and sundry weapons did not imply that he could handle Julia any better than anyone else could. Obviously she had come to hate him to such extremes that she was taking it out on her own family.

That was not a good sign.

If Lone Wolf had harbored the slightest hope that Julia would be elated to see him it died a quick death. He halted at the head of the steps and gathered his composure. Then he inhaled a fortifying breath and reached for the doorknob.

His hand stalled in midair when he heard a door slam in the near distance. It sounded as if it might have been the closet door or terrace door in Julia's suite. Lone Wolf dragged in another deep breath and mustered his resolve again.

Then he eased open the bedroom door to face his wife.

Chapter Twenty

When Lone Wolf saw Julia leaning against the terrace railing, wearing nothing but a skimpy chemise, her curly hair glistening with the colorful rays of sunset, he forgot to breathe. He stood there, spellbound. His hungry eyes roamed over every inch of her exposed flesh. His fingers itched to touch her as freely and intimately as he once had. He yearned to reacquaint himself with the silky texture of her skin and savor the unique taste of her, to hold her close and ease the emptiness that had become his constant companion.

She whirled abruptly to reenter the room and Lone Wolf froze to the spot. When she noticed him hovering beside the door, her brows snapped down in a sharp vee. Her unwelcoming expression caused his heart to slam against his ribs and his stomach to drop to his knees.

He was pretty sure this was not going to be a cheerful homecoming. She didn't look the least bit pleased to see him.

He wished *he* could have said the same. Unfortunately, he had never been so relieved to be anywhere or so overjoyed to see anyone in his life. Her injuries and bruises had healed and she looked as strikingly beautiful to him as ever.

Julia crossed her arms beneath her breasts, drawing his rapt attention to her cleavage. "And to what do I owe this unexpected visit?" she asked icily. "Nothing better to do, is that it, hmm?"

Well, so much for his fantasy of Julia spontaneously dashing into his arms the instant she laid eyes on him and showering him with kisses. Disappointed, he watched her give him the cold shoulder as she stamped over to grab her robe. He was sorely disappointed when she concealed her luscious body from his appreciative gaze.

"It's good to see you again, Julia," he murmured.

Bristling with hostility, she muttered, "What do you want? Whatever it is, be quick about asking for it. Then get out of my room. We might still be married, but you can no longer come and go as you please."

Her terse tone put him on defense. "I rode three hundred miles to tell you something," he said as he watched her pace from one side of the room to the other like a caged cat.

She stopped short. Her green eyes flashed with barely suppressed anger. "You have nerve showing up here unannounced, just *to tell me something.*" She whipped around, thrust out her arms in agitated gestures and resumed her pacing. "You waltzed out of here without looking back. For two and a half months I had no idea of your whereabouts. The *least* you could have done was send a note, in case I needed to contact you."

"When?" he countered sarcastically. "After you broke both arms and possibly a leg while trying to

be a roughrider for those broncs?" He flashed her a re-
proachful look. "That's men's work, Julia, and you
could have gotten hurt."

"I didn't think you cared what I did with my time or
how I felt about you," she snapped back at him. "If you
cared you wouldn't have left me in the first place."

The way she worded the comment—*not* the harsh
tone with which it was delivered—prompted a small ray
of hope to flicker to life inside him. Maybe she was happier to see him than she let on. Maybe wounded pride
was responsible for her waspish disposition, he thought
encouragingly.

Lone Wolf lingered too long in thought and Julia
began muttering and pacing again. "You lost the privi-
lege of lecturing me about what I should and shouldn't
do when you walked away," she said with a scowl. "No
man is going to control me or dictate to me!"

While she rattled on, reading him every line and paragraph of the riot act, Lone Wolf watched her agitated
movements and caught sight of the bare legs and enticing cleavage that peaked from the edge of her silk
robe.

Wanting her became such a tangible thing that it was
nearly impossible to resist the temptation to stride over
to scoop her into his arms and kiss the breath out of her.

Enough was enough, Lone Wolf decided as he
squared his shoulders and made a slashing gesture with
his arm to cut off Julia's tirade in midsentence. He had
come a long way to speak his piece and he was ready
to get at it.

"Julia, you told me once that you expected me to be
honest with you at all times. I'm sorry to say that I
haven't been."

The comment caught her attention and brought her to a halt in front of him.

He grabbed a quick breath and marshaled his resolve. "I came here to tell you that I want this to be a *real* marriage and I would like to live here and share the responsibilities of this ranch."

There, he had said it. Whether the admission was well received didn't matter, because he felt as if he had been holding back the truth so long that he would burst if he didn't get it out in the open.

Julia's jaw dropped and she staggered back a step. Then she recovered from her surprise and eyed him suspiciously. "You left me twice and you broke my heart both times. Why should I believe that you aren't going to walk away again when the mood strikes?"

He cupped her face in his hands and the pads of his thumbs brushed gently over the lush curve of her bottom lip. He stared down at her, willing her to believe him. "I want to be with you because when I'm with you there is more to my life than just survival. You make my life interesting and you make me happy. I've even reconciled with Sol, to some extent, so we can be neighborly. I want to invest my savings in this ranch and make it my home, too."

He drew a deep breath and put his heart on the line. "The truth I concealed from you is that I'm in love with you. I think I have been since the night you came barreling into my camp, but I fought all the unfamiliar emotions that wouldn't go away," he confessed. "I tried to give you enough time to sort out your true feelings instead of holding you to what you said while your life was in turmoil. If you've come to your senses and have realized that what you thought you felt for me was merely gratitude, then I'll turn around, walk away and never bother you again."

It would kill him, of course, but he wouldn't stay where he wasn't wanted.

"You love me? You really love me?" she choked out incredulously. "You left me to give me time to evaluate my feelings for you?"

He nodded his raven head and smiled crookedly. "I wanted you to be sure that you meant what you said. You've had fortune hunters trying to take advantage of you. I sure as hell didn't want to be one of them."

All the confusion, torment and frustration that had been roiling inside Julia for two months and sixteen days fizzled out in the blink of an eye.

"You left because you were trying to do what you thought was best for me?" She rolled the bewildering thought through her mind while she stood there studying the ruggedly handsome face that had haunted her dreams. "*Not* because you didn't love me back?"

"Loving you was never the problem, Julia. Loving you *too much* for my own good was."

When his hazel eyes flickered with undisguised emotion she knew that he spoke from the heart.

With a shriek of delight Julia launched herself at him without one smidgen of restraint. She hugged the stuffing out of him while her heart filled with so much pleasure that she thought it might split wide open.

"Say it again," she insisted in between ravishing kisses.

"I love you, hellion, and that is the honest truth. I want to have children with you and I want to be here with them. I want to grow old with you and I don't ever want to leave you again, because I was miserable without you. I want this…*us*…to last an eternity."

Julia leaned back in the sinewy circle of his arms as he carried her toward the bed. An impish grin pursed her lips as she traced the bronzed features of his face. "I am all in favor of an eternity with you, Lone Wolf, but *there's just one catch.*"

He tossed back his head and chuckled at the devilish gleam in her eyes. "Damn, I should have known that was coming. Okay, I'll bite. Just what's the catch, minx?"

Julia looped both arms around his neck to bring his head steadily toward hers. "You have to promise to love me forever, just as deeply and devotedly as I love you. Can you do that?"

"Yes," he assured her as he bent his knee to tumble her onto the bed, and then followed her down. "I'm anxious to take this assignment of *forever*…because that's how long I'll love you. I promise I'll never leave you again."

And then he kissed her with all the love and affection that he had locked in his wounded heart for half a lifetime. He knew beyond all doubt that this vibrant, wildly passionate woman loved him the way she loved no one else. It was in her answering kiss and in her cherishing caresses. It echoed in her voice, which had called him back to this place where he knew he belonged.

"You are my heart and my soul, Julia," he whispered as his body joined intimately with hers, physically expressing his unfaltering devotion to her in the throes of mindless passion.

"And you are mine," she whispered back to him. "For always and forever, Lone Wolf."

She gave herself up wholeheartedly to her soul mate…and he kept his promise of always and forever and never went away again.

* * * * *